INTERSECT

THE PARALLEL SERIES, BOOK 2

ELLE O'ROARK

1

QUINN

The woods behind Nick and Ryan's house are finally free of snow. There are buds on the trees, tiny green shoots poking out of the dirt.

"I can't believe your parents let you do that," I say, watching Nick hammer a nail into the wood. Our treehouse steps took a beating over the winter, but my mother would never allow me to use a hammer like he is.

"My dad had a treehouse when he was a kid," he replies. "And he built the whole thing himself."

"Does he still go in it?" I ask.

"Adults don't like treehouses."

"I will," I insist. "I'm going to keep coming up here, no matter how old I am."

He thinks for a moment and then shrugs, as if he's announcing a decision he was already pretty certain of. "I think I'll marry you when I grow up," he says.

I bite my lip to hide the sudden burst of delight in my chest. "Okay," I tell him. "Sure."

I go home to my mother and report what Nick has said as I'm falling asleep. "Maybe I'll go to the future and see if it happens," she says. She's teasing me. The room is so dark I can't see her face, but I hear the smile in her voice.

"You're not supposed to go to the future," I remind her. The stories she tells me each night about time-traveling are always about the past, because she says jumping to the future is dangerous, and you may learn things you wish you didn't know. She promises when I'm old enough she'll take me with her, but until then, I can only live through her adventures. "Tell me about visiting the soldier. That's my favorite."

"That's my favorite too," she says, her voice a little sad. "But you'll have stories of your own someday. Better ones."

My fears creep in. She's so certain I can do what she does, but if she won't jump to the future, how does she know for sure? "What if I can't jump like you?"

Her laughter fills the quiet room. "Oh, sweet girl. Your abilities will make mine look childlike by contrast."

"But when?" I plead.

She pulls the covers up to my chin and plants a kiss on my forehead. "You'll jump," she whispers, "on the day when you need it most."

My eyes open. I see moonlight washing over new Ikea furniture, a Monet poster in a plastic frame...my mother's guest room, no more real to me than the room in that dream. If I close my eyes it's almost as if I'm still there: the smell of my sheets and my mother's perfume, the sound of tree limbs sweeping the roof overhead, the soft brush of a cat walking past the bed—they all still linger. *Your abilities will make mine look childlike,* she'd said.

Yet it *had* to be a dream. The house was unfamiliar. We never owned a cat. And most of all, my mother can't time travel. Even if she *could* time travel, she would not. She'd be terrified of the ability, the way she's terrified of pretty much everything that is outside the realm of the normal. I'm willing to suspend disbelief about a lot of things, but it's a struggle to believe the woman in the darkness was my mother.

~

TAPPING.

My mother's voice outside the door wakes me. "Quinn?" she asks tentatively. "It's 10:00 a.m." I hear the worry that underlies her words. *Quinn never sleeps this late*, she is thinking. The brain tumor, unfortunately, has become the filter through which every unusual behavior must be viewed.

If she could see me at this moment she'd know that I do not look like a dying girl. In the mirror I see eyes that glow and a warmth to my skin that's long been absent. Nick is undoubtedly responsible for both.

And he is mine now. He's mine *again*, corrects some other, wiser voice in my head. I replay it all like a favorite movie montage—ending my engagement at the airport, his trip here last night. In twenty-four hours I changed my life, entirely for the better. Maybe I am dying, but if that's true, why does it feel like my life has just begun?

~

I WALK into the kitchen where my mother sits, clutching a cup of coffee between both hands. She offers me a weak smile, but the skin beneath her eyes is dark, smudged with the hours of sleep she didn't get last night.

"I didn't know you'd turned into such a late sleeper," she says, rising from the table.

"It was a pretty...difficult weekend." My mother knows about the difficult part already. The magnificent part—the hours I spent with Nick at the lake on Saturday, our time together last night—will have to wait. If she learns I've already moved on from the man she considers a son, calling off my wedding will get a lot more divisive than it already is.

She gets out a pan. "I can make pancakes?" she offers. "Or French toast?"

I could be sixty and my mother would still want to take care of me. That fact goes a long way toward easing my irritation about yesterday's argument. "I'm fine," I tell her. "I'll get something later."

"It's already 10," she frets. "Any later and you'll have skipped breakfast."

I laugh. "I skip breakfast almost daily, Mom. It's fine."

She frowns but puts the pan away, going to the counter instead and returning with a stack of mail. "We'll need to contact everyone and tell them the wedding is off," she says. "And then return the gifts that arrived here. If you're sure you want to do this."

I meet her eye. My conversation with Nick last night eradicated any lingering concern I felt about calling things off. "I'm sure."

She glances at me with something that looks an awful lot like suspicion. "You seem pretty lighthearted for someone who just called off her wedding," she says.

Guilt makes my pulse go from a slow march to a jog. I hate lying, and it's impossible for me to pretend I'm anything but thrilled right now. Not when Nick waits back in D.C. Especially not when every time I close my eyes I'm seeing him shirtless, muscles straining as he pulls the trailer out of the water. Or remembering the way he kissed...and if his abilities there are any indication, he's going to be very good at *everything*.

～

I SPEND the morning sending emails, calling all the vendors to cancel, and my mother helps where she can. As I'm shuffling through the RSVPs, looking at names of distant relatives I barely know, I think once again of the Rule of Threes. Even if there can't be more than three time travelers in one family, I still don't see what that could have to do with *us*. My uncle is gay, so I seriously doubt he's accidentally sired a time-traveling daughter. That only leaves my dad's sister, who ran off to Paris after high school and was never heard from again. The way she left the farm behind always made her a bit of a hero in my eyes, growing up.

"Did Dad ever look for Aunt Sarah after she left?" I ask.

"I'm not sure," she says briskly, staring at her computer screen. "I know they spoke, but he never wanted to talk to me about it."

My eyes lift from the RSVPs. My father wasn't an evasive person by nature. Why was he where his sister was concerned? "Did she stay in Paris? She never came back to visit?"

My mother's expression sours a bit. "If she did, she never came to visit *us*."

In a way it seems as if she didn't even exist. My father almost never mentioned her, even when he discussed his childhood. "I've never even seen a picture of her. Have you?"

"No," she replies, her fingers flying over the keyboard. "Damn these people to hell. They haven't shipped anything yet but they're refusing to cancel the order."

"You've never seen a *single* photo?" I ask.

"She was strange about it apparently, hated having her picture taken."

I freeze. Rose refused to have her photo taken too—with her favorite band, no less. It didn't occur to me when it happened, but what teenager refuses a photo with her favorite band? Maybe one who wants no photographic evidence that she existed in any time at all. Does that mean my aunt can time travel? It could, but it still feels like a huge leap to take. It's just as possible she simply hated something about herself—crooked teeth or a big nose—and refused to be photographed. And even if she does time travel, the bigger question is this: what is my mother capable of? In last night's dream it seemed that she didn't just carry the mutation...she time traveled, and did so enthusiastically. So if that really happened, in some other life, what would have changed it so much this time around?

"What do you think about time travel?" I ask, watching her face closely.

She frowns, her brows coming together, her mind still on her irritation with the vendor. "I liked *Outlander* well enough, but I'm more of a mystery person I guess."

I hear nothing hidden in her response, but surely there's some piece of her that at least responds to the idea of it when she did it so gleefully in another life. "I was just kind of wondering if you think it's possible?" I persist.

Her mouth sags and then her eyes brim with tears. "Oh honey," she says, as the tears start to fall. "No, I don't think it is."

"I'M STAYING ANOTHER NIGHT," I tell Nick.

I hear his disappointment in the ensuing silence. "Why?"

I laugh miserably. "I made the fatal error of asking my mom what she thought about time travel to see if she'd react in some telling way. Now she's convinced Jeff is right about the tumor making me crazy. She can't stop crying."

"Has she stopped trying to convince you to go through with the wedding at least?"

I lean back against the headboard of my bed and close my eyes. "More or less. She obviously still wishes I would, but it's hard to argue with a dying girl."

"Don't say that," he snaps. "You have no idea if it's true."

My heart twists a little. The closer we become, the harder it will get knowing I'm going to have to say goodbye to him. Which means it will become harder for him too. But I don't want to think about that right now. I want to enjoy this.

"How are things there, with you?"

"Yeah," he says slowly. "About that. Something happened this morning. I was going to wait until I saw you in person but... I went in early today, and inside my locked office, which only myself and one other person have a key to, was a woman looking at your file."

I grip the nightstand, as if the world has suddenly turned over, and I'm about to be spilled from its surface. "You're kidding."

"That's not even the weird part. She looked up at me and then she vanished, sitting right there. Just like Rose did." He draws in a breath. "I think she's the one behind all this."

Fear opens wide in my stomach. Having a brain tumor is bad enough, but the threat this woman presents is far more imminent. "God. Nick, all she has to do to separate us is go back a few months. It would just take one little tweak—"

"She won't," he says, with a certainty that makes no sense to me. Even his size and strength can't combat a superpower. "And we're going to figure this out. There are no security cameras in my office but since she was wearing scrubs, I knew she must have been in the hallway at some point, so I analyzed the hospital's security footage and found her. I'll forward you the picture in case you recognize her."

He texts the photo and I pull away from the phone to look at it.

And then my breath stops.

The same white-blond hair. The same beautiful, severe face. "It's her," I finally whisper. "The woman I've been dreaming about since I was small. She's the one who took me away from you."

"This time we have her, though," he says. "We've got a picture and we can track her down."

Except I seemed to know exactly who she was in London too, and it didn't appear to do me any good. Which makes sense, because how the hell do you stop someone who can vanish at will?

2

QUINN

I leave my mother's first thing in the morning, before she can guilt me into staying another day...or another two years, like she did when my father died. I get back to Caroline's apartment just after ten. The old Quinn would use this day off to pay bills or organize paperwork or get her car washed. The new one, the one who suddenly realizes time is fleeting, chooses to do none of those things. It's entirely possible this could be my last summer. If I'm on my deathbed next year, am I going to wish I'd spent today paying bills or getting my car washed? I doubt it.

Instead I lie out on Caroline's balcony. I start off in the red bikini, as I'm still limited to the clothes I brought for the trip to Vegas, but then, on impulse, I remove the top. Not a soul can see me since she's on the highest floor and faces the woods, but I feel rebellious for the first time in my life. It's Nick. Something about him makes me feel safe, willing to take risks, even when he's not around.

I'm too drowsy to read so I find myself thinking instead, my mind returning again and again to what my mother said: that she thought my father knew something about my future, some terrible outcome that marrying Jeff would help me avoid. I know it's related to Nick somehow, but I just don't see how it's possible. Being with him makes me feel like a better person. It makes me want to run out to the street and hug everyone that passes—clothed, of course.

I just don't see how it's possible something so good could turn bad.

I WAKE SLOWLY to the sounds of Nick getting ready for work. Outside our flat the sky is winter gray, though it is, theoretically, spring, and the light is so dim it must be early. I vaguely wonder how far along he is in the process of dressing...if I catch him early enough I can almost always convince him to get back in bed. I roll over to check, and instead wind up lunging forward, barely making it to the toilet before I expel the contents of my stomach.

Nick follows me in, looking more like a worried husband than a doctor who's seen everything. And in spite of the fact that he's seen far worse, I wave him away. "Don't look at me," I plead. I flush the toilet and he comes and sits on the edge of the tub.

"We're married. I was going to see you throw up eventually."

I shake my head. "You're not going to want to have sex with me after this."

He laughs low. "I fucking guarantee I will still want to have sex with you."

I sit up, leaning my head against the cool tile on the wall. "What if I was pregnant? Would you want to have sex with me then?"

His eyes widen a bit. "Of course I would," he says, tensing. I hate the hint of dread I hear in his voice. "Why?"

I reluctantly meet his eye. "Because I threw up yesterday too."

The next day, after three positive pregnancy tests, an obstetri-

cian tells us we are about ten weeks along, which means we got pregnant pretty much the first time we slept together.

"We were so careful," Nick says, as if he might persuade the doctor she's wrong.

The two of us come home from the appointment, looking at our small one-bedroom flat in dismay. I'm on the cusp of apologizing, though I took that pill every day as if my life depended on it, but before I can he wraps his arms around me.

"Do you think the baby will be more comfortable sleeping on the terrace, or on top of the washer?" he asks with a laugh. "Because that's pretty much the only space we have left."

A sob wells in my chest. He's joking but it's true. We've got no space for a baby. He's just started his residency and I've just started grad school and—my God—we've barely been married a month. "Is this going to be okay?" I ask, as my tears start to soak through his shirt.

"It's going to be better than okay," he whispers, tucking me closer, pressing his mouth to the top of my head. "I'm so happy right now I can't even put it into words."

I continue to cry, though. There's so much he doesn't know.

He tips my chin up with his index finger. "Honey, I know the timing isn't perfect but we'll figure it out. My parents will lend us money for a bigger place. We'll get someone to help with the baby so you don't miss class. It's going to be fine."

His joy hurts, twists something inside me, because I want this. I want it for him, I want it for myself. I can't bear the idea of telling him we're having a baby and tearing it all away from him, but I'm worried that's exactly what I'm going to do.

"I think this has happened before. When we were teenagers," I whisper. "That dream I always have, where you're in the convenience store and I realize I'm going to lose you? I think we were running somewhere because I was pregnant. And I feel like we got pregnant right away then too."

He's silent, and when I look up at him, his smile has disappeared. "Why does that worry you?"

I swallow down the lump in my throat. "Because if it happened before, how come I don't remember a baby?"

I WAKE with a start on Caroline's deck, my chest as tight as it was in my dream. I sit up, putting it all together, and the pain gives way to shock. Nick and I got pregnant the first time we were together, and it possibly happened in two different lives. Not just as young, stupid teenagers, but as adults who would have been extremely careful about contraception. With anyone else I'd attribute it to chance, or to carelessness, but this feels... unnatural. Rose said there were other qualities that accompanied the mutation—could some kind of super fertility be among them?

I spend the day able to focus on little but that dream. I'm not sure why, but it feels like a warning somehow, just like my father's dying pleas did. Our lives end before we have a child, and we seem to follow the exact same steps every time.

The real problem is that I think we're following them now too.

Now that I've seen it unfold, I want that future we had ahead of us as badly as I did in London. I want to be the one who makes Nick's face light up when he gets the news. I want it to be *our* child he holds for the first time. But it won't be. All those firsts will go to someone who comes after me.

I force the thoughts out of my head as I start to get ready to see Nick. I could very easily be newly married to Jeff right now, stuck at *Washington Insider* for the rest of my short, miserable life. But instead I'm with someone who is more than I could ever have imagined, and I'm going back to school. I need to appreciate what I have.

Caroline comes home just before I leave. Having no respect for personal boundaries, she pulls at the neckline of my dress to see which bra I'm wearing without asking, and then demands I go change it. "No dude wants to see that thing when he's undressing you for the first time. Put on something lacy or freeball it."

I laugh. As much as I wish the bra I'm wearing would be an issue, I don't see how it could be, given that there's no place we can be alone. "No one is getting undressed," I tell her primly. "This is only our second date."

"I've had sex on a second date," she argues.

I grin. "That would probably carry more weight if you didn't also have sex when there's been no date at all. I'm sleeping on your couch and he's got his ex-girlfriend dropping by all the time, so it can't happen."

She frowns. "That is a huge red flag, by the way. Why does she still have a key?"

"She's taking over his lease," I reply, rubbing lip balm on. "It's really not a big deal."

She ignores me. "Remember Russell? The guy who always had an excuse for why he needed to stay here instead of his own place? He was homeless. I didn't find out until a few months later."

I laugh again. Caroline has had some good experiences with men and a wealth of abysmal ones. I'm sure she has a horror story for every possible situation. "Nick is a neurologist. Russell wasn't employed. I feel like their situations are somewhat different."

"I'm just saying that no matter how hot the guy is, you've got to watch out for red flags. Go change your bra."

I push her away from me as she reaches for my zipper. "He's not going to see my bra! Where would that even happen?"

"Public restroom, back of his car, parking garage, mail room, alleyway, that couch because I'm happy to clear out on your behalf..." she says, ticking them off on her fingers. "Shall I continue or are you going to change your bra?"

I stick my tongue out at her. "Fine, but the joke's on you when nothing happens."

Her face grows grave. "Oh Quinn, that won't be a joke at all. That will be a tragedy, because you need a good shag more than anyone I've ever known."

I don't argue. Given how I respond when Nick merely *kisses* me, I have no doubt she's correct.

BECAUSE I'M a little unnerved by what might come out of Caroline's mouth when she meets Nick, I tell him to meet me in the lobby rather than the apartment. He's already there when I walk off the elevator, his eyes lighting up as I approach.

He rises, towering over me even in my heels, and places his hands on my hips, pulling me toward him for a brief kiss. Closed lips, held there just long enough for me to breathe him in, relish the way his hands tighten. I may not be the only one in need of a good shag.

"You're tan," he says, pulling back just enough to meet my eye. It's clear from the way he's looking at me that this is a *good* thing.

"I spent most of the day lying out on the deck."

He raises a brow. "Red bikini?"

I feel my cheeks heating a little. "Yeah. Well, half of it. No one can see onto her deck and I wanted to see what it was like to have no tan lines for once."

He grows still. "You're saying you laid out topless." He closes his eyes. "Jesus."

You'd think I just told him I ran down the street naked. "You're way more puritanical than I thought you were. Than you used to be."

His eyes open and there is something feral in them that wasn't there just a moment before. "I'm not puritanical at all," he growls. "Believe me. I'm just trying not to picture it because it's having an effect on me I'd like to avoid in a public place." He pulls me closer until I can feel exactly what he's referring to, and desire snaps in my belly, so sharp it's almost painful. If Caroline weren't upstairs I think I'd be tempted to skip dinner. Except until I've told him about the dream, no one is skipping anything.

THE RESTAURANT IS FANCIER than any place I've ever been, the kind where all the food looks like art. Even my margarita comes with leaf-shaped foam floating on its surface. Yet it's a struggle to pay attention to all the careful details with Nick sitting a foot away, creating this painful need in my stomach, making my heart skitter in my throat. I think about the way he pushed me to my back in his Jeep last weekend—his fervor, his lack of restraint—and I want him so badly I feel like I can barely function. Not once, in all the years I've known Jeff, did I ever feel this way.

I stare at the open collar of his shirt, imagine popping the second button, the third, as my mouth moves over his neck. "What are you thinking about?" he asks.

I'm blushing again. This has to stop. "I don't think you want to know."

He winces. "Quinn," he says, exhaling, "you're killing me. Talk about something please. Something normal. Or I'm going to drag you out of this restaurant and take you to the nearest hotel."

Fuck. Yes. Please. He's watching my face, and I'm pretty sure he's seriously considering the hotel plan. Except I still haven't told him about that dream. I can just imagine his reaction to learning I will probably get pregnant the first time I sleep with him. He won't run, necessarily, but he's sure going to think about it, and I'm not ready to watch it all unfold.

Instead I ask about the woman who was in his office. It seems like a sad state of affairs when the woman who wants you dead is the easiest thing to discuss.

"I talked to the police today," he says. "Security gave them the photo and they're searching the database."

I can't say this inspires much hope. "A woman who can vanish at will doesn't seem likely to have ever gotten caught in the past."

He leans back in his chair, blowing out a breath. "I know."

I run my finger over the glass's rim, pondering the situation again. "What I don't understand is why she's going to the trouble. I'm already dying. What more can she want?"

"You're not dying," he says sharply. "And if nothing else, the fact that she can time travel and she's still bothering to break into my office and look at your file should reassure you. If you weren't a threat for whatever reason, she'd know, right?"

I glance at him, wondering if he could be right. I'm not sure what she thinks I'm going to do to her in the future, but she must still be seeing it happen somehow. "I suppose. But if she can do what Rose does...why hasn't she killed me already? She got into your locked office. She could find me anywhere I was alone and kill me with ease. So why doesn't she?"

"We don't know all the rules," he says, his mouth slipping up at the corner. "Maybe she needs to wait for the full moon."

A low laugh slips from my throat. "You're confusing your supernatural beings."

"At the rate we're going," he says, "I'm going to end up fighting a werewolf over you."

"*Would* you fight a werewolf over me?" I ask, reaching across the table to swipe a grain of salt off his lower lip. The change in his expression holds me there for a moment. His eyes are dark, drugged, focused on my mouth. Finally he blows out a slow breath. "In a heartbeat."

I laugh, the sound slightly too high, thrown off kilter by a sudden surge of desire. I would follow him to any of those public places Caroline suggested without a second thought. *Pull it together. You still haven't told him.* "I won't make you do that. We've got enough problems with the exes we already have."

He frowns. "Which reminds me—Meg knows about you. She got wind of stuff from the nursing staff and I figured it was best to get ahead of the story."

I freeze. We just began officially seeing each other two freaking days ago and people he works with already know. That *can't* be a good thing. "What did you tell her?"

"That you were a friend from college," he says. "She wasn't happy but she seemed to believe it."

A friend he's gotten pregnant. *Twice.* I wanted to put it off but I have to tell him.

I take a deep breath and stare at my plate. "Speaking of our time together in the past—I had another dream last night." I glance at him warily.

"Yeah?" His mouth edges up. A dirty smile that makes me want to change the topic entirely.

"I dreamt that we got pregnant."

His smile fades. "That's not where I hoped you were going with that," he finally says. "Which time was it?"

"I was dreaming about London," I reply. "But when we were in London I knew it had happened before, when we were teenagers. And here's the thing: both times it was an accident, and in London, at least, it happened fast, probably the very first time we slept together, even though we were careful."

His wariness turns to open-jawed shock faster than I ever could have imagined. "A teenager's version of 'careful' is probably very different from yours or mine," he says after a moment.

"Believe me, if we dated when I was a teenager I wouldn't have been capable of 'careful' with you." His gaze flickers to my mouth. "I'm not even sure I'm capable of it now."

I shake my head. "We were adults in London—you were doing your residency and I was in grad school. *And* I was on the pill there. It just didn't work. It's like we can't avoid getting pregnant no matter what we do."

"We must have done something wrong," he says. There is desperation in his voice.

I want to let him believe it, but I can't. I lived through London. I remember it in detail. We did nothing wrong. "So you're willing to believe in time travel but not that some kind of super fertility accompanies it? Dr. Grosbaum said I was a different *species*, remember?"

He scrubs a hand over his face. "I'm able to believe it but...I just don't know what the hell this is with us. It's not like anything I've ever experienced before."

The way he phrases it makes it sound like a bad thing, but at least he's not calling for the check. "In what way?"

"There's something going on here I don't understand," he says, leaning toward me. Beneath the table his hand squeezes mine. "I had this connection to you from the moment we met. That's easy enough to explain away... If we really had these other lives together, it makes sense to me that the connection would remain. But it's more than that. It's not about our past lives or our present one. It's like we're both being led toward something."

Another piece of the puzzle clicks into place. I hadn't thought about it consciously, but I know exactly what he means. "There's some purpose to all of this."

"Yes," he says. "And it really bothers me that we don't know what it is."

It bothers me too. And thanks to this brain tumor, I'm not sure we'll get a chance to figure it out.

WHEN DINNER ENDS he drives me back to Caroline's, which I guess means my roommate's long list of places where I could potentially show him my bra won't be coming into play, not that I expected they would.

We walk into the building slowly. He stops when we reach her door and hesitates. *Is he even scared to kiss me now?* He leans down, his mouth brushing mine, but there's a tension in him I haven't felt before. It's not until my mouth opens under his, that he finally gives in to it, his kiss harder, needier. The hands that kept their distance land heavily on my hips and my back is pressed to the door as we strain for more friction, more closeness. His mouth moves to my neck, tugging at the skin in a way that makes me gasp. The bulge, currently pressed to my abdomen, seems to pulse with need, and his hand slides under my dress, slips beneath the elastic of my thong. I'm already soaked, gasping at the briefest touch, and he groans above me.

"God I want…" he begins, and suddenly he pushes away with something close to panic on his face. "Sorry," he says, running a hand through his hair. "*Fuck.*"

I stare at him, dizzied by the change of direction, longing for him to come back and resume what he was doing seconds before. "What's wrong?"

His tongue pokes out between his lips and then he shakes his head. "Nothing. I'll see you tomorrow?"

I nod, bewildered, as he presses a kiss to my forehead and waits for me to unlock the door. What the hell just happened? And what did I do wrong?

"YOU LOOK DAZED," Caroline says with a grin as I stumble into the apartment. "He must have done something right."

I lean against the door. "He didn't do anything at all."

"What are you talking about?"

It just ended so abruptly. After all the build-up between us over these long weeks, how could he just walk away like that? "I'm saying he walked me to your door, kissed me, then apologized and *left*."

She is outraged. "Why the fuck did he apologize?"

I huff in frustration, slumping into the chair across from her. "Exactly. I don't get it."

"And you're sure he's single?" she asks. "Because this exact thing happened to me with that douche Eric. Remember him? He told me he was single and then he was all weird about it during sex and it turned out he was fucking *engaged*."

I close my eyes. "Yes, I'm sure he's single."

"Maybe he's visiting here from the Victorian age, where you only kiss a woman you're engaged to?"

I laugh, the sound stilted and uncertain. It's a little unnerving to hear time-travel jokes under the circumstances. "I am going to go out on a limb and say I don't think that's it."

"Then what was it?"

I'd assume it was just what I told him about my possible super-fertility, but it's not like we were going to get pregnant *kissing*. And why apologize? I was embarrassingly wet, which he seemed to like well enough for a second but, God, who even knows? I've only ever been with Jeff. I know nothing about what men like. "You know how inexperienced I am. Maybe I'm just...bad at it?"

"If this is your way to get me into *Cruel Intentions*-style girl-on-girl action, you need to say so outright."

I laugh, and this time it's a real one. "Fuck off. You know what I mean."

She throws a pillow at me. "I know what you mean and you're being an idiot. You kissed plenty of guys while we were in school and there were never any complaints. Maybe he's just old-fashioned."

He didn't used to be, I think to myself. I have a very distinct memory of waking up beside him after our first date. And maybe that's the issue—those other times he didn't know where sex with me would lead, and there was nothing at stake. This time, he's risking his career to enter a relationship that may never get past third base. If he changes his mind, I'm not sure I could even fault him for it.

3

NICK

I feel like there's a target on my back.

I can tell by the lingering looks as I pass the nurses' station, the conversations that stop when I walk up, that Meg has been talking, and I'm guessing she didn't leave out the fact that I'm now dating a patient. This is definitely going to get back to the administration and when it does, things will get complicated.

The conversation with Quinn last night is never far from my head either. Her words replay again and again, like clues that are out of order or missing some key piece.

There's some purpose to all this.

It's like we can't avoid getting pregnant no matter what we do.

You're willing to believe in time travel but not that some kind of super fertility accompanies it?

Regardless of how many times I think about it, though, it doesn't come together. She's been with Jeff for years and managed not to get pregnant. What is it about *us*?

Jace is waiting when I return to my office. "Lunch?" he asks, in a way that sounds more like a demand. I guess he's heard about Quinn too. He's one of my oldest friends and it's going to all come out sooner or later, but there's no way he's going to be okay with me dating a patient. Especially a dying one.

We go up the road from the hospital to a sandwich shop we used to frequent when we were in med school. The place is as packed as it ever was. "I'm starting to remember why we stopped coming here," I tell him after a woman with a stroller runs over my foot.

He frowns. "I figured this is a conversation that should be held outside the hospital." I hear condemnation in those words. Jace is not a guy who's grave all that often, but he sure as shit is right now.

He waits until we're sliding into a booth before he shakes his head and looks directly at me. "Okay let's hear it."

I lean my head back against the seat with a sigh. "Sounds like you already have."

"What I've heard is that you were cheating on Meg with a dying patient," Jace says. "I'm hoping your version makes you look a little better."

Fuck. Meg is making sure everyone hears the absolute worst version of this story. I should have expected it, but it's still a blow. "I broke up with Meg before anything happened."

"Yeah," he says, arching a brow, "it wasn't the timing of it that bothered me. Are you really fucking a terminal patient? Seriously?"

My eyes close. The lie is necessary, even with Jace. "It's not as bad as it sounds. We dated in college and lost touch until she came to the hospital."

"Dude," Jace groans. "It still looks bad. You should have transferred the case. She's dying and you're her doctor, which makes you a port in the storm. It's fucking wrong to sleep with her even if she's willing."

I blow out a breath. He's not saying anything I haven't said to myself a thousand times. The guilt I thought I'd moved past comes tearing back. "I didn't transfer her because I don't trust anyone else to take care of her. And I know what you're saying and all I can tell you is that this is different." If I could utter the term *soul mate* without sounding like a complete pussy I would. Unfortunately, that's not possible.

"Let's say you're right. Let's say you're her everything and she's yours and this was written in the fucking stars. The girl's still going to die, Nick. You're putting your professional reputation in serious jeopardy for a relationship that can't go anywhere."

My anger is probably more at the situation than him, but it's a struggle to rein it in. "I don't need a lecture. And if you learned Julie was dying would you just take off?"

"Of course not," says Jace, "but Julie's my *wife*. This is some girl from college you forgot about."

"I never forgot about her. Not really," I tell him. "And it's different with her. Night and day." I wish I could explain what it's like—that it feels like a compulsion, that I feel out of control around her in ways I never have before—but it wouldn't exactly help my case.

"Of course it's fucking different. Sex with someone new is always going to be more exciting, but that doesn't mean you're meant to be with her."

My shoulders sag at the introduction of yet another sore subject. "I haven't even slept with her yet."

Jace's eyes widen. "You're risking your career for someone you're not even sleeping with? Dude...really?"

"Which one is it?" I snap. "Is your problem with the fact that we're together at all, or is it that I'm not sleeping with her?"

He sighs. "Neither. Both. Look, before this goes any further I just hope you really give it some thought. She's relying on you to save her life, so you may be really into this girl, but you need to ask yourself why she's really with *you*."

ASK yourself why she's really with you.

I gnaw on that phrase the whole way back to my office. It's not that I actually doubt Quinn is with me for the right reasons. Our connection was there long before she needed to worry about the tumor. But if there's really some greater purpose to our union, why *me*? She has a super power, even if she doesn't use it. But I'm a normal guy. Why would nature or God or whoever is orchestrating this need me involved too? If her purpose is to change the world or stop some terrible evil from happening, shouldn't it be fucking Superman by her side? She definitely needs someone who can do more than diagnose neurological disorders and swim a fast 400. But it is me, and I feel certain there must be a reason for that. I've just got no clue what it is.

"Reilly," barks a voice. I turn to find Ed Philbin, the head of the department, coming up behind me quickly. "We need to have a chat."

I thought I had a few weeks to get this figured out. Apparently not.

"Hey Ed," I say, turning toward him reluctantly. "What's up?"

"There've been some rumors going around," he begins and my stomach sinks. "Heard you're single now."

My tongue pokes at the inside of my cheek. I'm not sure if he's leading up to my relationship with Quinn or hoping I'll cop to it myself. I shrug. "Not exactly. I just started seeing someone. Why do you ask?"

His gaze is steady. It could be his gaze is always steady, or it could be he's trying to hint that he knows more about the situation than he's letting on. "We have our rec league basketball playoffs Friday. Could use your help." Ed's asked me about this more times than I can count, I suppose because I'm four inches taller than anyone on the team. But this time it feels different—it feels a bit like a quid pro quo: *you scratch my back and I'll scratch yours.* I'll come help them out, and he won't look too closely at the rumors.

Which means I really don't have a choice.

4

QUINN

I rise, trying to put Caroline's ridiculous doubts from last night out of my head. She left a note this morning that she was "plotting" to get me laid on tonight's date with Nick. Her goal is over-ambitious, obviously, but I'd settle for a kiss that doesn't end in an apology.

I walk down the street to get a bagel. Maybe there are some imperfect things in my life at the moment, but I'm out and about on a Wednesday morning without a single responsibility and it's hard not to feel pretty good. Nick texts as I walk, making my heart take another small leap. The mere sight of his name stirs something giddy and ebullient in my chest. I've heard other girls describe this phenomenon, but it's a first for me. All he's said is *good morning* and I want to break into a song and dance number right here on P Street. Maybe he's freaked out about the pregnancy thing but he's still texting me. It's got to mean something.

Nick: Any dreams last night?

Me: I'm not sure it's something I should be putting in a text while you're at work.

Nick: Okay, I absolutely need to know right now. Were we naked?

Me: It would take all the fun out of it if I told you that.

Nick: I had some dreams too. I have no problem telling you we were naked. We'll compare notes tonight.

Not the response of a guy who isn't interested. I'm smiling as I walk into the lobby, so unaware of anything but my own happiness that I don't even notice Jeff until he's standing right in front of my face.

He's unshaven, wearing jeans and a T-shirt instead of work clothes. I've been letting his calls go to voicemail, so I suppose I owe him a discussion of some kind—I just really don't want one.

His face is tight, a vein throbbing in his temple. "Can we talk?" He glances toward the front desk. "In private?"

A week ago, I wouldn't have hesitated to be alone with him. But I don't know the person who stands in front of me, looking like he wants to put his fist through the wall. I don't know the guy who called so many times he filled up my voicemail twice. And I haven't mentioned it to Nick, but this is also the guy whose messages have grown increasingly furious. He's said things on my voicemail I never dreamed I'd hear him say. I know people can behave badly when they're wounded, but listening to those messages makes me feel like I never really knew him at all. "We're good here."

His jaw drops. "You were ready to marry me four days ago and now I'm some kind of deviant you can't be alone with?"

In the last voicemail he left, he called me a lying bitch. I'm not feeling any guilt about refusing to be alone with him. "I never said that. But given how you've been acting, I'd prefer to discuss this in a place where I have the option to walk away."

He blows out a breath and folds his arms across his chest. "How *I've* been acting?" he demands. "Are you fucking serious right now? You dumped me at the airport after more than six years together and won't even pick up the phone."

"Think about what you've said on my voicemail. Can you blame me?"

"I just want an answer. I just want to know how you go from being perfectly happy with someone you're about to marry to miserable overnight?"

I raise my eyes to his, and though I'm stunned by how badly he's reacted to our break-up, I still wince at what I'm about to say next. "That's just it, though. We weren't perfectly happy."

He narrows his eyes. "Don't you dare say *we* because you don't get to speak for me. I was fine."

I sigh. Jeff always was a bit oblivious about things, so it shouldn't come as a surprise that he's oblivious here too. "You learned I had a fatal illness, and you continued on with your job like nothing had changed." It's strange to me now that I didn't see how wrong it all was, but that was before I knew what it was like to be with the *right* person. The one you can't live without. It's so clear to me now how different Jeff should have been, because I see how Nick *would* have been in his shoes. "I'm not faulting you for it. But the point is this: when the person you are supposed to love above all others tells you news like that, you stop worrying about whether the suppliers in Ithaca are going to meet their shipping deadlines."

"So that's what this is? You're punishing me for leaving? For trying to support us both?"

I feel the tiniest spark of irritation at *trying to support us both*, as if I didn't work too, but I force myself to let it go. "I'm saying that if you felt the right way about me, you would not have been willing to leave. Knowing I'm dying...it's just put a lot of things in perspective. And we're one of those things."

"Your father begged me to take care of you," Jeff says. "You know that? When he was dying he begged me to make sure you were safe. And I know he spoke to you too. It was his final wish. Doesn't that mean anything to you?"

Will the guilt over that ever go away? Until it does I just have to pretend it isn't there. "The two of us together is nothing he'd have wished for before he got sick. So no, I'm not going to let that be the thing I base my future on."

His whole body softens as he changes tack. He reaches out to grasp my arms and it's a struggle not to shrug him off. "Can we go to dinner tonight, hon? Just to talk. We can go to Zatinya. You always wanted to try it."

The suggestion makes me long to roll my eyes. I begged him to go there for six years, but suddenly he's someone who cares about what I want? "No," I reply. "I don't want to go to dinner. You aren't going to change my mind. Please just let this go."

"Never," he says. "I made your father a promise. And I intend to see it through."

My stomach drops. Now that it's over, I just want to be done with him, and the look on his face tells me I won't be for a good long time.

THAT AFTERNOON, Caroline and Trevor walk in carrying garment bags. "We're here to play fairy godmother," says Caroline.

"Unless you think he's gay," says Trevor. "In which case, you can play fairy godmother to me. *Literal* fairy godmother."

Caroline slings the hanger of her bag over the closet door. "Shut up, Trevor," she says. "You know he's not gay."

He hands her his garment bag and pulls a blind down to keep the bright afternoon sun out of his face. "Maybe it wasn't lust like we thought. She's beautiful. Maybe he's just fascinated by her the way I am with that Renoir at the National Gallery of

Art. I could stare at it for hours but I don't want to put my dick in it."

"You're making me feel worse," I tell him.

He sits beside me and pats my leg. "You know I'm just kidding. I promise he wants to put his dick in you."

I laugh and rest my head on his shoulder. "That's sweet. Thank you."

He gets out his phone and I hear the ping of a text arrive on my phone and Caroline's a moment later. "I'm sending you both the deets on my date tonight, by the way. He looks like a criminal."

"Which is your type," I add.

"Yes. But it also means he's slightly more likely to kill me after sex than Nick is likely to kill you after sex," he replies. "Perhaps because *you're* less likely to have sex in the first place. Anyway, if I don't turn up at work tomorrow, avenge my death."

I lean back on the other end of the couch. "You do realize we're the most ill-equipped people ever to avenge you if something goes wrong?" I ask. "I've never hit anyone in my life. And Caroline talks a good game but she'd mostly be worried about protecting her designer shoes if there were an altercation." Caroline ignores this, unzipping the garment bags with a reverence normally reserved for the Mona Lisa and religious artifacts.

"You're right about Caroline," he agrees. "But *you've* got hidden scrappiness. Like Jennifer Garner in *Peppermint*. One day you're just plain old Quinn and then some senator will kill me to cover up our affair and it brings out your inner badass. Next thing you know you're walking down the street with a loaded shotgun."

"So just to be clear, you're saying that when you are killed, you want me to engage in maybe a year of martial arts and weapons training, and then go kill a US senator?"

"Okay," says Caroline, clapping her hands to get our attention. "Enough irrelevant chitchat. Trevor is likely to die on one of these dates and neither of us plan to lift a finger because it's his fault for choosing criminals." She looks at the outfits she's pulled out and hands me a jumpsuit. "Try this first. It's perfect."

I gnaw on my lip, taking it in. It's sweet that she wants to help but I'm a pretty conservative girl, nude sunbathing aside. And this is not a conservative jumpsuit. The whole back is bare, and I'm not sure it wouldn't give a complete view of my breasts in profile either. "It looks, um, *revealing*. It's basically an apron."

Her eyes roll. "Maybe the problem isn't *him* after all, Virgin Mary. Go try it on."

I stick my tongue out at her but take the jumpsuit, my hand brushing over the heavy, luxurious fabric almost against my will. It looks expensive. It even feels expensive. I go into the bathroom and slip it on. It shows as much skin as I thought. And yet, as always, I feel glamorous in a way I never do when I dress myself.

"Stop overthinking it and come out here!" Caroline shouts.

Warily I emerge. "It shows too much side boob. And I won't be able to wear a bra with it."

"Isn't that the *point*?" asks Trevor.

"I want him to *want* to see my boobs," I argue. "I'm not trying to expose myself to him against his will."

"We'll use double-sided tape on the outside to make sure there's no nipple reveal, but let's let him have a tiny hint of side boob," says Caroline. "Men go nuts for that. It reminds them of being horny teenagers desperate to see a hint of cleavage."

Once I'm dressed, the two of them take over my hair and makeup, and when it's all done, they've given me red lips and what *appears* to be naturally glowing, bronzed skin. "If he can resist you looking like that," says Trevor, "then I really *am* going to take a shot at him."

～

I'M STILL SO unnerved by Jeff's visit that I make up an excuse to meet Nick out rather than having him pick me up. I Uber to the address he gave me, experiencing a moment of shock when I discover it's a hotel before someone points toward the bar on its roof. I take the elevator up way too many floors and emerge to a panoramic view of D.C., along with an even better view—Nick standing in a ray of sunlight, looking slightly too godlike to be real. He's in a white button-down and jeans, a head taller than any other guy here, not noticing that half the wait staff is looking him up and down like something they plan to divide and consume in its entirety.

He glances in my direction as I begin to walk toward him, and when I see that look in his eyes—surprise, followed quickly by joy and something far more carnal—I forget all my earlier angst. This is Nick. We've somehow come together no matter how many times we were separated. He's not going to let a little thing like excessive fertility get in our way.

"Hi," I say, sounding a little breathless. I go on my toes to kiss his cheek, and he pulls me close, wrapping his entire arm around my back, his mouth to my ear.

"You're killing me," he groans. "You know that, right?"

I gaze up at him. "Is that a good thing or bad?"

His gaze flickers over the low V of my top, catches there for a moment, and he flinches. "Both," he says, wrapping an arm around my waist as we walk toward the hostess stand. "I got us one of the private areas."

I have no idea what he's talking about but at the moment I'm pretty content just to be plastered to his side. He speaks to the hostess and she leads us through a door at the north side of the bar, and onto a terrace with a vine-covered trellis on either side and an amazing, unimpeded view of D.C. from the front.

She takes our orders and points to a button on the table. "If you need anything else, just hit this," she tells us, and then she leaves, shutting the door behind her.

My eyebrows go nearly to my hairline. "What *is* this?"

He gives me a sheepish smile, complete with dimple. I want to eat him alive because of that smile alone. "It's just one of those bullshit VIP things so we don't have to fight for space out there." His hand wraps around my hip and he pulls me closer. "Which enables me to do this." He leans down, grazing my lips with his, holding them there a moment. My eyes flutter closed. I don't want him to stop. *Please, please don't stop.*

His hand releases my waist and his fingers twine with mine. "Let's sit."

Restraining a sigh, I follow him to the couch, curling up in one corner of the loveseat while he sits beside me. Off to the west I see the Pentagon and feel something sink inside my chest, the way it always does. 9/11 was one of those days, one of those days I knew what would happen before it did. When I saw footage of the first plane hitting, I *knew*. I knew more planes would hit. It was on the tip of my tongue to say it aloud, but I took one look at my mother and closed my mouth. I was all too familiar with the way she would look at me for weeks if I was proven correct...as if she was scared of me. And while no one would have listened to the premonitions of a ten-year-old, the fact that I stayed silent has always made me feel complicit somehow.

"Everything okay?" he asks.

I'm tempted to tell him the story, but that old fear creeps into my throat. I never want him to look at me the way my mother did. I smile. "Of course."

He rubs the back of his neck, a gesture I find unbelievably hot for some unknown reason. "Why did you insist on meeting me here instead of letting me pick you up?" he asks.

I hold my breath for a moment, trying to come up with a plausible excuse. I can't claim I didn't want him to go out of his way...he only lives a few blocks from Caroline. My breath releases. I don't want to lie. "I went to get a bagel this morning.

Jeff was waiting in the lobby this morning when I got in. I was worried he'd come back."

His eyes widen. "And you really thought the solution was to not have me there if it happened?"

The waitress taps on the door at that moment and delivers our drinks. I wait until she's gone before I answer. "I don't want you to get into trouble for this. Jeff's...hurt. And angry. And he's not being rational. He's saying things on my voicemail I never imagined he was capable of saying. There's not a doubt in my mind he would try to create problems for you if he had a shred of proof."

He runs his hands through his hair, tugging at it. "I don't give a shit if Jeff creates problems. But I don't want you dealing with him by yourself."

I sort of love that Nick wants to protect me, but I'm not letting him get fired over this. "He's not violent," I reply. "He's just upset."

Nick's expression sours. "The last two times I saw him it nearly turned into a fist fight. So don't pretend he's not violent."

I smile and squeeze his hand. "And you were just as eager to fight him. Doesn't that make *you* violent by definition too?"

He laughs reluctantly. "No comment. But I want the truth about this stuff from now on, okay? And maybe you ought to share some of it with your mom, since she's still so convinced Jeff is perfect for you."

My mother's adoration of Jeff brings out the sullen teenager in Nick, which has me fighting a smile. "She just hasn't met *you* yet. Maybe she won't think my judgment is so impaired when she does." I wish I'd never asked her about time travel. Even when I left yesterday morning she was on the cusp of tears. "But that reminds me—I asked my mom if there were pictures of my aunt, the one who ran away when she was a teenager, and my mom said she doubted there were many because apparently Sarah was weird about having photos taken."

His brow furrows. "I'm not sure I'm following you. Lots of people don't want their photos taken. My mom will only get in front of a camera if she's got a full face of makeup and her hair is done."

"But remember Rose? I mean, didn't it strike you as weird... this 15-year old girl is hanging out with her favorite band but refuses to be photographed?"

"She was a total delinquent, Quinn," he argues. "She probably just didn't want her dad coming across it."

I lean forward. In the process of trying to convince him, I'm beginning to convince myself. "Think about it, though: why would a time traveler make a point of refusing to be in any photos? Because she doesn't want anyone finding her picture on two dates that are a hundred years apart. The safest thing to do would be to make sure you never leave a trail."

He takes a sip of his scotch, but I can tell he's pondering what I've said. "You might be right," he finally says, setting his drink down. "And if your aunt can actually time travel, then we need to find her. She might be able to tell us what to do. At least how to make the tumor stop growing."

I sigh heavily. "My mom's got no address for her, and I'm not sure looking up *Sarah Stewart* and *France* is going to yield a lot of useful results. I don't even know what city she's in."

"Your dad must have an address for her somewhere. Do you guys still have his old files?"

My father had tons of files. Are we really going to be able to find her address in all of that mess? It seems unlikely, but we can't just not try. "Most of them are in storage. Everything's in storage, actually."

"Then we should go up there this weekend and take a look. I have to play in this fucking basketball game on Friday, but we could go up on Saturday morning and spend the night at the lake on the way home." He hesitates. "You'd have your own room," he adds.

I frown. Any other guy would be capitalizing on the situation, and he's doing the opposite. He sure didn't seem this reluctant Sunday night in the back of his car. "We don't need separate rooms," I say quietly. I'm blushing, unable to meet his eye, as I utter the words.

"Yeah," he says, his voice hard. "I think we do."

I'm humiliated and annoyed at the same time. We're adults. I shouldn't feel like a slut for suggesting we stay in the same room. I slap a palm to my face in frustration. "What the hell is going on, Nick?" I ask. "You apologize for kissing me last night like it was a mistake and now you're acting like we're just...*buddies.*"

He laughs unhappily, which just frustrates me even more. "You think I don't want more? I want *more* so badly I'd cut off a limb to get it."

Then take it! I want to scream. Even if we don't have sex there are plenty of other options. "So what exactly is the problem?" I ask.

He sighs and clasps his hands in front of him. "Look, the truth is I'm worried I'm going to take it too far."

My brow furrows. "Take *what* too far?"

"You *cannot* get pregnant right now, Quinn. We can't risk anything exacerbating the tumor."

I'm blushing all the way to my ears but desperation drives me to persist. "There are lots of things besides intercourse."

I hear a groan stifled low in his chest. "I'm aware. But when I kiss you, I want so much more I stop thinking rationally. And if we're doing all the other things you're referencing, my guess is I'll stop thinking at all. At some point, it's going to lead to sex. It just is. We...need a plan."

"A plan?" I ask with a small smile. "I could put a note on my forehead that says 'don't fuck Quinn'?"

His teeth slide over his lower lip and he blows out a breath. "Even hearing you say the word *fuck* sends my mind down a bad path. Where I start rationalizing things. It feels predatory."

"Nick," I say, my eyes slowly raising to his. "I'm okay with predatory."

He inhales sharply, leaning his head against the back of the loveseat and squeezing his eyes shut.

"What—"

Before I can finish the sentence, he is pulling me over him, my legs on either side of his. His hands grip my hips, pull me down so that I'm flush against him. "Do you feel that?"

I nod. I couldn't miss *that*. It feels like he's got an extra limb pulsing between my legs.

The fingers of one hand slide through my hair, gripping it at the root. He does nothing more, but his eyes are on my mouth, dark and hungry in a way they weren't a moment before. His other hand curves around the side of my neck, his palm rough against the soft skin, drawing goose bumps to the surface. "You have no idea what you're saying when you tell me to be predatory, Quinn. Every bone in my body tells me to take from you until there's nothing left. So we need a plan."

I stop holding my weight and sink against him, leaving him pressed right where I want him, with no distance between us. A shudder begins in my center, radiating outward, and he pulls my mouth to his in a way that turns me wet and loose and desperate. I want more but before I can demand it of him, he demands it of me, groaning as his mouth opens, as his free hand cups my ass, squeezing it tight until he is all I can feel.

That hand moves straight to the bare skin on the side of the jumpsuit, as if it's a destination he's been thinking of for a very long time.

"Jesus Christ, this thing nearly killed me when you walked in," he grunts, his mouth moving over my neck. His index finger slides under the side, the tape there giving way easily, as if it were made of air. That finger brushes against the soft skin at the base of my breast then moves up, up, finding my nipple, which immediately grows so hard it hurts.

"Fuck," he groans. His hand slides free only to push the straps of the jumpsuit down, leaving me bare all the way to my rib cage. "You have no idea how badly I've wanted—"

His words are cut off by a quick tap at the door. There's only a moment for me to jump off his lap and pull at my jumpsuit before the waitress pokes her head in. Since our lower halves are blocked by the back of the couch, she can't see Nick's skyscraper-sized erection, but her eyes flicker to the one strap of my outfit that still hangs off my shoulder. "You hit the buzzer?" she asks.

"We did?" I glance at the table, realizing even as I ask that when his hand slid inside my top, my toes curled right along the table's edge. "Sorry. I think it was an accident."

"Do you want another round?"

I shake my head, thinking I need her gone as soon as possible, and also permanently, but Nick says yes.

When she leaves, he presses the base of each palm over his eyes. "Jesus Christ. We need a fucking chaperone."

My stomach sinks a little. That is not the direction I thought he'd go once we got rid of the waitress. "We apparently have very different views of what just happened."

"I just tried to undress you in a public place, Quinn." He waves his hand at buildings in the distance. "Anyone could have seen you."

I shrug. "They'd need binoculars to get a good view. If anyone wants to work that hard to see me half-naked, they've earned it."

He gives me a dark look. "No one but me gets to see what's under that outfit. No one." His bossy tone makes the blood in my veins hum, plucks that sharp note of desire at the base of my abdomen. I want to scale him like a rock wall.

I press my lips together. They feel raw, swollen from his kiss, and our eyes catch. "Don't look at me like that," he pleads.

"Why not?"

"First of all because I need this hard-on to go away before the waitress returns," he says. I glance down. The skyscraper is still standing firm. "Second, because it makes me want to do a lot more than we did, and being with you sends common sense out the window. The second we start, there's a serious lack of restraint."

It's not a lack of restraint. It's an *absence* of it. The minute he touched me I stopped caring about anything but shedding his clothes, feeling him push inside me, watching his teeth sink into that perfect lower lip as he tries not to come.

"We don't need a plan," I tell him. "You're like someone who decides not to eat at all until he's figured out how he wants to lose weight. There's no way it can work because the hunger is going to build up until he snaps."

His mouth twitches. "So you're proposing the sexual equivalent of a healthy salad with grilled chicken, whatever that is."

"That makes it sound way less fun than it should be. It's more like I'm proposing we eat one piece of pizza instead of the whole pie."

He swallows, his eyes halting on my mouth. "You think we'll be able to stop at one piece?"

"I was thinking of many, many pieces spaced out in small increments," I whisper.

"Fuck," he growls, pulling me back into his lap. "Yes."

"So you agree?" I ask.

"No," he replies. "I'm just not good at turning down pizza."

5

QUINN

I s it a bad idea? Of course it is. It's the worst possible idea. If he's right about his lack of control and it goes too far at the lake, he'll never touch me again.

However, thanks to my own lack of control, I just want it too badly to say no.

I try to convince Nick to meet me away from Caroline's on Saturday morning. I've caught Jeff following me twice since Wednesday, and though it's unlikely he'd be waiting this early in the day, I just can't be sure. He's unraveling, turning into someone I don't recognize.

I haven't told Nick about the incidents because I suspect he'd react poorly. My suggestion to meet in a neutral location fell on deaf ears, but he'd have refused whether he knew about Jeff or not.

He's idling outside Caroline's building in his Jeep when I get to the street. I never dreamed I could feel so excited about going on a trip to comb through a storage unit, though if I'm being honest, most of my excitement is reserved for what will come *after* the storage unit.

"Holy shit," he says. "If I haven't mentioned it before, you look really good in shorts."

"I'm a student now," I remind him. "Well, almost. Time to start dressing like one."

His eyes flicker over my legs. "I'd never have made it through college or medical school if you'd been back at my apartment dressed like that."

Immediately, I'm picturing it, all the things he might have done to me back then if our lives had gone differently. I lean over the console to brush my mouth against his. "If I'd been back at your apartment," I say low against his ear, "I'd probably have been naked."

"Fuck," he says with a heavy exhale, pulling onto the road, "you just guaranteed I will be thinking about you naked this entire drive, no matter what we're discussing."

"Current affairs?"

"Nope, still seeing you naked."

"Hmmm. Small children attending their first carnival?"

"At the risk of sounding creepy, I'm still thinking about you naked."

I eye the bulge in his shorts. "I like you thinking about me naked."

He raises a brow. "We need to change the topic," he says. "Or separate rooms isn't going to be enough to keep me away from you."

The idea of sharing a bed with him warms something inside me. Even if we never even touch. "We don't actually have to sleep in separate rooms you know," I tell him. "I trust you. And I trust myself, more or less."

"You shouldn't," he says.

I turn to face him. "I shouldn't trust myself or I shouldn't trust you?"

He glances over quickly before his eyes return to the road. "Either. There's something I never told you about that night in Baltimore."

Baltimore. A night in a hotel, in separate beds. Where I woke up in his and he woke up in mine. "Tell me," I whisper, trying to hold my dread at bay.

"We came extremely close to sleeping together," he says quietly.

My breathing comes to a halt. "*What?*"

"We were both asleep," he says hurriedly. "I was dreaming about you. It's *only* because something about it didn't make sense that I woke. And when my eyes opened you were sound asleep in my bed and we were seconds from having sex."

The idea that I fall asleep and dream about things that happened in another life is bad enough. The idea of falling asleep and actually doing things I don't remember—in this or any life—chills me to the bone. I dreamed about him that night. I dreamed I was the aggressor, the one who pushed him into the back seat of his parents' car and had my way with him, sort of. Was I dreaming or was I actually acting it out in real life? I press my hands to my face. "Oh my God."

His hand leaves the steering wheel and finds mine, giving it a reassuring squeeze. "I'm sorry. I probably should have told you, but I was just worried you'd feel guilty. And I guess if I'm being honest, I didn't know whether you'd blame me, or avoid me afterward."

I release a long breath, thinking of how badly that might have gone. The possibility that I could have gotten pregnant, obviously, but also...if I'd known it had happened, I'd have stayed a mile from him. There would have been no dance at the harbor, no talk in his office, no visit to the lake. I would have allowed my own guilt and shame and fear of him to lead me to all the wrong decisions. "Thank God you didn't. I think I'd have wound up married to Jeff, solely out of guilt, if you had."

His hand tightens around mine. "But that's why I think we need separate rooms. It's too out of control with us anyway, and if it can happen when we don't even know it's happening..." He takes another glance at my bare legs. "Yeah. You definitely need your own room."

I can't argue with him. And it's not even for my protection— it's for his. He's so worried about being predatory, but I'm no longer sure he's the one we should be worried about.

IT TAKES a little over two hours to get to the small town where I grew up. I point out the road to the farm as we pass. I have good memories of my childhood there, but the bad memories are enough to kill any nostalgia I might feel.

"I guess your mom is no longer there?" he asks.

"God no," I reply.

"Why so adamant?" he asks.

For a moment my pulse begins to trip and sputter, as I contemplate telling him the truth of what happened, but it's too engrained, this habit of keeping those secrets to myself.

"Farms are a lot of work. Although the storage-unit pass-code is our farm address so maybe she didn't hate everything." I inhale deeply. "Shit. I hope she didn't change the code."

He frowns. "Can't you just call and ask her for the new one?"

I take another deep breath. "No, because then she's going to want to see me, which means she'll see *you*."

"You're doing wonders for my ego here."

"You expect me to believe a super-hot neurologist who's also a former college athlete could get his ego damaged over *that*?"

He laughs. "It might take one or two more serious blows, but you do intend to introduce me to her at some point, right?"

I smile at him. It sort of thrills me to see *my* super-hot neurologist so adamant about meeting my mother. "Of course. Just not one week after I cancelled my wedding. Turn here."

He follows the direction of my hand and we pull up to the storage facility, me breathing a quiet sigh of relief when the code works. Nick lifts the rolling door and flips on the light... where we discover wall-to-wall boxes. My shoulders sag. "I moved most of these in here myself, but I forgot how bad it was."

He shrugs. "At least they're labeled." His face lights up as he grabs a box that says *Quinn Photos* on it. "I think we should start here."

"The sooner we get out of here, the sooner we get to the lake," I remind him.

"Right as always," he says, putting the box back where he got it. In the end I have him retrieve a box labeled *Photo Albums* and two boxes labeled *Files*.

I flip through the photo album of my father's family. There are pictures of my father and Sarah as toddlers, two towheaded babies with sunny smiles. And then nothing.

"Nick, look at this," I tell him, drawing him away from the files. "There are pictures of Sarah as a baby and a toddler, but then they just stop." His eyes follow mine to the remaining pages, which feature only my father, as if Sarah never existed. His life is documented thoroughly...each birthday party, his high school graduation and wedding.

But nowhere in the entire book is there a picture of Sarah past her babyhood. Nick releases a slow breath. "Okay, yeah, that's pretty weird."

I glance over at the stack of papers he's set on the floor. "How's it going with the files? You find anything?"

He shrugs. "Well, I've discovered that your parents have saved their tax returns going back to 1980, which seems a little paranoid. But I did find this," he says, handing me a file, labeled *Quinn, Psychologist Reports*. "I didn't look."

I hesitate and then hand him a sheaf of papers from it while I take the other. "I'm not too worried about you discovering my innermost thoughts when I was five."

I read through the first few pages of mine. It's mostly background and psychobabble about tests they performed. It angers me more than anything else. My parents didn't have two pennies to rub together during most of my childhood. Yet I'm sure this psychologist had no problem insisting I needed a bunch of irrelevant tests. My IQ? A cognitive-motor assessment? How could these things possibly have made a difference?

"Holy shit," whispers Nick.

My heart thumps hard in my chest. "What?"

He's still staring at the paper. "You really did remember everything." His voice is empty with shock. "You told them my name and that I was a doctor. You told them our address in London. You told them I swim. My name is all over this, and not in some vague way. I can *tell* it's me."

I still. Waiting for the look, the one I saw all through childhood. When these things happened, my mother would grow purposefully quiet, trying to hide her fear, and her eyes wouldn't meet mine for weeks afterward. But when he finally turns to glance up at me, his eyes are gentle, awed. "It's fucking amazing," he says.

The relief is so sweet and sharp, I have to look away from him, worried I might cry.

He continues to read, whipping through pages as if it's the most fascinating thriller ever created, and I return to mine, skipping ahead to the final few pages—a transcript of what appears to be my last session.

Patient was asked to draw a picture of her family, it says. *Unlike previous drawings, "Nick" is excluded.*

JC: Can you tell me who these people are?

QS: *That's Mommy and Daddy and me. And that's Cocoa (dog).*
JC: *You didn't draw Nick this time. How come?*
QS: *Nick can't be part of my family. (Patient evidences notable sadness at this statement.)*
JC: *Why can't Nick be a part of your family?*
5-sec delay.
QS: *Because Nick is going to make me do a bad thing.*
JC: *What kind of bad thing?*
Patient hesitates again, is uncomfortable.
QS: *I can't tell you.*
JC: *Did Nick ask you not to tell?*
QS: *Nick doesn't even know it's going to happen.*
JC: *Can you tell me more about this bad thing he's going to make you do?*
Patient begins to cry.
QS: *I can't. But it's very, very bad.*

Ice slips down my throat, fills my chest. It's impossible. I must have gotten something wrong. Nick would never, ever *make* me do something bad. Maybe I pictured sex and misinterpreted it. Except I told the doctor that Nick didn't even know it was going to happen.

Beside me he is still reading avidly. I take in his beautiful, bright face. I must have gotten something wrong.

He looks up. "Anything there?" he asks.

I slide the papers back into the folder. "No. All garbage."

WE LEAVE EMPTY-HANDED. Perhaps in one of the hundred boxes in that storage unit there exists a scrap of paper or an old envelope with Sarah's number on it, but we're never going to find it.

I wish hadn't gone, but Nick feels otherwise. He brings up the psychologist's report again and again.

"You even described your wedding ring," he says, glancing at me with those stunned eyes before they return to the road.

I hadn't remembered the ring at all until now, but the moment he mentions it, I can see it clearly. "It was your grandmother's," I tell him. "Don't ask me how I know that because I don't have a clue. This oval diamond with tiny diamonds all around it."

He frowns. "There's no ring as far as I know."

I grin at him. "Maybe the ring you gave me sucked so my imagination embellished things a little."

He gives me one long glance before his eyes return to the road. "The ring won't suck, I promise." My heart quickens and I swallow, uncertain if I'm thrilled or panicked by how serious we've gotten already. I suspect it's a little bit of both.

WE ARRIVE at the lake late in the afternoon. Nick's still insisting we sleep in different rooms, and after what he told me I don't have the heart to try to change his mind anymore. He shows me to the master bedroom so I can change into my suit—a red bikini, naturally. As I open my bag I notice a picture of Nick and Ryan as babies on a nightstand, and it makes my heart twist painfully. I miss Ryan and I barely remember him. How bad must it have been for Nick and his parents?

I change and head downstairs to find Nick standing just inside the pantry—and wearing nothing but swim trunks. My God. How much swimming does he *do*? Because I could swim twenty-four hours a day and not even approach a stomach like his. The brain tumor isn't what's going to get me in the end. It's *this*, trying to behave when Nick is shirtless.

"What are you doing?" I ask a little breathlessly.

He backs out of the pantry. "I thought we had more staples but—" His eyes sweep over me from head to foot. "Holy shit."

I grin. "It's not like you haven't seen it before. Sort of."

He coughs. "Let's just say the experience of the red bikini is a little different in person." He walks over to me but hesitates. I'm the one who bridges the distance, going on my toes to press my lips to his, waiting to feel his self-restraint lessen just a touch. When his hands grip my hips, pulling me tighter against him, the need for him sharpens—a pulse in my belly that is half pleasure and half pain. He breaks the kiss suddenly, breathing fast as he pushes a hand through his hair. "If you are going to make noises like that we will not get out of this house."

I'm dazed and desperate to continue. "I didn't make a noise," I argue weakly.

"Believe me. You made a noise." He blows out a breath. "Let me feed you before I take this in a very different direction."

I'm tempted to object, but lunch was hours ago and it's not going to hold us forever. I need to let him move at his own pace anyway. "So there's no food?"

"Yeah," he says. "My parents' housekeeper must have tossed the food I bought last weekend. I need to run over to the Captain's Market."

"I'll go with you," I tell him. "I have to call Jeff really quick but then—" His face falls and I put up a hand before he has time to object. "I have to. His mother texted twice today, begging me speak to him. He drove home yesterday, and it sounds like things are going poorly."

Nick's jaw hardens. "You don't owe them anything."

I wish I agreed with him. It would be such a relief just to wash my hands of the whole thing. Nick and I were meant to be. I just wish it hadn't left so many people damaged in its wake. "That's not true," I say softly. "Abby was there for me after my dad died. And Jeff was too. I...I do feel like I owe them this."

He sits on the counter, staring at the floor, his teeth grinding. "I can't tell you what to do," he says, a hard edge to his voice that wasn't there before. "But all these calls and these visits of his—he's not looking for you to *explain*. He's trying to bully you into coming back, and he'll use guilt and fear and anything else at his disposal to do it. He's gotten his way for a long time, just by playing on the fact that you were too nice to draw blood."

I think of the house in Manassas. The way Jeff returned to the topic again and again, trying to persuade me. Is this any different? "Maybe," I reply. "But I do still need to call."

"If he gives you shit," Nick warns. "Draw blood. Because if you don't, I will."

I WALK to the grassy hill leading down to the dock, taking a single deep breath before I hit Jeff's name on speed dial.

He answers immediately, and my stomach sinks a little. I guess I was hoping he might not answer at all. "Are you fucking kidding me?" he asks, in lieu of greeting. His words are over-loud, slightly slurred as if he's been drinking. "Six years together, our wedding invitations already out, and all I get is a two-second conversation in your lobby? That's all I deserve?"

No matter how much I wish it wouldn't, guilt is mounting inside me, a small shrill alarm in my blood that is only going to get louder. "I'm sorry," I begin. "I—"

"No," he cuts in. "It's not your turn to talk, it's mine. And this is some crazy fucking bullshit. You're going to tell me to my face you don't love me. Do you? Do you love me or was it all a fucking lie?"

I've never thought of Jeff as a bully before, not until Nick said it, but as Jeff unloads on me it's striking a chord. "I don't love you in the right way," I reply, each word meted out care-fully. "I care about you, but this isn't what I want."

"What, precisely, don't you want? Name one goddamn way in which I'm not what you want."

A voice inside me whispers *bully, bully, bully*. And it's not

Nick's voice, oddly enough, but my own...a voice I didn't know existed until this moment. "I—"

"Because everything I am I did for you. I moved to D.C. for you. I took this job for you. I gave up everything for you and you don't even appreciate it."

"I never asked you to do those things," I tell him. I didn't want him to do those things. I remember the sick resignation I felt when he showed up on my doorstep, telling me he'd gotten a job in D.C.

"You sure didn't complain about it, though, did you? You were more than happy to let me give up football and move from one shit job to the next, all so you could stay in D.C. So I want you to tell me what's so wrong with our life. What is suddenly, out of nowhere, so terrible you just can't stand to be with me anymore?"

I never asked you to give up football. If you hadn't moved to D.C., I'd have gone back to school. I wouldn't have gotten talked into a mortgage I wound up paying on my own most of the time, a mortgage that took school off the table entirely. All the things I thought during our worst moments but kept to myself...those words are bubbling in my throat, demanding to be released. But I've done him enough harm without that, so I force them back down. "Nothing is terrible," I tell him. "It's just not what I want."

"Then what *do* you want? Because I think you don't have a fucking clue. That brain tumor is making you crazy and you're the only one who doesn't see it."

I pushed everything down for so long, and when I finally act on my own behalf he tries to convince me I'm not sane? For some reason *this* is the last straw. "What I don't want," I hiss, "is someone who insists on moving to Manassas or back home when he knows I've got no desire to do either one, and who discourages me from following my dreams. I don't want to be with someone who talks over me in the hospital and tries to start a fight with my doctor. I don't want someone who suggests

I'm insane the second I speak up for myself. And you know what, Jeff? *No one* would want that. So instead of blaming the brain tumor, take a look in the mirror." The words tear out of me, with a thousand more behind them that I manage to keep to myself, and I don't feel scared, the way I thought I might. I feel strong.

"Do you hear yourself?" he demands. "Tell me you hear yourself, because this is not you, and if it's not the tumor I don't know what it is."

I laugh. It's his default, I realize. Blaming me, blaming my tumor, is way easier for him than accepting a shred of responsibility. "I can assure you it's me. You just might not recognize it because I haven't *been* me in a long time with you, if I ever was."

"Believe me," he snarls, "if it weren't for that tumor, you'd be humiliated by what an absolute cunt you're being right now."

I'm so stunned I nearly drop the phone. I've known him since I was a little kid, and I never dreamed he'd use that word, much less direct it at me. But it's freeing, seeing how low he will sink when he doesn't get his way. Any lingering guilt I felt releases into the air like a balloon. "You have no idea what a cunt I can be. Keep harassing me and you'll find out."

I hang up and turn to find Nick standing a few feet behind me with a shirt on and keys in hand, eyes narrowed to slits.

"Tell me he didn't just call you that," he says, his voice flat. It would be easy to mistake him for calm, but there's nothing calm about him right now.

"It doesn't matter."

His nostrils flare and his fist is clenched so tight I'm worried the keys are going to cut into his palm. "The fuck it doesn't."

"Believe me—if you intervened, it would just make things worse for everyone involved." My mouth twitches upward. "And I took care of it."

"Why are you smiling?" he demands. "Because I'm fucking

pissed."

I laugh and close the distance between us, wrapping my arms around his neck. "Did you hear me? I was kind of a badass for the first time in my life. I was feisty."

He grins reluctantly. "Yeah? And? Did you enjoy it?"

I go on my toes to press my mouth to his once, quickly, before I drop back to the ground. "Yeah, I really did."

He pulls me back to him. "Good," he says, his lips a whisper from my mine, "because I think seeing you feisty is unbelievably hot."

Desire spasms low in my stomach at the look on his face. "You might not like it so much when it's directed at you," I reply, my voice suddenly breathless.

His lips graze my temple, my cheek, the corner of my mouth. He teases me, avoiding them, moving down to my jaw and my throat. "I think I'm going to like that even more. But I'm going to fuck you until you can't climb out of bed afterward, so wait until that's an option."

I groan. The combination of his mouth on the side of my throat, and his words, and the image of him doing exactly what he said...I want it so badly I don't know how we're ever going to avoid it. "You can't say things like that." I feel *winded*. "Or I'm going to beg you to do it."

He is hard against me, and his hands now contain a tension on my hips they didn't have before. As if the rage that was boiling in his blood only moments ago has suddenly been channeled elsewhere. "Jesus. You have no idea how badly I want you to."

I vibrate with the need for more. His hand slides from my hip to my thigh, beneath the bikini bottom. His fingers glide over me, slip inside, and he groans low in his chest—a stifled, desperate sound. This isn't carefully planned like we'd intended, but it no longer matters. I can't be content with just his fingers. He could make me come ten times, just like this, and it still wouldn't be enough. My hands are at the button of his trunks, sliding them down even as he lowers me into the grass. On an open hillside, in daylight, for all the world to see, and it just doesn't matter.

He looms over me, his eyes heavy-lidded and hazy. He pulls my bottoms to the side and his cock rests between my legs. "Jesus, Quinn. You have no idea how hard it is not to push inside you right now." I want to beg him to do it. The need pulls every cord of my body tight, except there's a tiny voice in the back of my head, warning me. "We can't."

His mouth finds mine as he glides against me. The head of his cock bumps my entrance and I gasp—90 percent want and 10 percent fear. Our eyes lock. The strain of holding back is written in every line of his face. "We can't," I repeat, "but I just need...just don't stop."

He flinches and continues to glide against me, faster, harder. He unties the sides of my bottoms and pulls down the top before his lips fasten on one nipple, hard. "Faster," I plead, my legs wrapping around his back. He complies and the sight of him above, his face strained and desperate, unleashes something inside me.

I shatter without warning, crying out so loudly I can hear the sound echo down the hill, over the water. He jerks away and spills across my stomach. "Fuck," he growls. His eyes are squeezed shut, his jaw taut with the strain. We aren't even done and I already want more.

His eyes open slowly, still in a haze. "Jesus Christ. The last time I came from dry humping someone was the day I got my learner's permit."

He presses his mouth to my forehead and then pulls away, preoccupied and unhappy, only now glancing toward the lake to make sure we didn't have an audience. He hands me my bikini bottoms and pulls up his trunks, then strips off his T-shirt to wipe my stomach—all of it in complete silence. "That's exactly what I was talking about," he finally says, collapsing on the grass beside me. "If you'd told me to go for it, I would have. I'd halfway rationalized it before we hit the ground. If it was anything like this before, I understand how you wound up pregnant so fast."

Except I was on the pill in London, and it's worked without exception since I started dating Jeff. I assume Nick's managed not to impregnate anyone either—so what is it about the two of us together that causes the problem? And the woman I always see in my nightmare—is it a coincidence that she appeared in his office mere hours after the two of us got together?

Of course it isn't.

I can't believe I didn't see it sooner.

"It's not about us," I gasp, sitting up. "It's about the baby. In that dream I always have of us in the hospital? We're there because I'm delivering, and that's when she stops us. She doesn't want us to have the baby."

He sits up too, looking at me warily. "Why do you say that?"

"Neither of us have a single memory of me that goes past the point when I was pregnant, right? That's where our story ends both times. I remember feeling panicked in the hospital. Scared something bad was going to happen, even before she came in, and also desperate to get through it before she could stop us." I'm talking so fast I'm barely stopping to breathe. "She keeps changing aspects of my life so we don't meet at all. The first time we grew up together, were children together, and so she changed it. The second time we grew up apart but found each other in London, and she ended that too. But she doesn't care about the two of us being together. It's only when we get pregnant that she tries to change things."

Nick stares at the water, frowning, his expression grim. "It has to be related to the Rule of Threes, right? The baby must make the fourth in the line."

"Yeah. And you know what this means, right?" I ask. "If this is related to the Rule of Threes, this kid we have must be a time traveler. And for that to be the case, *you* have to carry the mutation as well. Which means it's just as likely to be someone in your family behind this as it is mine."

He cocks a smile. "She's not even your mother-in-law yet and you're already blaming shit on my mom." I'm so startled by that *yet*, as if it's a foregone conclusion, that my mind goes blank for a moment. Fortunately, he doesn't seem to notice. "I wondered what my role was in all this, why it's the two of us who keep being brought together, and I guess the mutation would explain it. But I don't have a lot of family either. I'm not seeing an obvious culprit anywhere. I can't picture my mother having some kind of supernatural power, and I don't have any sisters."

I pull my lip between my teeth. "You should probably ask her, though. Your mom, I mean."

He laughs. "You want me to ask my mom if she *time travels*? And I thought telling her I broke up with Meg was going to be the most awkward conversation I'd have with her anytime soon."

My gaze flickers to his face. "I guess she liked Meg, then? Is she going to be upset?" Her son *was* dating a beautiful doctor who will probably lead a long and healthy life. I'm not sure what exactly he got in exchange for that. His mother will probably blame me, and I won't be able to fault her for it.

His fingers slide through mine. "She's going to love you. It wasn't anything about Meg, necessarily. She just wants grandkids." He grins. "Believe me, if she had any idea how easily you can get pregnant and how badly I seem to want to do it, she'd be sending us upstairs to a bedroom right now."

Just the mere suggestion of it has me feeling needy and overheated. I lean back on my elbows, gazing up at him from beneath my lashes. "So, just out of curiosity, how badly do you want to do it?"

He groans. "Quinn, stop looking at me like that or I'm going to show you exactly how badly I want to, and I think we've both just realized how excruciatingly careful we need to be."

My tongue slides over my lower lip in anticipation. "Baby steps."

His eyes close and suddenly he's on his feet. "Fuck it," he says, grabbing my hand. "If we're going to take baby steps, we're going to start right fucking now."

WE GET TO HIS PARENTS' room. The moment he kisses me I start sinking into a darkness I don't want to come back from. I only know his mouth, his hands, the rasp of his five o'clock shadow against my skin and the sound of his sharp inhale. My bikini bottoms and his trunks are pushed to the floor and I'm not even sure how it happened.

He winces. "I'd like this to last longer than five seconds this time."

I would too. But there is absolutely nothing rational about us right now.

I step away from him and go to the bed, pulling down the covers before I lie on one side. "Come here."

He turns. It's my first real look at him completely unclothed, and the sight leaves me purring...and intimidated. He's so beautiful, but Trevor's guesses about the size of the *package* were absolutely on the mark, and something that size will be a novel experience for me if we ever get around to having sex.

He gets in on the other side of the bed and rolls to face me. My fingers tentatively press to the center of his chest and roll down an inch or two. "We were here before. Just like this," I tell him.

"Was it good?" he asks, his voice strained.

"What do you think?" I allow my hands to slide outward, to

the curves of his triceps, up to his perfect shoulders, over his clavicle. His eyes flutter closed and he swallows. There is nothing hotter to me than the way he is struggling for control. "Too much?" I ask.

He pulls me against him, where he is every bit as hard as he was earlier. "No," he says between his teeth, pressing his mouth to mine, his body taut with restraint. I want to dig my hands into his hair, wrap my leg over his hip, but I sense there's something so tightly coiled inside him it could snap with very little effort.

His hand skims the outside of my bikini top, which is the only shred of clothing still separating the two of us. "Too much?" he asks.

"No."

He swallows. "You need to tell me when it is." His fingers glide over my skin—up the curve of my hip to the dip in my waist, my body strung tight with anticipation. His hands span my rib cage. His index finger moves, drawing a smooth line up my breast until he reaches its tip, already hard, waiting for him. "I need to see you."

He unties the bikini. His eyes find their destination, and then he leans down, taking my nipple in his mouth—pulling with his teeth, soothing with his tongue—until I am flat on my back and gasping, arching fruitlessly for more. He moves his hand down my belly, slipping between my legs to find me slippery and ready for him, while I let my own hand wander, skimming that line of hair below his belly button. When my hand wraps around him, the air hisses between his teeth. "Jesus," he groans.

His fingers glide against me, infuriatingly slow. My grasp on him is harder, from his base to the tip, which leaks copiously enough that my palm slides easily, and faster.

"Fuck," he gasps, rolling me to my back, pulling at my knees so he can push between them.

"Nick," I whisper, and at the sound of his name his eyes open, hazy and unfocused. "Don't."

He gives me the smallest nod, as if some distant part of him has heard what I said. The pace of his hand between my legs quickens and we begin to kiss. No longer careful, but sloppy, voraciously.

"Oh God," I whisper. The moment I start to come he does too. And the world is still dark and full of stars but I already want more from him in a way I cannot explain. As if one orgasm was merely foreplay.

He supports his weight, still breathing heavily, before he finally flips onto his back, pulling me with him. "Jesus Christ," he says. "I told you it was going to be slow and I lasted about twenty seconds."

"As long as you keep your super sperm away from me, we'll be fine."

He grins. "You realize we were young and stupid those other times, right? God only knows what we were doing."

I raise a brow. "We weren't that young in London. And it sounds like someone's making excuses to do something he wants to do."

He laughs hard, as if relief and happiness have twined together. "There might be some of that going on." He climbs out of bed and grabs a towel, wiping my stomach off, and then he is back under the blankets, pulling me against him.

"You okay?" he asks, pressing his mouth to the top of my head.

"I'm so much better than okay."

"Me too," he says. "Although I think more baby steps might be necessary."

The mere suggestion of it is all I need. "How soon?" I ask, my hand sliding beneath the covers. Already he is coming back to life.

He groans. "Right now works."

～

HOURS LATER, the room is only illuminated by moonlight and I'm cuddled up against him. Sometime between the second orgasm and the seventh—we ordered a pizza in the hours between them—things changed between us. I've never felt more naked or vulnerable, but his faith in me is a solid thing at his very core. Nothing I say to him is met with fear or disdain. It feels like I don't have to be careful around him the way I did before, as if I finally know I'm safe.

"I lied to you," I whisper.

"You did?"

My tongue darts out, tapping my upper lip—one of a thousand nervous gestures left over from childhood. "Earlier today I told you my mom hated the farm because it was a lot of work, but that's not why she left." I hesitate. That old warning in my head echoes: *don't tell, don't tell, don't tell.* But I'm tired of keeping secrets, and he is not like my mother. There is nothing conditional in his acceptance of me. My heart is tumbling and tripping in my chest and yet I know this is going to be alright.

"I told you about the murders on the farm. It was awful, obviously, but what really upset my mom was—" I stop as fear begins to crawl in, replacing my newfound bravery.

His hand cradles the nape of my neck, slides into my hair. "It's okay, Quinn. Just tell me."

"She thought I had something to do with it," I whisper, raising my worried eyes to his.

He looks every bit as stunned as I imagined he would. But not scared. "*What?*"

My nails dig into my palms. It's the first time I've ever repeated this since it happened, something my parents made me swear I'd never tell.

"The morning after Jilly died, I came downstairs and told my parents I'd gone to her house in the middle of the night and tried to stop them from being murdered. My parents had no idea what I was talking about. I was insisting it was Thursday, and that Jilly had died the day before, but they showed me the calendar and I was wrong. It was still Wednesday, and they kept telling me Jilly was fine, that it was just a bad dream. But I kept insisting. I remembered all of it. The police and the caution tape the day before, how I snuck to their house during the night and one of our dogs followed me but I was too late."

He's so still he barely seems alive. "Then what happened?"

"My parents told me it was just a dream. I started to believe them…"

My breath is coming in small pants now. His hand slides over my back. "And…?" he prompts.

"Our dog was missing. My dad heard him barking in Jilly's house, and went to check. When no one answered, he unlocked the door and discovered Jilly and her parents in there, dead. My father was the primary suspect for a while, because the dog was in there and his footprints were outside." I'm not sure I'll ever recover from the guilt I felt when the police took him in for questioning.

"Jesus," he whispers. "You must have been terrified. And that means…you must have entered the house and seen them yourself, right?"

I shake my head. "I don't know. It's like I blacked a lot of it out. But I told my parents I'd had to leave really fast. That's why I couldn't get our dog. My mother…she never looked at me the same way again."

I venture a glance at him, waiting to see condemnation or fear or uncertainty. But his eyes are the gentlest gray.

"You time traveled."

I shake my head. "I didn't know how to time travel. I still don't. I think I just kind of *knew* things as a kid. I had a premonition and created a story to explain it. Maybe I remembered it happening before. From one of these other timelines I have memories of. Like 9-11. When I saw the footage of the first plane hitting I knew what would happen next. I was just remembering it from before."

"You know you don't need to make excuses for it to me, right?" he asks. "Your mother's response was just...wrong. She never should have reacted like that."

"I can't blame her. Anyone would have been scared of me."

"I'm not," he says.

I glance at him and feel a small crack, a sliver of light entering that dark place inside me. "Yeah," I reply, smiling. "You're not."

He presses his mouth to my forehead. "I hate that you seem so surprised by that. You deserved to spend your entire life surrounded by people who treated what you could do like a gift instead of a curse."

My heart stumbles and falters. *He's wrong.* I bury my head to his chest and try to ignore the thought. But it remains anyway, a tiny undercurrent of guilt I can never quite place. There's the dread I feel when he mentions Ryan's name. And in that dream about the hospital in London, my certainty I'd done something Nick wouldn't forgive me for—it means something. At some point, in one of these lives, I think I may have done something very wrong.

"I HAVE TO PEE." I mean to whisper but it comes out loud enough for half the room to hear. "I think I'm drunk," I add.

Nick's eyes crinkle at the corners, his dimple coming out as he tries not to laugh. "Yeah, I think you might be," he says. "And you're a cute drunk, but my brother isn't, so maybe we should find him and get out of here."

My stomach sinks at the mere mention of Ryan. He was once my

closest friend, after Nick—I still remember the kid who sat under my
window when I had mono and played chess with me, moving pieces
as I instructed. The little boy who brought me tulips when I broke my
arm...tulips he cut from his mother's garden without permission, a
move he'd later be punished for. But now his bitterness about the situation has ruined everything, no matter how hard he tries to restrain it.

"Hey," says Nick, tipping my chin up. "What's up?"

It's something we don't discuss, normally. But alcohol has loos-
ened my tongue. "He hates me now," I whisper.

Nick pulls me toward him. "No, it's me he hates. He thinks I stole
you. And maybe I did, but I'd do it again in a heartbeat."

He kisses me, tasting like beer and spearmint, which is oddly not
an unpleasant combination, but he ends it with a reluctant sigh.
"This isn't a good idea when you're drunk," he says.

I step into the space he's created between us. "I think it's an
amazing idea."

He groans and closes his eyes. "No, it's not, because you won't
make the same decisions you would if you were sober, and if we keep
going I'll be tempted to let you make the wrong ones." He pushes
away from me, his shoulders set in a way that means there's no
arguing with him. "You pee while I go find Ryan. I'll pull up the car
and meet you in front."

Somewhere in the far recesses of my inebriated brain I know he's
right, even if I don't like it. I promised my mother I'd wait until I was
out of high school. It's just getting harder and harder to keep that
promise.

He leaves in search of Ryan while I move through a dark hall
and into an even darker bedroom in search of an unoccupied toilet.
When I'm done I stumble blindly back through the bedroom, running
my hand along the dresser to find my way to the door.

"There you are," says a familiar voice, pulling me against him.
"I've been looking for you."

I press my head to his chest. Now that I've peed all I want in the *world is to go to sleep. I'm so tired I'm not sure I'll even make it to the* *car. "I thought we were meeting in front,"* I murmur.

"I'd rather meet right here," he says, as his mouth lands on mine. *Even inebriated I recognize it's not his normal kiss. It's harder,* *pushier, needier. He stumbles a little and my hip slams into the side* *of the dresser, but he doesn't seem to notice. Something is wrong with* *him and I can't quite form the words to ask. His hands are on my ass,* *gripping me the way they do when we've taken things too far and* *he's desperate to come. I don't understand what's happening, but* *when he pops the button on my jeans, it triggers an alarm inside me:* *Nick wouldn't. He wouldn't be like this. He wouldn't do this here.*

"I don't think we —"

"I wanted you first," he says.

My blood turns to ice and I put a hand on his chest to push away *from him. "What?"*

The door opens. Light from the hallway illuminates the room, *and Nick stands there, the blood draining from his face as he takes in* *my open jeans and my hands on Ryan's chest.*

"No!" I cry, jolting myself awake. I sit up, struggling for air, and press my knees to my chest, my forehead between them, forcing myself to take controlled breaths. Beside me, Nick —*grown-up Nick*—is in a deep sleep. *What did I do? Did Nick* *understand? Did he forgive me?* Unlike all the other memories, even the bad ones, I feel tainted by this. I want it just to be a dream and I know it wasn't. My head bumps against the frame of the bed and Nick rolls toward me.

"You okay?" he asks.

"Yeah," I whisper. He pulls me down beside him. My leg slides over his and, half-asleep, he rolls toward me, pressing his mouth to my neck, his body far more awake than his brain. It distracts me from my panic of a moment earlier. I want him to keep distracting me. I want to forget it entirely.

6

QUINN

"Well, we made it through the night without having sex," he announces over breakfast.

In the bright light of morning, with Nick here, grinning at me like something miraculous has occurred, the dream last night feels distant. I tell myself it was just a nightmare, a figment of my imagination. I ignore the part of me that knows it wasn't.

I smile back. "As far as we know, anyway."

"If I managed to have sex with you while I was asleep I'm pretty impressed with myself, given everything else we did last night."

I look at him under my lashes. "I think you should be impressed with yourself either way."

"Keep looking at me like that and I'm going to insist on impressing you some more," he says, shoving his plate to the side.

The memory of Ryan hisses in my head, a poisonous snake I want to lock away in some dark corner and forget. I push my plate to the side too. "You say that as if you think I'd be threatened by it."

"You might be," he says, pulling me into his lap, "if you had any idea how much more I'd like to do to you."

I feel a hum of pleasure in the middle of my chest. "Tell me more about these things you'd like to do."

"I'd like to have dinner with you every night," he says softly. "And wake up with you every day."

My head tips back to look at him. "That's way less filthy than I was expecting."

He grins. "There are plenty of filthy things I want too, but I'm trying to focus on the bigger picture at the moment. I want you to move in with me."

I blink, wondering if I've misheard him or if I'm somehow misunderstanding him. "*What?*"

"Move in with me," he says, pulling away just enough that he can see my eyes. "I want your face to be the last thing I see every night and the first thing I see every morning. I haven't even been trying to find a new place and I just realized it's because I want it to be your choice too."

My heart begins to trip in my throat, excitement that is joyful and frightened all at once. "We're not supposed to be dating in the first place. Sharing a home might make it a little hard to keep this a secret."

"We'll figure something out. We'll get a house with a back entrance and I'll sneak in at night."

I allow myself to picture it, him coming home to me, sliding between the sheets of our bed in the darkness the way he did in London. I want it so badly I can taste it, but this isn't London and there are so many consequences this time around. "But we can't even *be* together," I reply, flustered. "Physically. You know what I mean."

"That isn't going to last forever," he says. His eyes darken in a way that makes me momentarily forget we were ever discussing anything other than sex, and us having it. "It can't. And we've found plenty of other ways to deal with it."

We've found so, so many ways to deal with it since yesterday. Desire flares again and I struggle to ignore it. "But we're only on, like, our fifth date. You cannot ask me to move in on our fifth date. God, I can't even imagine how everyone would react if I moved in with you right now."

"Fuck everyone else. And this is more like our 15th date," he argues. "What about the night we danced at the harbor, or when we went to Baltimore, or sat up all night at the hospital?"

I laugh. "Okay. You cannot ask me to move in because it's only our 15th date."

"Fine," he says. "You're right. I'll wait til our 16th. Which is tomorrow, just so we're clear."

I shake my head, but I also don't say no. The sensible thing would be to wait...until we see where this goes, until my fear recedes. But I no longer have forever to put the things I want on hold.

WE SPEND the day out on the water. He teaches me how to paddleboard and standing there, watching him restrain his grin as I struggle to maintain my balance, it's easy to forget about the dream last night. It's in the quiet moments, when he's pulling the boards out of the water and I'm standing idly by, that I'm struck by a fresh wave of guilt.

"What's wrong?" he asks, studying my face when he returns to the dock. I want to tell him the truth. He wouldn't hold it against me, would he? It's not even *this* version of me that's responsible for what happened, if he even blamed me in the first place. Does it count as cheating if you don't know you're doing it?

I smile. "Nothing. The wind is picking up. You think we'll be cold on the boat?"

"Why don't you grab a sweatshirt while I store this stuff?" he asks. "There's one in my bag. It's still in the other room."

I make my way back into the house. The room he once shared with Ryan rests at the end of the long hall. A part of me doesn't want to set foot inside it, wants to avoid any other memories that linger.

The room is bathed in sunlight yet feels dangerous to me. Two beds sit there, with matching navy-and-white quilts, pillows shaped like footballs. It's still the room of children. One of whom is no longer alive.

A framed photo rests on the nightstand between the two beds. Nick and Ryan as boys. Baseball uniforms and big smiles. I put the photo back where it was, wrestling with this sense of dread in my chest. There's more here, I know there is.

And I'm scared to learn what it is, because I'm pretty sure it was my fault.

7

QUINN

It's dark when he pulls up to Caroline's apartment on Sunday night. The streets are quiet and the air is balmy but not hot, and I wish we could just stay right here and not emerge from our bubble a little longer. He climbs out of the Jeep and grabs my bag for me.

"Don't walk me in," I tell him. "Just in case Jeff is in the lobby."

He raises a brow. "You really think that would *discourage* me from walking you in?"

There's no arguing with him, but my stomach doesn't relax until we've reached the elevator. He wraps an arm around me as we ascend and I rest my head on his shoulder, wondering what comes next. He hasn't brought up moving in together since this morning. Maybe he's giving me space, or maybe he's come to his senses. It would be best for both of us if he had, but it depresses me all the same.

When we reach Caroline's door, sadness hits me hard, out of nowhere. I don't want him to leave. He sweeps the hair that's escaped my ponytail behind my ear, his fingers and his gaze lingering on my face. "What's the matter?" he asks.

"Nothing." My smile is forced, fleeting.

He presses his mouth to mine and in seconds I give into the pressure of his lips. Wanting more, as always. I arch against him and my bag falls to the floor as his hands grab my hips to pull me against him.

His mouth is on my jawline, my neck. I purr like a cat in heat.

"More," I whisper, grabbing the neck of his T-shirt and pulling those perfect lips of his to my own.

I feel the groan of need rumbling in his chest, feel the moment something snaps inside both of us and we stop caring that we are in the hallway. His hands pull at my ass, so that he is pressed to the junction between my legs. My dress slides up and all that separates us are his shorts and my panties.

My leg wraps around his hip and my hand is on his zipper when the elevator dings and unloads a carful of laughing twenty-somethings. It's the splash of cold water we need. In an instant my leg is back on the floor and he's pulled my dress down, but by their suppressed laughter and raised brows as they pass, I intuit they got an eyeful of something.

He presses his forehead against mine. "Jesus Christ," he whispers. "I'm sorry. I—"

"Stop apologizing," I say, pressing my mouth to his. Within seconds his hands are sliding up my thighs again and almost as fast he pushes away, pinning me to the wall so I can't chase him.

"I'm not going to ask you to move in again," he says, pulling his lip between his teeth.

I nod, swallowing hard on my disappointment. "It's probably for the best." I stare at the floor to avoid his eye.

His index finger tips my chin up to meet his gaze. "I want to move in with you more than I have ever wanted anything. Okay, there's one thing I probably want more." His eyes flicker over me, a half-smile on his face. "But I'm not going to be Jeff. It was pretty easy to figure out what he was saying to you on the phone yesterday. I'm not going to be one more guy who tries to push you into doing what he wants. Just know that I hate that I'm going home without you."

And then, pressing his lips to my forehead, he turns and walks away.

INSIDE THE APARTMENT, Caroline is lying on the couch with a huge smile on her face. "You look like you had a very *satisfying* weekend," she says.

I sink into the chair across from hers. "Not entirely the way you're thinking, but yes."

Her mouth falls open. "You went away for the entire weekend and didn't sleep with him?"

I would like to tell her everything, but it sounds too far-fetched, even for a best friend inclined to believe anything I say. "We're just taking it slowly."

"Oh my God," she says, flinging herself dramatically across the couch, "a whole weekend with a gorgeous man and not a single orgasm? That's *terrible.*"

I grin. "I didn't say there were no orgasms. I just said we're taking it slowly."

She rolls toward me so fast she nearly falls right onto the floor. "I need details."

I laugh to myself. She's going to be so uninterested in the detail I'm about to share. "He wants me to move in with him."

All the delight is sucked straight from her face. She sits upright. "*Not* what I was looking for. Tell me you're not considering it?"

"I am," I admit. "I'm just concerned—"

"Of course you're concerned!" she shouts. "You've only

dated him for a fucking week!"

"That's not what bothers me," I reply. There are things I've been keeping from her and Trevor, but it's gotten to the point that I need to come clean. I'm no longer optimistic Nick and I are going to discover some magical cure. "It's mostly that it's not fair to him, because I have—" I stop to take a deep breath. "I have a brain tumor."

Caroline's ever-present insouciance fades. "What?" she whispers. "If this is some kind of joke it's not funny."

My eyes shift away from hers. "It's not a joke. I've known for a few weeks, but I didn't want to mention it because I was worried you and Trevor would treat me differently. And I was sort of hoping I'd find a cure."

She stares at her knees, her cheeks sucked in hard. "I guess you didn't, then, if you're telling me now," she finally says in a tiny voice.

My heart aches. She's been my best friend for a decade. I wish I'd found a better way to break the news. "Right. I didn't."

She presses her fingers to her temples. "I can't believe you didn't tell me." Her voice is barely audible.

"I didn't want everyone being upset and serious and talking in hushed voices, reminding me something's wrong. I want you and Trevor to continue to be assholes whether I'm dying or not."

She heaves a sigh and throws her head back against the cushions, looking at the ceiling instead of me with eyes that are suspiciously bright. "I promise I'll go back to being an asshole. Just give me a minute."

I wait for her to pull herself together. "This is bullshit, Quinn," she says through a raspy voice. "You're finally going back to school and you've jettisoned your loser fiancé and...this is just bullshit."

My throat tightens a little. I sort of agree, but I'm realizing life really doesn't work out like the movies do. Sometimes things are unfair, and they just remain unfair. "But you see the issue," I finally continue. "Nick should be finding someone he can have a future with, and that person might not be me. It probably *shouldn't* be me, given that it could impact his job."

"He's a big boy," she says dismissively. "Just think about if the positions were reversed: if he had the tumor, would you want to be moving on, or would you just want to capture every day with him you could?"

I know the answer in my very bones without even considering it. I'd want to capture every day and I'd be in agony if he wouldn't allow me to do it. "I'd want to be with him," I admit. "But even with that, I'm still scared. This won't make sense, but I just feel like I might...care about him too much."

"That is literally the stupidest thing I've ever heard, aside from a minute ago when you said you were going to move in with a guy you just met. You might care about him *too much*? What does that even mean?"

I curl into myself. "I don't know." I really don't. I only know it feels dangerous somehow to get even closer to him than I already am.

Caroline shakes her head. "I can't believe I'm encouraging this, because I think it's fucking insane, but you've spent most of your life cowering and—"

"I haven't been *cowering*," I argue.

She arches a brow. "Really, Quinn? Dropping out of college because your mom was a mess? Getting back together with Jeff just because he quit his job to follow you here? For whatever reason, you have been shying away from greatness your entire life. So tell me something: how's that worked out for you?"

My arms fold across my chest. I can't really argue. I just hate what she's saying. "Not especially well."

"No, it's worked out fucking *terribly*. So I say if something you want scares the hell out of you, go for it. Because the other way isn't working."

8

QUINN

The following afternoon, Nick steps into one door of the imaging waiting room just as I emerge from the other. Despite his sweet, lopsided grin, he looks more like an Olympic athlete about to take over a press conference than a doctor collecting a patient. My eyes move straight from his face to his shirt to his belt, cataloguing what I'd like to remove in precise order.

"Escorting me back to your office?" I ask under my breath. "Don't you have people for this part?"

For just a moment he allows the back of his hand to tap the base of my spine before it falls away. "Yes, Miss Stewart, I do," he says quietly. "But there are a few patients I escort from imaging personally."

I glance up at him. "The ones you're moving in with?"

His smile lifts high on one side and I get a glimpse of that dimple I love. "Yes. Those. The agent is meeting us at five."

He holds the elevator open for me and I walk in, shaking my head. I looked at the listings he forwarded. They're way too expensive. I knew housing in Georgetown was insane, but I didn't know it was *this* insane. "I could pay four months of my mortgage for the rent on a fixer-upper here. We should just look at apartments."

He bends toward me and his laughter brushes my ear, husky and warm. "I am a neurologist with no kids and no debt and nothing I would like to blow my money on more than this."

I purr under my breath at his nearness and he moves away, leaning against the opposite wall of the elevator. It's a respectable distance for any security cameras, but the look in his eyes is positively filthy. Or maybe that's just where my mind had already gone, because his shirt is unbuttoned just enough to get a glimpse of that chest I so enjoyed this weekend, and already I am picturing my mouth pressed to the hollow in his collarbone as I pull his belt loose.

"I don't know what you're thinking," he says, "but if these elevators weren't monitored by security I'd make you demonstrate every one of them."

The doors open and I slide past him. "You're all talk," I say over my shoulder.

"Such a smart mouth," he replies, the words half spoken and half growled. "Let's see how smart it is when I get you alone."

I raise a brow. "Easy to say when there's no place we *can* be alone."

"You think?" he asks, opening his office door and pulling me inside. The moment the door shuts, I'm wrapping my arms around his neck, pressing my face to his blue oxford, and breathing in the smell of his skin beneath the starch of his shirt.

"God, I've missed you and it hasn't even been 24 hours," he says, seeking my mouth. My hand palms him outside his khakis, and his fingers slide up my inner thigh, beneath the elastic of my panties. "You're already wet," he says with a quick, rough breath. "Get on the desk."

As much as I would love to do just that, I have something else in mind. "Maybe I feel like being the one in charge today," I reply, dropping to my knees. I slide his khakis down and then slowly pull him free of his boxer briefs.

His head falls back against the wall. "Fuck."

I saw plenty of him this weekend but it was mostly prone, in the dark. Seeing him like this, in a well-lit room, is another thing entirely. His size is...intimidating, which should probably make me nervous but instead only makes me want all the things we *can't* do even more.

The hallway outside echoes with footsteps, chatter, the wheels of a gurney. Inside here, though, it is is whisper-quiet, his small sharp breaths the only sound as I begin to tease him with my hands and my tongue.

For so much of the time I've known him, Nick has been the expert, the one leading the charge—calm, responsible, stoic. But here he's at my mercy, and I can feel his desperation in the hitch of his breath, in the way his fingers—already tangled in my hair—struggle not to press to my scalp, to demand more. "Jesus, Quinn," he finally begs, "you're killing me. Stop playing with it."

I obey, finally giving him what he wants. The heat of my mouth, my hand firm around his shaft, his hips bucking to chase me whenever my head backs away. His fingers lose their restraint, begin to press. He looks down at me and then his eyes squeeze tight. "You have no idea how badly I want to fuck you right now," he grunts. "None." I try to take more of him, until he hits the back of my throat. He gasps and I do it again.

"Oh fuck," he says on another gasp. "I'm gonna come." With the smallest pained cry he lets go, my head held tight in his hands until he sags backward against the wall, his chest heaving.

I rise from the floor, unsteady with want. I've never been the girl who licks her lips after giving a blow job like some porn star but he's made me into that girl and I'm not ashamed of it. He watches me through eyes that are heavy-lidded, drugged. "Holy shit," he says, pushing both hands through his hair. "Get on the desk."

Watching him come just now left me so worked up I can barely stand it, but I force myself to be responsible. "We need to meet the realtor."

"Get on the fucking desk," he growls. He backs me into it and lifts me himself before I can even think of arguing, shoving my sundress around my thighs and dropping to his knees. His mouth is between my legs, against the cotton of my panties, inhaling me, his tongue pressing against the fabric but not moving beyond it.

The tables have turned and it's me who's desperate now. I throw his words back at him. "Stop playing with it."

I feel his low laugh against my skin, but he slides the panties down, kissing along the inside of my thighs, nipping the skin a little, before he pulls a knee over each shoulder to hold me open. His tongue flickers over my clit—fast, hard, relentless—and just as I feel myself getting close he changes tact—long sweeps of his tongue like I'm a melting ice cream cone in the heat of summer. He increases the pace, groaning over my skin, and then slides a single finger inside me.

I come before I even have time to warn him it's going to happen, with a small cry I barely manage to muffle. My eyes are still closed, my arching back hasn't even fallen back to the desk, I'm still *coming* and I already want more. I want the feel of him inside me like I've never wanted anything in my life, enough to beg, to bargain with God, to do whatever is necessary.

He apparently does too. When my lids finally flicker open, he's rising with that drugged look on his face once again, pushing me farther back on the desk, so hard it's almost impossible to believe he just came five minutes ago. He stands between my legs, the tip of his cock resting in precisely the right place. I feel the first hint of pressure, the fullness that will come, and I know I should stop him, but *God* I don't want to. I've never seen him look quite as desperate, as needy, as he does right now. He wants to shove inside me as badly as I want him to. His nostrils flare, the tendons in his neck strain, and then he leans down and rests his forehead against my chest, trying to regain control. "God, this is hard," he whispers.

"I know." It just doesn't seem to ever be satisfied—the need. No matter how many times he makes me come, in the end I find myself exactly where I am right now—trying to justify doing the one thing we cannot do.

He finally backs away, leaning against the wall while I brush my hands over my sundress and pull my hair back again.

"Am I presentable?" I ask.

He grins at me as he pulls up his pants. "Are you asking if you look like you just came?"

I laugh. *He* certainly looks like it—his eyes are glazed over, his cheeks flushed. "I'm pretty sure there aren't a lot of moments I *haven't* looked like that of late, but yes."

He pulls me against him, pressing his mouth to my forehead. "You just look hotter than hell. You're lucky we have to meet that agent or I wouldn't be letting you out of here today."

I straighten his tie and then, with his hand at the small of my back, he opens the door and we step into the hall—where we come face-to-face with a woman in scrubs who goes pale at the sight of us. With a sinking stomach I realize the woman is Meg. She isn't done up like she was at the market a week ago, but it's almost easier to appreciate her perfect skin and bone structure without the makeup and curls. It's petty, but I wish his ex was less attractive. Especially since she'll be the one who's still here when I'm gone. And based on the look in her eyes, I think she'll be more than willing to take him back.

Nick exhales. His shoulders relax but it's a forced gesture, the same thing he used to do before swim meets. His hand falls away from my back but it's too late. She saw how we emerged from the office and her nose crinkles in disdain at his attempt to cover it up now.

"Hi Meg," he says. "This is Quinn."

Her eyes move toward me, not nearly as full of loathing as I'd expect. She's angry, but there's something else there too. It takes me a moment to realize what it is: pity. Did Nick tell her about my brain tumor? Does she know I'm dying? I'm not sure why it bothers me so much, but it does.

She says nothing. Just stands still as a statue and then steps around us. Nick pulls my hand and leads me to the elevator, while I grapple with a stew of sick thoughts I wish I was not having. I stare at the floor, wanting to pull my shit together so when I voice a thought, it's the right one.

"Hey," he says, pulling me to him. "I'm sorry about that. Are you okay?"

I press my head to his chest and close my eyes, needing comfort and distance at the same time. My imagination is off to the races now. She's moving into his apartment after all. She thinks their lives might just pick up where they left off when I die, and I wonder if, at some level, he's thinking they will too. If I were a better person I'd want that for him, wouldn't I? I'm not a better person. The idea of him with anyone but me makes me feel like I'm going to be sick. I step away from him, leaning against the wall. "You told her, didn't you?"

"Told her what?"

"You told her I'm dying."

He swallows. "She knows about the tumor."

She doesn't *just* know about the tumor. That look she gave me wasn't the kind you give a person who might recover. "And is she just...waiting for you?" I ask. My words snap like lightning but there's grief behind them. "Letting you go spend time with the dying girl, knowing the two of you will pick up where you left off in a few months?"

I'm not sure what I expect from him in response, maybe blithe reassurance, a little pat on the head. Instead, he stops the elevator entirely and closes the distance between us until I'm pressed to the wall and so close to him I can barely breathe. "Are you serious right now?" he asks. "Please tell me that was not a serious question."

I exhale. "I wouldn't fault you for it," I reply, my voice small. I think it's true, although the pain is so fresh right now it's hard to imagine. "I mean, you deserve to have a life after I'm gone. But..."

"It may have escaped your attention," he says, voice low with fury. "But I am crazy about you. I'm so crazy about you I seem to care very little about everything that mattered a month ago. Not my reputation. Not my job. Not my future. All that exists for me is the time we have left, and after that, honestly, I can't imagine wanting to go on."

The pain swells and releases, and I weep, my face pressed to his shirt. It can't all be about seeing Meg or the possibility that he'll move on. I've been building to this for a while. Every day I spend with him just makes it hurt even more that it can't last. "I'm sorry."

He holds me tight to his chest. "Not as sorry as I am."

9

NICK

Our talk in the elevator lends our house-hunting trip a new gravity. *This is probably the last place she will ever live.* It focuses me. I want to choose the perfect home for us. The one where we might have stayed forever.

We follow our agent over the cobblestone streets. She's talking on the phone, so I tug Quinn closer and press my mouth to her hair. She's recovered from the incident in the elevator but I'm not sure I have. *It's actually going to end*—for some reason, it didn't seem real until now. She's already preparing herself for the day when I'm here without her. The emptiness I feel at the idea of it terrifies me.

"Like anything yet?" I ask.

We've seen two townhouses and a few apartments. They were fine, but none of them were *enough*. I'm beginning to wonder if I'm just asking too much.

"They're all great," she says. "I just can't get past the idea of spending that much on a place."

"It's really not that much," I counter. "Everything we've

looked at isn't a ton more than I'm paying for a one-bedroom right now."

"I guess you take the girl off the bankrupt farm, but you can't take the bankrupt farm off the girl," she says with a small laugh.

I raise a brow. She's implied before that she grew up without money, but she's got this inheritance and her mother's new home couldn't have been cheap. It doesn't add up. "Your definition of bankrupt and mine must be different. Your mom looked like she was living pretty well to me."

She shrugs. "My dad had this massive life insurance policy. About two million. And 200 grand of that was earmarked for me. That's what I'll be using to pay for school."

I shove my hands in my pockets, thinking. People who are broke don't take out insurance policies that size. He'd have had to pay premiums on it he could have barely afforded. "Doesn't it seem a little strange that your dad would have taken a policy that large?" I ask.

She nods. "Yeah, especially because my father was the cheapest man alive. He once went an entire day in Philly in the summer without anything to drink because he couldn't find a water fountain and refused to pay for a bottle." She smiles a little at the memory. "But thank God he did. We found out about it at the last possible moment, right before the bank was going to foreclose."

"It wasn't in his will?"

She shakes her head. "Nope. If I hadn't dreamed about that policy I think we still wouldn't know."

The agent is on the phone again so I stop, tugging her hand to face me. "You dreamed about it and then it happened?"

She laughs. "I see where you're going with this, but no. I just had a dream in which I remembered talking to him about needing a policy and when I woke up I knew where to look."

"Rose said you may be time traveling in your sleep without even realizing it."

She shakes her head quickly. Too quickly. For some reason her default position is to deny that there might be anything supernatural going on, no matter how bizarre the circumstances. "My friend Caroline dreamed her missing passport was under her toaster once and found it there. Does she time travel too? Sometimes we just forget stuff, tuck it away some place we can't reach it when we're awake."

I'll table this for now but we're coming back to it later. I have a feeling her mom did a number on her where this stuff is concerned, and I need to rectify that immediately.

We arrive at the next house, a single-family Cape Cod on Q street. "The owners have spent the whole year redoing the interior," the agent tells us as she opens the door.

Given how many "redone interiors" we've seen that have fallen short today, it doesn't mean all that much, but I'm more willing to keep an open mind once we get inside. It's in better shape than a lot of the places we've seen, and the owners have put in wide-plank hardwood floors and a new kitchen. Quinn's unwilling to tell me she likes anything simply because she's worried about the money, but I see the way her eyes soften when we enter, and once we pass through the kitchen I know for certain. The back of the house is a wall of windows, looking out on a private garden. It reminds me of my flat in London. Quinn stands at the French doors with this look of wonder on her face, taking it all in. And that's the look I've been waiting for from her.

"This is it, eh?" I ask, smiling.

She forces her mouth into a straight line. "How do you know that?" she asks. "I haven't said a word."

I twine my fingers through hers. "How do I know anything?"

"Yes," she replies with a small laugh. "This is it."

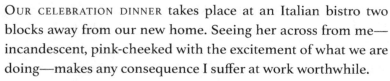

Our celebration dinner takes place at an Italian bistro two blocks away from our new home. Seeing her across from me—incandescent, pink-cheeked with the excitement of what we are doing—makes any consequence I suffer at work worthwhile.

Beneath the table her legs cross, brushing mine by accident. I try to ignore the images that flash through my head. This afternoon in my office took the edge off but that edge is back, and it's multiplied. What we're doing was supposed to quench the fire but instead it just seems to spread and spread. I've been picturing her bent over this table at least once a minute since we sat down. I was picturing her bent over my desk until we got here.

"What's the matter?" she asks, tilting her head, brow furrowed. "Are you worried about moving in together? Please be honest."

"I was thinking about how badly I wanted to fuck you on my desk this afternoon," I reply, watching the pink in her cheeks deepen. She's a little shocked but there's a gleam in her eye that tells me she likes it too. "How I wanted to bend you over and push that dress around your hips and pound you loud enough for the whole fucking floor to hear. Honest enough for you?"

She tucks her head, smiling. "That was pretty honest."

"Sorry," I reply. "To use your diet analogy, anything I do with you is like eating a single potato chip. All it does is remind me how much I love potato chips."

"And then you want to fuck them over your desk."

I laugh. "Exactly. I want to fuck the potato chips into oblivion."

"Is it weird that this conversation is turning me on?" she asks. "I'm picturing your dick in a bag of Ruffles and I'm a little wet."

And all she has to do is use the phrase *I'm a little wet* and I've got an erection that will make leaving the restaurant impossible. I shift in my seat. Adjust myself. It doesn't help. "We need to talk about something else," I plead. "Something that will not make me think about what you just said."

"You mean that I'm *wet*?" she teases. "So wet you could slide right—"

"*Stop*," I say with a low groan. "Please."

She laughs. "Fine. Then we can talk about logistics. That's a boner killer if there ever was one. What happens when the hospital finds out we share an address? I could just have my mail sent to Caroline's, I guess."

It's occurred to me too, but I refuse. I get one chance at this life with her and I'm going to do it right. "No. We aren't half-assing this. Look, I've told the few people I've discussed this with that we dated in college. If push comes to shove, it's what I'll tell the administration too. We'll just hope for the best."

It's on the tip of her tongue to argue. I can see the struggle in her face. She wants to remind me it might not last that long. It feels like she's always trying to remind me of that, as if I could possibly forget it. "God, I wish we could find Rose and just ask her a few more questions," she says instead.

"You know," I venture. "There is one way we could talk to her."

Her brows raise nearly to her hairline. "There is?"

"You could time travel back to her."

A laugh escapes, and then she sees my face. "Oh my God, you weren't joking."

I don't know why she persists in acting like this is some crazy impossibility. Haven't we had enough proof she's capable of doing *something*? "Rose said you could do it. She said you've *been* doing it."

She shrugs. "They're just memories though. I mean, you've remembered things too."

"Not like you do," I argue. "Not with that level of detail. And what about the insurance thing? Don't you find it pretty freaking hard to imagine you completely forgot a conversation like that with your father? And then the new policy turns up the very next day?"

She waves her hand. "Coincidence."

"That's one hell of a coincidence. All these things you just know too. Think about the story you told me about your neighbor: you dreamed you'd tried to save your friend and the dog followed you. What if it wasn't a dream? What if you really did travel backward to save her?"

She pauses. For a moment I see a hint of fear and then she shakes her head and laughs. "Come on, Nick. If I'd tried to go back to save her, I'd probably have died too. Yes, there've been times when I've known stuff I shouldn't, like about architecture, about you and London. But that's because we lived them before, somehow. The thing with the neighbor was...I don't know what it was, but there's no way I actually went there. If I don't know how to time travel now, I sure as hell didn't know how to then. It's like I told you before. If we actually existed in some parallel time, maybe I read about the murder there."

Her refusal to believe she's capable of doing this is almost pathological. If I, the biggest non-believer of all time, can buy into it, why the hell can't she? "Dreaming you had a conversation with your father about life insurance and waking to discover he actually acted on it is a once-in-a-lifetime," I tell her. "Dreaming your neighbor has been murdered and that the dog followed you when you went to save her—and being right? Another once-in-a-lifetime. So how many other times did you dream something that came true? Don't just reflexively argue with me. *Think* about it."

She folds her arms over her chest, and I see the temptation to argue written all over her face. But she doesn't. And after a moment her shoulders sag, as if she's finally admitting the truth to herself. Another second passes, and then her eyes go wide and she gasps. "Oh shit."

I look behind me, expecting to see Jeff or Meg or my boss. "What's wrong?"

"It's possible."

She looks so shell-shocked I reach across the table and grab her hand. "I didn't expect you to come around to my viewpoint so quickly. What's the matter?"

She takes a single deep breath and a controlled exhale, her eyes wide. "I just remembered something that happened. It was so weird at the time that I didn't even tell my parents about it and then I lied so they wouldn't know." She looks up at me in shock. "I think I might have shot a kid out of a tree."

I had no idea what she might say but it wasn't that. "You *shot* a kid?"

"With a slingshot," she amends. "This little asshole, Robby Harding. He used to sit in this tree, shooting birds with his BB gun. And one day he threw the dead birds at my back as I ran home, trying to get away from him. I fell and was all scraped up afterward, bad enough my mom thought I might need stitches. But that night I dreamed..." She flushes, looking anywhere in the room but me. "I don't know. It will sound ridiculous."

"Tell me," I urge. "You dreamed what?"

"I dreamed that I waited in a tree behind him and shot him with my slingshot, and he fell. When I woke in the morning, all my cuts had healed. It was as if they'd never happened. I wore pants for a week just so my parents wouldn't ask how I could have healed overnight like that. And Robby..." She flinches. "Robby was in the hospital with a broken leg, because he'd fallen out of a tree the day before. He told everyone he got hit by something. I thought it was karma. But maybe it was just me."

I laugh. Maybe it's wrong, but the idea of little Quinn shooting a kid out of a tree is so damn cute. "You're not going to start telling me about all the people you wished dead who died the next day, right?"

She squeezes her eyes shut. "Don't even joke about it. I mean, what if I did?"

I grab her hand beneath the table. "You aren't a murderer."

"I may have shot a kid out of a tree," she argues. "He could have broken his neck. But if it's true, if I'm really doing this," she says, "why can't I do it when I'm awake?"

The question is a relief. I've been convinced for weeks that she is time traveling, but I needed her to actually believe it before I could push her toward the next step. "Have you *tried* to do it when you're awake?"

She looks at me blankly. "Of course I haven't."

I lean in and tighten my hands around hers. "Then maybe it's time you did."

10

QUINN

That night, and into the following morning, I'm still thinking about what Nick said. About Robby and the life insurance and all the other bizarre incidents in my childhood. Maybe it should be enough to convince me I can time travel, but it really isn't. There have been a thousand things in my life I'd have changed if I could. If I really had the ability, it would be more than some shadowy thing that occurs when I'm asleep. Nick is pushing this because he needs something to believe in. I suppose I need that too. But it's not going to be this.

The next day I go to campus to fill out some last-minute forms. I've always loved the Georgetown campus. Half of it is deliciously old and reminds me more of Hogwarts than anyplace else I've ever been, although I suppose that's no longer true if you count London.

Nick meets me when I'm done, bringing us lunch from the hospital deli, and we sit under a tree, hidden from passersby and the blinding August sun. When we're done eating, we lie side-by-side while I geek out over the courses I'm signed up for and he tries to get me to admit to shooting children other than Robby.

"Just give me a number," he says. "Approximately how many kids do you think you've shot?"

I narrow my eyes at him. "One, at best."

He bites his lip, trying hard to keep a straight face. "Okay, maybe I'm being too specific. How many kids have you injured, stabbed, maimed, decapitated, or otherwise wished ill upon?"

I roll my eyes. "*Wished ill upon* is a ridiculously broad term. I'm guessing I *wished ill upon* plenty."

"In ways that led to their deaths?" he asks with a cheeky grin and I swat him with the folder I got from Admissions.

"You're a terrible human being."

His smile fades. "Speaking of terrible human beings, have you heard from Jeff?"

I wish he hadn't brought it up. Discussing Jeff is definitely not how I want to spend the only time I'll be with Nick until this evening. "He showed up at Caroline's this morning on his way out of town. Building security finally asked him to leave."

His jaw grinds. I know he hates the idea of me being confronted by Jeff without him, but the alternative—me *with* him—is so much worse. Jeff would love to find someone to blame for what's gone wrong. "When are you picking up your stuff?" he asks with a heavy sigh.

"Tomorrow," I reply. "He has a meeting in Harrisonburg every Wednesday, so I know he won't be home."

His frown deepens. "Wait til I get off work and I'll go with you. I don't want you over there without someone, and besides, you'll need help carrying stuff, right?"

I shake my head. "I don't think I will and the absolute last thing I need is for him to see you involved in any way. Besides," I add with a grin, "at least he doesn't sit around accusing me of killing children."

He gently pushes me to my back, looking around before he leans down and bites my lower lip. "That's for comparing me unfavorably to Jeff. And I'm joking about the kid thing, but have you given anymore thought to it?"

"Killing a child?"

He laughs. "No. Time travel. Just try it."

I squint up at him in the sunlight. "Kiss me again nicely and I'll consider it."

I hear his small hum of satisfaction as he leans back to me, pressing his sun-warmed mouth to mine, which opens and begs for him to sink farther, do more. "Please try," he whispers.

He pulls away, leaving my body thrumming with a desire to skip this time-travel nonsense and yank him back to me. Except if I skip it, we probably have no future. "I have no idea how."

"Rose said something about fastening on a memory, right? So try that. Lock onto a memory and see if you can move toward it."

I desperately wish he'd drop it. I probably won't succeed, and if I do, there's so much that could go wrong. "What if I wind up somewhere naked?"

"Good point," he says, his thumb brushing my lip. "Go somewhere you can land naked safely. Like the dock last weekend."

The sun flickers through the trees overhead and his hair glints gold, his eyes a dusky blue I could never replicate. There are moments, like this one, where I wonder if he can even be real. "Landing on your dock naked seems like the most dangerous thing I could do."

His mouth curves upward. "True. I promise to behave," he says with so little sincerity that I'm chuckling as I shut my eyes.

"Fine. If I succeed, do you have any special requests? I was going to offer to go meet you back in the treehouse until I realized how creepy it would be, given that I'm now 28."

His eyes light up. "I assure you, 16-year-old me would be

willing to overlook that fact," he says. "But if it's off the table, go buy stock in Apple and Microsoft."

I arch a brow. "That seems slightly...I don't know...unethical?"

"Please don't let your ethics get in the way of us owning a Caribbean island once it's all figured out," he says. "But I'd rather just find you on my dock. Naked is preferable. That bikini was easy to remove, so that's also an acceptable option."

"Your erection is making it hard for me to think about time travel," I reply.

He laughs. "I'm not thinking about time travel so much at the moment either."

I picture that weekend anyway. It feels safe here, with him beside me. I picture him shirtless, those navy swim trunks hanging low. I picture the perfection of his stomach, the small trail of hair just below his belly button that I wanted to trace with my tongue.

My eyes open. He's watching my face, his eyes dark with want. "It's not working," I tell him.

"What were you just picturing?" he asks. He knows. Maybe not the specifics but I can tell just by the look on his face, the twitch of his lips, that he knows where my mind went.

"You in your bathing suit. You have this tiny little trail of hair right here," I reply, running my finger just above his belt. "I was imagining tracing it. With my tongue."

"Fuck," he whispers. "I shouldn't have asked." His eyes are hazy as he leans down to kiss me. My hands slide into his hair, tugging at it, and with a low groan, his mouth opens, pressing mine to do the same. My fingers slide over his warm skin and land at his waistband before I even realize what I'm doing. I flinch and break the connection, feeling the hum of his skittering heartbeat pressed to mine. We move in together next weekend. I hope I learn a little more restraint before then, or we are really going to be in trouble.

11

NICK

After lunch, I get back to the office and call my mother. I don't even fully admit to myself why I'm calling because it's insane that I'm already thinking the things I am with Quinn.

My mother, as always, sounds both relieved and irritated when she answers. I try to be decent about calling home, but it's never enough—especially the past month. I should have been better about it. If things were different, she'd have two sons and possibly a few grandkids. I'm sure her retirement is a lot less full than she imagined. "I haven't heard from you in ages," she says. "You're avoiding us."

I can't deny it. Her questions always seem to focus on my personal life, and for the better part of the past month I wasn't sure how I'd answer. "I texted."

"That's not the same. When you don't call it's because there's something you don't want me to know. So go ahead and give me the bad news."

I laugh wearily. "There's no bad news. I just had a question.

I was wondering if you or Dad might have inherited a ring from Grandma Reilly or Grandma Sawyer?"

"What kind of ring?"

I feel idiotic even bringing it up. But Quinn hasn't been wrong once. "An engagement ring."

"*Engagement?*" she asks, her voice kicking up an octave or two. "Finally! If you need money for a ring you know we're happy to help, although with as much as you make I can't imagine you need it. Does Meg have any idea? I thought this day would never come."

I sigh, rubbing the back of my neck. How could I have forgotten what a big deal this will be to my mother? She's had her hopes pinned on Meg for a long time, no matter how many times I told her to unpin them. "I broke up with Meg."

"*What?*" she cries. "*No!* Meg was perfect for you."

I lean back in my chair and close my eyes. "You never thought she was perfect for me, Mom. You just thought she was good enough to provide you with a grandchild someday."

She exhales heavily. "At the rate you're going I might as well stop hoping for that at all. What happened? I thought every-thing was going so well."

"I met someone," I admit. "Before you jump all over me, I didn't cheat. I didn't even think she was a possibility...but meeting her just confirmed I didn't feel the right way about Meg."

"So you're already with someone else and you want to *propose*?"

Yes. I'd marry Quinn tomorrow if I thought she'd say yes, if it wouldn't be so fucking insane to ask when we haven't even been together for two weeks. I don't expect my mother to understand this, and while I'm slightly embarrassed by how irrational it must seem, I'm not embarrassed enough to drop it. Quinn will want that ring and no other. I'm sure of it.

"It's kind of complicated, but...it's something I can see happening."

"Nicholas, I cannot believe you're this serious with someone and you never even *mentioned* her to us."

Part of me wants to keep Quinn a secret and part of me wants to tell everyone I meet that she is mine. I opt for the middle road with my mother. "Like I said, it's been...complicated. Her name is Quinn. She—"

"*Quinn?*" my mother demands. Her voice is sharp, startled.

I sit bolt upright in my chair. "Yes. Why?"

She is silent for a moment. "No reason."

She's lying. She wouldn't have cut me off like that if it was really nothing. "Mom," I plead, "is there something you're not telling me? Did you already know about her somehow?"

"No," she replies. "I just...I have dreams occasionally, about you and Ryan, fighting over a girl."

I inhale deeply. Somewhere inside, my mom holds memories of Quinn too. There's not a doubt in my mind that Ryan and I would have fought over her. We fought over everything. "And the girl's name is Quinn?"

There's a long moment of silence. "Yes," she finally says. "I'm sure it's nothing. It's just an unusual name so it's kind of odd."

"What happens in these dreams?"

She hesitates again, reluctant to say it aloud. "They're just a combination of make believe and real life, like all dreams are. You and Ryan are younger at first and you're in this fistfight over her, and then all of a sudden Ryan is older and getting in that truck with Tyler, but I know it's because of her. I always just figured she was kind of symbolic."

"Symbolic how?"

"You and Ryan were at each other's throats once you hit adolescence. I never knew what exactly you were competing for, if it was recognition from us or from your peers or something else. But I thought maybe she was the symbol of whatever it is you both wanted."

Fuck. It's a gut punch, those words. Because I think maybe Quinn was more than a symbol. I think of the immediate spark of rage I felt when she first mentioned dreaming about Ryan at the homecoming dance, before I knew anything else about it. Was our belligerence in this life just some remnant from another one, with Quinn at its core?

My mother begins to cry. "It's my fault. I should have found a way to make it stop."

"Mom," I say softly, "no one could have stopped us. It wouldn't have made a difference anyway."

"You don't know that. If you'd just gotten along…" She trails off but I already know what she thinks. If Ryan and I had been getting along I'd have gone to that party with him. I'd have carted his drunk ass home before he got in Tyler's truck. I know what she thinks, and what's worse is I agree.

After a moment she coughs, clears her throat. "So when do we meet this new girl? We're leaving for Brazil this weekend but maybe we could drive up when we get home?"

"Sure," I reply. "And you're positive there's no ring? Something in the family?"

"Nick, are you having money issues?" she asks. "We're going to have a long talk about finances if you're outspending *that* salary."

"No. I just think Quinn would prefer a family heirloom over something new. That's all."

"Well, my mother's still alive and they never found your father's mother after she disappeared, so I assume that means they didn't find a ring either."

There's a chill at the base of my spine. My grandmother died long before I was born, when my dad was small. But I never heard she'd *disappeared.* "I thought she drowned."

"No one ever knew for sure. They never found a body... Everyone's best guess is that she drowned in the river."

I'm struck silent by the admission. I think of Grosbaum telling us about his missing wife. Is it a coincidence my grandmother disappeared too?

"YOU'RE *WHERE*?" Quinn asks.

I push my way past the crowd heading to baggage claim. Given I left straight from the office with nothing but my gym bag, I won't be needing to join them. "Florida. Sorry...I tried to call on the way to the airport, but I got your voicemail."

"I heard your message but I just don't understand. You left town just because your grandmother disappeared decades ago?" she asks.

I expected her to be as excited as I am, because this is our first real lead since Rose. She very clearly is not. "Quinn, she *disappeared*. Think about it. Your aunt disappeared too, right? And Grosbaum's wife? Disappearing isn't a standard way for people to die. And if she was a time traveler then my grandfather might know something. Or at least he might know someone who can help us."

She sighs. "Okay. I'm just...well it's stupid but I'm just disappointed. I was really looking forward to seeing you tonight."

"I was too," I tell her. "You have no idea how much. But we don't have time to waste. Any information we get could be the piece we need." And I really hope to God I find that piece here.

IT's dark by the time I arrive at my grandparents' house. In the moonlight, I see the banks of the small inlet where my grandfather took me and Ryan fishing when we were kids. It's easy enough to imagine how someone might disappear around here. Between all the water and the gators, I'm certain my grandmother isn't the only person in town who just never made it home.

Grandma Sue, the woman my grandfather married a few years after his first wife disappeared, is the only grandmother I've ever known. She's always doted on me to such an extent that it was a shock when I learned we aren't actually related. She flutters around me from the moment I walk in the door. "Why didn't you tell us you had a meeting down here?" she asks. "My friends will be so upset they missed your visit."

"Sorry. It was just kind of last-minute." It feels a little disloyal that I'm here to ask about her predecessor. My grandfather has been a good husband, I'm certain, but there's apparently never been any doubt where his heart lies. Sue deserved better than second place.

We eat dinner while Sue grills me, asking in every roundabout way possible when I'm going to settle down. "We need babies running around the house again," she says. "How much longer are you going to make us wait?"

"I don't know," I reply. I think of Quinn pregnant; I think of us raising a child together. That it will probably never happen makes my chest tighten. We'd have been good parents. "I'm not sure that's in the cards for me."

I call Quinn after dinner but only get her voicemail. I know she's out with Caroline, but I call it again, just to hear the sound of her voice, that tiny rasp when she says her name, the sweetness of it. I just saw her a few hours ago and I already miss her. What's it going to be like if she leaves me for good?

~

THE NEXT MORNING, my grandfather and I head out on his boat, just as the morning sky morphs from black to lavender. Fishing has always been more his thing than mine, but the traditions involved—waking up at dawn, the thermos full of coffee, and a small cooler with the breakfast my grandmother prepared for us—brings back memories.

"Don't imagine you do a lot of this in D.C.," my grandfather comments as we cast our lines.

"I don't think I'd want to eat anything that came out of the Potomac."

He nods. "So why don't you tell me why you're really here," he says. "Because no one travels to a medical conference with nothing but a gym bag. Did your dad send you to check up on me?"

I laugh to myself. My grandfather never did miss much. "No." I close my eyes and take a deep breath. "I did want to ask you some questions, though. About your first wife."

A shadow crosses his face, a kind of sinking, deep-seated grief I suspect is always present, just hidden.

"What do you want to know?" he asks, his voice slow, gravelly with caution.

I lean forward, my elbows pressed to my knees, and turn my head toward him. "Do you really think she drowned?"

There's a flash of something in his eyes, *knowledge*, gone nearly as soon as it appears. "No one knows for sure," he replies. "Why do you ask?"

I hesitate. There is a ninety percent chance he's going to decide I'm nuts by the time we get off this boat. "The woman I'm seeing, Quinn, may have a genetic mutation, one I think I may have as well. And I'm trying to figure out where I got it."

He grows still. "What kind of mutation?"

I adjust my line, as if his question or my response are casual. "The kind that might be responsible for someone's disappearance. Something not a lot of people seem to know about."

My grandfather is silent, staring hard at the water. "I'm not sure what you mean."

"Quinn has a brain tumor," I reply quietly. "Unlike anything I've ever seen. Growing with no sign of blood flow to the site. We've been told she can do things other people can't."

"What sort of things?" my grandfather asks.

I'd hoped to get him to talk without being forced to admit what I'm getting at. If I'm wrong he's going to think I'm crazy. "Time travel."

He's quiet. He's quiet for so long I grow certain he's looking for a diplomatic way to end our fishing trip entirely before he goes home to tell my parents I need medication. "And you're wondering if your grandmother did it too," he says. "Because she disappeared."

I run a hand through my hair, realizing how insane it sounds when stated outright. I jumped on a plane and flew down here like a fucking lunatic because a woman who lived next to the water disappeared over fifty years ago. "I know it sounds crazy," I tell him. "We're just a little desperate."

He doesn't look at me but stares straight at the water. "It doesn't sound all that crazy to me," he says quietly.

My head jerks toward him. "Are you saying she *did* it?"

He sighs. "She did."

I grip the fishing rod, stunned into silence. I came here because I thought it was possible, but learning it's true still shocks me. It also means Quinn's theory may be right—I carry at least one mutated gene and she carries two. Which means there's a 75 percent chance any daughter we have would be able to time travel.

"It's funny," my grandfather muses, "how you can convince yourself of anything until you learn otherwise. Once I knew the truth about your grandmother, I couldn't believe I hadn't wondered. She had these eyes like nothing I'd ever seen before, and she was so beautiful we couldn't walk down the street without getting stares. But I never questioned it."

I didn't either. I noticed the same things about Quinn—the way people stare as she passes, the color of her eyes—and it never occurred to me that she was anything more than genetically blessed. I guess it's human nature to explain away the unusual. Quinn denies all these strange incidents in her childhood meant anything, my mother and I both have these bizarre dreams we rationalize away. We've spent our lives insisting unusual things were normal. Maybe it's time we stopped.

"So when she disappeared," I ask, "did you know what happened? Do you know where she went?"

His face sags. He stares ahead at the water, but his mind is somewhere else. "I was trying to save money for medical school and she kept saying she could go back a few years. Make an investment for us. I always said no. I didn't want her to do it, not until your father was grown, because it was a dangerous business, time travel. Never know what you're going to find or where you're going to get stuck. And I think she mostly didn't do it, but the temptation was just too strong I guess. A few months after she disappeared I got a financial statement from a broker. We somehow had 400,000 dollars in stock, which was a fortune back then. I researched it, of course. It looked like the original investment was made in 1921. I kept hoping she'd come back—" He flinches. After all this time, the memory still hurts. "Obviously, it didn't work out that way."

I can already feel it, the sick turning of the gut I'd have in his place. That could be Quinn. She could go back and I'd have no fucking way to find her. "How would she have gotten stuck there? Couldn't she just time travel right back out?"

He pulls off his hat and straightens it. "She once told me if you go back a ways, it sometimes takes all you've got. You're so exhausted you have to recover before you can jump back. And if you stay someplace too long you weaken until you *can't* get back. But I don't think that's what happened to her."

"No?"

He shakes his head. "She was only 25 when it happened. If she somehow just got stuck in 1921, she'd have still been alive when she got to 1962. Even if she didn't want to come back to us, she'd have let me know somehow that she was okay."

I'd pictured it as something simple, like a jump over a yardstick. It's not simple at all. It's deadly, and here I've been pushing Quinn to try. "I'm so sorry," I whisper.

He looks over at me for the first time since the conversation began. "I've had almost sixty years to get used to it. Sounds like you're the one in need of sympathy. This girl of yours—there's no other way to cure the tumor? Radiation? Chemo?"

I grit my teeth as I realize I'm going to lose her whether she time travels or not. "No," I reply. "And maybe I'm fooling myself, thinking that if we can just talk to the right person, someone who knows what's going on, we can solve it. But I have to try."

"I wish I could help," he says. "But your grandmother was the only person I ever knew who could do it."

"She never mentioned anyone? A friend? A family member?"

He shakes his head. "There are rules," he says. "I don't understand them, but there are rules about who you tell. She never even told me until she was pregnant—said we had to share a blood relative."

I think about Rose and her initial refusal to help. "What would have happened if she'd told you before?"

He shakes his head. "I never knew a lot about it. Didn't want to know. But she implied if you got caught it was bad for everyone involved."

I try to ignore the twist of guilt in my stomach. If any teenager was duplicitous enough to get away with breaking some time traveling code of ethics, it was Rose.

We sit in silence for a while longer. Nothing is biting, so eventually we turn toward home. It's only as we're climbing off the boat that my grandfather's hand lands on my shoulder. "I hope you know what you're doing. It's a hard life."

"Time traveling?"

He shakes his head, staring at the rope in his weathered hands. "No," he says. "Being the one who has to stay behind."

12

QUINN

It feels like days since I've seen Nick and it hasn't even been twenty-four hours. Caroline and Trevor took me out last night, but even they couldn't cheer me up. He'll be back tomorrow. It's pathetic how badly I want to beg him to come home tonight instead.

It will be an unpleasant day on so many fronts, I think, as I pull into the driveway of the house I shared with Jeff. It's probably the last time I'll ever come here, but what makes me unhappy right now is the fact that I wound up here in the first place. I never wanted this house. I never wanted the furniture we bought. I never wanted to live in the suburbs. The thrilling part of being in D.C., after my years on the farm, was how lively it was. I loved that I could walk to restaurants, that I never had to drive anywhere if I didn't want to. It was Jeff who wanted what we had, and I gave up everything again and again, without a fight. It's almost as if I was scared to ever want anything of my own too much.

I walk back into my former home, uncertain where to start.

It would be frugal for me to take some of the furniture, but I really don't want it. I go through the kitchen and find that I don't really care about anything there either, even though I purchased most of it myself. They were *supposed to's*. Because you're supposed to have a fancy cappuccino machine, even though I rarely drink cappuccinos. You're supposed to have the panini press, the salad swiveler. They were things I chose in an attempt to fill the hole in my life, but it was like pouring water into a pit made of sand...far too soon the space it took up siphoned into nothing and left me empty again.

I move to the closet instead, carefully folding the clothes I wore to work, the T-shirts I bought on sale at the J Crew outlet or Ann Taylor Loft. After about ten minutes I dump them out of my suitcase and put them in a bag of donations.

I'm not taking anything into my new life with Nick that I don't absolutely love.

The suits go, as do the blouses, the heels I spent too much on but never wore because they killed my feet. I throw in the pantyhose, the slips, the worn, old bras I held onto for no reason other than frugality. Caroline was right when she said I'd spent my life cowering. From my career choices to my boyfriend to the clothes I wore, my whole life has been about shrinking myself, trying to become less than what I was because it felt like the safest course. With Nick it no longer seems necessary.

In the end it only takes two suitcases and a few boxes to hold every single thing I actually love: my favorite jeans, my softest sweaters, the dresses and shoes I can't live without. A few books, a few photos. It's astonishing, and depressing, that in a two-bedroom home crammed with stuff, I loved and wanted so little. All of it fits tidily in the trunk of my car. I think I had more stuff in the college dorm room I shared with Caroline than I have right now.

I arrange for the bags of clothes I'm giving away to be

picked up, and I'm in the process of dragging the last one outside when Jeff turns into the driveway. I freeze, rooted to the spot as if I've been caught breaking in. I wasn't really scared of him before, not the way Nick thought I should be. Now I realize how foolish that was. There's no reason for him to be home today at all—and certainly not at this hour—unless he somehow knew I was here.

He climbs from the car, stalking toward me with narrowed eyes. "What the fuck do you think you're doing?"

Inside, I quake, but I refuse to let him see it. "Why aren't you in Harrisonburg?" I counter.

"What's the point?" he asks. "I was only at that job because of you. And you didn't give a shit."

The guilt trip he's given me over the jobs he's held here is getting a little old. It's not like I pushed him, and in fact with his current job I lobbied against it because it was such a bad fit. "I never asked you to take that job."

"Don't try to act like it had nothing to do with you. You could have told me no at any point and you never did."

I swallow and stare at the ground. He's being an asshole, but he's also right. I should have shut him down when he first came to D.C., but I was so desperate to keep the peace, to do what my father wanted and to feel safe, that I wound up doing something so much worse: I stayed with someone I was never meant to be with. "I'm sorry," I say quietly. "And I know an apology makes up for nothing and can't give you those years back, but I'm truly sorry I put you through this."

He steps closer. I fight the urge to back away. "Tell me something. How much of this bullshit is about your tumor, and how much of it is about Nick fucking Reilly?" His arms cross over his chest, his legs spread wide as if he will actually block me from heading to my car. "I knew he was after you from the first fucking moment he looked at you. You weren't even *conscious,* and I knew. That's what this is about, isn't it?"

My heart beats faster. I'm shit at lying, and he's right. If I'd never met Nick, I probably would have continued with my blinders on, marrying a man I didn't deeply love, going through the motions of a life I never wanted. But the truth won't work here, not with him as angry as he is. "No. It's not." Liars look up and to the left, as I recall, which is probably why my gaze desperately wants to veer away from his. "I just want this year, if it's going to be my last, to be perfect."

"Bullshit," Jeff hisses. "You're covering for him because you know how much trouble he could get into for this. You're his patient. I'll bet he's not even allowed to date you, is he?"

My hands start to tremble, and I shove them into my pockets in case he notices. "Is it really so hard to accept that I don't think you and I are meant to be together? We don't like the same things; we don't want the same things from our future. You've been unhappy with every decision I've made for months. Don't start trying to make this about someone else."

His nostrils flare. "You know why I know it's about someone else? Because you're too goddamn weak to have ever left on your own. You'd never have been willing to hurt me and my family and your mother unless there was someone else. And the second I get proof I'm going to make that asshole pay. He's taking advantage of a dying girl. You're probably not the first one he's done it to, but you'll definitely be the last because when I'm done with him, he'll be out of a job."

My stomach starts to spin, whipping fast and faster until the knots are tied so tight I'm not sure they'll ever come loose. "You sound insane," I reply, doing my best to sound flippant when it feels like I'm about to vomit on his shoes. "And you're just convincing me I made the right decision."

I walk away, swallowing my pain and my terror until I'm behind the wheel of my car. And then I drive exactly one block away, press my face to the steering wheel, and cry, wondering exactly how much of Nick's life I'll have ruined before this is through.

13

NICK

My grandfather and I enter the house after what could only be considered an unsuccessful trip— no fish, no information that can save Quinn. Just a new kind of anxiety eating at my gut when I imagine losing her the way my grandfather lost his wife.

It's barely been twenty-four hours since I saw her, but it's already been too long. I miss the curve of her lips, the way her lashes lower when she's thinking something she shouldn't. The raspy note at the base of her laugh, the velvet skin on the underside of her wrist. I want to hear about her day and tell her about mine. In an ideal world I'd do a whole lot more than all of that.

Just after lunch I call her. My relief when she answers fades the moment I hear the choked sob in her voice. "What's wrong?" I push the bedroom door closed behind me. "What happened?"

She takes a deep inhale, trying to pull herself together. "I went to go get my stuff from Jeff's. He showed up as I was leaving and..."

I'm going to break every bone in his goddamn body if he laid a finger on her. "I thought he was out of town."

"I did too." Her swallow is audible. "But he's convinced I broke up with him over you. He didn't seem to have any actual proof, but he said he could get some and that he'd ruin you."

The news tires me more than anything else. Neither of us has time for this bullshit right now. I sink onto the bed. "I knew the risks when I started this with you."

"Nick," she whispers, "I can't be the reason you lose your job."

I pinch the bridge of my nose. God, I wish we weren't having this conversation over the phone. "You won't be. Let's just cross that bridge when we come to it."

"We've already *come* to it!" she cries. "Jeff is going to do whatever it takes to find proof. And there's nothing about this that is good for you. I'm just taking up a year of your life that should be spent finding someone you can actually end up with. It was selfish of me to even consider it. And I definitely can't let you risk your job over me too."

I grip the phone tightly, appalled by the shift this conversation has taken. I thought I was on safe ground but it's as if I've suddenly found myself scrambling up a crumbling rock wall instead. "Quinn—"

"No. Don't try to convince me." Her voice breaks. "When you care about someone you want what's best for them, and I'm definitely not what's best for you. I'm trying to do the right thing here. And I need you to let me." She hangs up the phone and I sit here in shock, staring at it in my hand.

She's crazy if she thinks I'm going to let her walk away over this.

〜

I've told my grandparents that something came up. We say our goodbyes, and my grandfather walks me to the car, resting a hand on my shoulder as I reach for the door. "Are you sure you want to get involved with this girl? Even if you save her, it's not likely to end well."

As if I wasn't painfully aware of that fact. "It's too late," I reply. "It was too late from the day we met."

He sighs, reaching into his pocket. "I thought you might say that," he replies, holding out a small black velvet box. "It was your grandmother's. I never told anyone I had it because I'd have to explain why her ring and her clothes were still here the day she left. But she once told me that if something were to happen to her, I should hold onto it for the right time. She never told me when it would be, exactly, but I feel like it's probably now."

I pop the box open. It's a very large oval diamond, surrounded by tiny ones. The exact ring Quinn described.

Which means my grandfather and I have had this conversation before.

14

QUINN

I've managed to stop crying but just barely, and my tears threaten to return every thirty to forty seconds. Trevor and Caroline gather in the apartment with a bottle of wine in an attempt to cheer me up. I appreciate the effort, but the truth is there isn't enough wine in the world to make me anything other than despondent right now.

"You're being ridiculous," says Trevor. "Jeff can't follow the two of you everywhere."

"That's what I said!" Caroline shouts. She's been drinking at a much faster rate than the rest of us.

"He wouldn't *have* to follow us everywhere," I say quietly, staring at my glass of wine. "He'd just have to follow us *once* successfully."

Caroline throws her hands in the air. "This guy is obviously your soul mate! And when you find your soul mate, you can't just curl up in a ball and decide to skip it because you've hit a little roadblock. Especially with a dude who looks like *that*."

I wish they'd leave so I could sleep. I want to sleep until this is over with, whatever *this* is. Grief, pain, shock. Except it's not going anywhere soon. "It's not a *little* roadblock," I reply. "He's going to lose his medical license because of me if this continues. Do you know how many years he's invested in this? How much money? Four years of college, four years of med school, four years of residency. All to end up empty-handed because of me. It would be selfish to even allow him to continue this."

"Well, I think it's selfish of you to try to make his decisions for him," replies Caroline.

I swallow hard, running a finger over the rim of my wineglass. "I hung up the phone earlier today and he never called back, so he must agree at some level." It's for the best he didn't argue with me about it, even if it sort of hurts at the same time.

The two of them continue to argue until the doorbell rings. Then they exchange a glance and jump to their feet.

"You invited someone else?" I ask.

They both ignore me. "Get your purse," Trevor says to Caroline.

"Wait..." I demand, rising. "What's going on here?" I start moving farther from the door. Knowing Trevor, he's called a male prostitute to cheer me up.

"You, my little sad sack, are going to do some chatting," says Trevor, heading toward the door with Caroline at his heels. They open it and walk out, which is when I hear a voice I'd recognize anywhere.

Nick.

He walks in, so beautiful I want to weep at the sight of him. He's wearing a navy-blue tee that makes his eyes look impossibly blue and ends right at his biceps. An arrow saying *look at my magnificent arms* couldn't do a better job of calling attention to them. "It's ridiculously unfair that you're wearing that shirt," I whisper, my voice hoarse with the need to cry.

His eyes move over me—hair, face, moving down to the floor and back up—before he remembers to shut the door. "I needed to use every advantage available," he says, with the barest of smiles.

I want nothing more in the entire world than to fall into his arms like this is some dumb movie, but it's not. "I assume Caroline and Trevor are behind this?"

He shakes his head, his eyes never leaving mine. "Nope, this is all on me. Fortunately, they both agree you're being insane."

I groan. "It's easy for them to say that. They're not the ones who will lose a medical license because of this."

He crosses the room and presses me to the wall. "I'm not going to lose my license either." His mouth lands on mine, hard. He kisses me with a desperation I feel all the way to my bones, one that matches my own. His hands move from my hips, slide into my shirt and it's only when I gasp—the good kind of gasp—that he backs away.

"Fuck," he groans. "What am I doing? I'm trying to persuade you to take me back, but not like this."

I inhale sharply, wishing I could regret it as much as he seems to. So far, my attempt to do the right thing is going really poorly.

He pulls me against his chest, tucking my head safely beneath his chin. "I've been sick to my stomach since you called."

My breath hitches, a small sob trapped in my throat. "If I were healthy it would be different. But I'm not. How can I let you risk everything for what will amount to a year or two of your long life?"

He pulls back just enough to see my face. "I can only assume you don't feel nearly as much for me as I do for you or you'd get this. I don't care about the years after you're gone. I'm not even sure I *want* those years. I just want the time you have left, every fucking minute of it."

I feel light entering more of the dark space inside me, as something that's waited a lifetime to blossom begins to unfurl.

But this isn't about me. "That's exactly how I feel too, but Nick... you should have seen the look on his face. He was really determined. He's going to stop at nothing until he has proof."

He gives me that cocky grin of his. "We'll just need to be a little cleverer than him which—no offense—shouldn't be that hard. He might try to trail you for a little while but eventually he's going to tire of coming up empty-handed. In the meantime, we figure out what's behind the tumor and if we can cure it, and maybe we find your aunt or somebody else who can fabricate a past for the two of us."

I sigh. "Okay. I'll try harder—to time travel, I mean. Maybe I can—"

"No," he says fiercely. "I don't want you to try anymore."

My eyes widen. "Why the sudden change?" I ask. "A day ago, you were pleading with me to try."

"That's before I talked to my grandfather. We can discuss it later, but suffice it to say, it's a lot more dangerous than I realized. We need to find another way."

"What if we don't, though?" I ask.

"We will," he says. "We'll find another way because there's no other choice. You're my life. You're the only part of it I want. And we will find a way to fix this." I love his words and they break my heart at the same time, because there's this deep sadness to his eyes as he voices them, a sadness I can't explain. Maybe he's finally decided I'm not going to beat this. Whatever the reason, I have no doubt I'm the source of his pain, and that I'll continue to be for a long, long time.

15

QUINN

Three days later, the perfect little house becomes ours. I oversee the delivery of our new bed and couch, then wait impatiently for Nick to get back from packing his place so we can christen one, or both. The last time we were alone for any extended period of time was last Monday in his office. Needless to say, we are both about to burst.

"Honey, I'm home!" he calls. His voice echoes over the bare hardwood floors.

I lean over the upstairs railing, smiling down at him. "I think we might need some rugs."

"It's perfect like this," he says, taking the stairs toward me, two at a time. "I can demand a blowjob from any room of the house without even raising my voice."

He walks right into me, lifting me as he continues on a path to our room. "Are you planning to demand a blowjob?"

He grins. "Of course not. I'm assuming you'll offer one long before I get to that point." He presses his mouth to mine and holds it there a moment before he sets me down in our room. "So this is the bed."

"This is the bed. Is it everything you hoped it would be?"

"All I hoped for was a flat surface big enough to pin you to, so yes, it's perfect." He glances at the corner of my room, to the boxes I carried in from the trunk of my car, and frowns. "You already started carrying stuff in from Jeff's? I told you I'd get it."

I shrug. "There wasn't much. I'm already done."

His frown deepens. "Wait. You're saying that's *it*? That can't possibly be all of your stuff."

I slide my hands into his. "The tumor kind of brought everything into focus. I decided I was only bringing the things I really loved."

This, to me, is a good thing, but when he averts his gaze I remember how much he hates even the smallest reminder this is all going to end. "Nothing about your tumor is normal," he says, turning away to drop his wallet, phone and hospital ID on one of the boxes. "Your last MRI showed it hadn't grown at all. Possibly it was even smaller. And also—it's not affecting you. At all. I mean, aside from those seizures, you haven't had a single symptom, right?"

"I guess not."

"You should have," he says, turning back to me. "So maybe it's...this is going to sound crazy, but maybe it was just some weird time-traveling thing and it's all solved now that you're doing what you were supposed to. We're back together, you're getting your degree...maybe that's it."

There's a desperation in his voice that saddens me. It's what he wants to believe. And, God, I want to believe it too. I wish I'd never said anything—today is a day for us to enjoy what we have, not destroy it with thoughts of what's to come. I slide my shorts off as he watches. "I feel pretty healthy at the moment," I reply. The T-shirt is removed next.

His eyes flicker over me, gone sharp and feral in the blink of an eye. "You *look* exceptionally healthy."

I walk over and lie back on our brand-new mattress. "How do you feel about taking advantage of an exceptionally healthy girl?"

He runs his tongue over his lip and unbuttons his shorts. "I'm feeling better about it by the second."

THAT NIGHT we order Chinese food and eat it in our garden, on a blanket under the stars—a romantic way to deal with the fact that our kitchen chairs are backordered for the next month.

"When was the moment you knew you'd break up with Meg?" I ask him.

He sets his plate off to the side and leans back on the blanket. "That night in Baltimore. Sometime between leaving the diner with you and jerking off in the shower at 3:00 a.m. because of you."

"You didn't," I gasp, wide-eyed and completely turned on by the idea at the same time.

He grins. "Are you kidding me? We were two seconds away from having sex when I woke up. There was no way I was falling back asleep without taking care of it. What about you? When did you know you were breaking up with Jeff?"

I try to focus on the question, but really I'm a little too busy imagining him in the hotel shower. I might need him to stage a reenactment. "It's not nearly as exciting as your story. There's almost no jerking off in it at all."

He pulls me down beside him. "I kind of figured that much. But seriously, when did you know? I mean, you went to the airport with Jeff so it had to be kind of last-minute, right?"

I stare at the sky, wondering if I'm looking at the Big Dipper or just a bunch of random stars. "My dad told me this story when I was a kid, about the good wind and the bad wind, and how you had to let them both in. I always thought it was his way of telling me not to be scared of storms, but that morning on the way to the airport, I finally realized it had nothing to do with weather. It was about opening yourself up, risking all the bad that can come along with the good, because without it you will suffocate. And I knew I was suffocating."

He gives a low laugh. "Wait, are you saying I might be the *bad* wind?"

I roll toward him, taking in the upward curve of his generous mouth. Right now, it's hard to imagine him being the bad *anything*, but that's precisely what makes him so dangerous. "You're both, potentially. Because the more you let someone in, the more they're able to hurt you, or drive you to do something terrible." I get a sudden flash of Nick's face when he walked in that room and saw me with Ryan, the agony there, and there's a tightness in my chest—dread. Is it just residual guilt, or is it because I made a mistake after that, a grave one? That party was the night Ryan died. I already know I shot a kid out of a tree. What else might I have done that I couldn't take back?

"I'm never going to hurt you," he says, pressing his mouth to the base of my wrist.

I focus on the warmth of his mouth against my skin, trying to drive away thoughts about Ryan. "People hurt each other all the time without meaning to. It doesn't have to be malicious. Like Darcy. When she dies it will destroy her parents. I'm not sure how anyone recovers from that."

He brushes the hair back from my face and lifts my chin toward him with his thumb. "That's why you're hedging your bets," he says. "You dumped Jeff and you were willing to risk being with me, but you're still scared. You're still trying to hold a little of yourself back."

I'm on the cusp of arguing when it strikes me: he's right. I agreed to *marry* Jeff but for some reason that never seemed risky, while with Nick it feels like I've gotten behind the wheel for the first time, and the only way I can stay safe is by riding the brake the whole way. "A lot could go wrong with us," I whisper.

He pulls my head onto his shoulder. "And a lot could go so, so well. I can wait. You're going to let me in eventually."

That's what I'm scared of. Because it feels dangerous, being with him.

And I'm worried I won't find out why until it's too late.

16

QUINN

We spend a blissful week acting like newlyweds. He goes to work, and I putter around the house, putting our meager belongings away, going to the store every five minutes for mundane things like trash cans and spatulas, the sort of stuff that doesn't seem important until you discover it's missing.

I've also tried to time travel a bit, without success. I know Nick doesn't want me to—he's too worried about what happened to his grandmother. Every night he comes up with some new way to find Sarah's address: he tells me we should check my dad's will, go to the state department, search my parents' computer. But it seems like it would be so much easier if I could just go back and find Rose myself, and it's frustrating when I come up empty, time and time again.

For the most part though, we exist in a happy little bubble, and it's easy enough to shrug off my fears. We cook together, shop together, sit out on a picnic blanket under the stars each night to eat our dinner. We could have gotten plastic chairs until the real dining chairs arrive, but I sort of like our little tradition. I like that there is no TV, that we aren't on our phones, that I get his full attention and he gets mine. And then we go to bed, where we do a lot of things, but we don't have sex.

Which is getting more difficult to deal with by the day.

It shouldn't be. We should be fine just as we are. But I miss it, desperately...not with Jeff, but with Nick. I miss something I don't even remember having and he does too. Each night I see the toll his restraint takes, the way his teeth clench as he tries not to head in directions we can't go.

We are in bed and he is above me, separated only by the paper-thin fabric of my boy shorts, and he's got his eyes squeezed shut, wanting the feeling of being pressed against me and tortured by it all the same. "Maybe we should," I whisper. I'm not sure if it's logic or desperation speaking.

His eyes open, a hazy blue, with that drugged look they get when he's in this exact position. "What?" he says.

"Maybe we should just do it," I whisper. "We have no idea what will happen this time and I'm on the pill. So maybe we should."

He is hard as steel against me the second the words emerge, and then a sort of panic comes over his face. "God, Quinn," he groans, pushing harder against the fabric, burying his face into my shoulder. "Do not say that to me right now." His leg swings off me, and in a flash he's gone, nothing but a blur walking straight out the bedroom door.

I guess my timing could have been better, but I don't feel like it was a mistake. I'm no longer sure what I believe in, but I know being with Nick makes me happier than anything in my life ever has, and every step we've taken together has only improved things. It's just hard to imagine sex would be any different. It's hard to imagine something so good could end up going bad.

Nick returns a minute later, and lies down beside me. "I'm sorry I left like that."

"Why did you?"

He laughs unhappily and pushes his hair off his forehead. "Do you have any idea how hard it is for me to stop every time? Suggesting it might be okay at *that* moment, when my defenses are down...could have been disastrous. I had to get out of here because it was the only way to make sure I didn't lose it entirely. I mean, what were you thinking?"

"What I'm thinking is that we don't know everything," I reply quietly. "And that we are supposed to be together, and there is obviously something driving this. Fate or history or something else. Maybe it knows more than we do."

His hands go to his hair again. "*Don't*. Don't go down the path of justifying it. It fucking kills me, the fact that Jeff has had something I want this badly. And every day it gets harder. But until something changes, until we know you could actually survive a pregnancy, we cannot take that risk. Because as badly as I want it, I want you more. I want you to survive and be here with me for the next seventy years."

I don't realize I'm crying until he pulls me against his chest and brushes away my tears. I want everything he does. I want to give him those seventy years. And I'm so bitter right now about all the things—fate, the crazy blond lady, whatever—conspiring to separate us again.

～

THE NEXT AFTERNOON I go to the hospital to visit Darcy. I've been in a few times, but this is the first where I can say definitively that she's getting worse. She's thinner and pale and the circles beneath her eyes have gone from lavender to a bruised sort of blue. There's a wheelchair in her room permanently now, which leads me to think she no longer roams the halls freely dragging her IV behind her.

It's late in the day when Nick walks in to join us for the cutthroat Connect Four tournament now underway. He smiles at Darcy and Christy before he allows himself to look at me, but when he does there's a single long moment where I forget there's anyone else in the room.

"Who's winning?" he finally asks.

"Darcy. Never bet her money on this game." I'm not trying to pump her up—she's truly unbelievably good at it, and every time she wins I'm swallowing down a lump in my throat. It's so fucking unfair that I'm dying now that I've found Nick. And it's so much *more* unfair that she's dying before she's experienced anything at all, before she's gotten a chance to even uncover that amazing potential inside her. I hate that she's getting worse. Even over the course of our game she's been falling asleep and then jolting awake a minute later, without seeming to realize she was asleep at all.

Christy smooths a hand over her daughter's head, where only tiny wisps of light hair remain. "That's exactly what Darcy's father says."

Nick raises a brow at her. "Any progress with that?"

Christy shoots a wary glance at her daughter, who's dozed off again. "Nothing yet."

I know, from Nick, that Darcy's father was stationed in Afghanistan and is recovering from serious injuries there. The hope is he'll be stable enough to be transported back to the States before Darcy gets too ill. Except, based on how thin she is and those circles under her eyes, I'm beginning to wonder if he's going to be too late.

"Quinn," Darcy says, opening her eyes as if nothing's happened, "what's Prom?"

My lips press together and I try not to think too hard about why she's asking me this. "It's a dance. In high school. Girls wear long dresses and boys wear tuxedos."

She drops a yellow disc into a row, basically trapping me. No matter what I do, she will win on her next turn. "Who did you go with?" she asks.

Nick's eyes flicker to mine, waiting for my answer. "Um...his name was Josh. Josh Casey."

"Did you kiss him?" she asks. "Was he a football player?"

"Darcy," her mother scolds softly, "that's a little personal."

I smile at them both. "It's okay. Yes, I kissed him. And no, he played hockey. He still does, actually. He plays for Vancouver now."

"I just won," she says, dropping in her last yellow disc. Her eyes close for a long moment, but then open again. "Are you still friends?"

I shrug. "I guess. He moved away so we only see each other at Christmas." When I glance up at Nick, I find his jaw is set. And he looks absolutely miserable. He can't possibly be jealous of someone I dated a decade ago, but it would certainly appear, to look at him, he is exactly that.

HE SAYS nothing about it as we leave the hospital. We maintain a safe distance between us until we're outside and have crossed to Reservoir Road. That's when his fingers twine with mine. "I hate that," he says quietly. "I hate that there were other guys. It feels like whoever's changing your life has stolen something from me. I should have taken you to Prom. I should have been your first kiss, your first everything, and I fucking hate that I wasn't."

I sigh. I've tried not to let myself think about it, but there's always a small weight in my chest, knowing he's been with other people. From the sound of it, a *lot* of other people. "I know. It bothers me too."

"And with fucking Josh Casey of all people," he mutters. "You went to Prom with Josh fucking Casey. I can't believe you never mentioned you used to date a pro athlete."

I shrug. "I don't think of him as a pro athlete. I just think of him as a nice kid from the town over who was obsessed with hockey. And I didn't sleep with him, if that helps. Jeff's the only person I've ever been with."

"It helps less than you think. No guy wants to picture his girlfriend with the center for the Canucks in any capacity."

I laugh and lean my head against his arm. "He was a kid, Nick. And actually...this is going to sound crazy, but I think it'll help both of us: I want to see pictures. I want to see who you took to Prom. I want to see the first girl you ever slept with."

He stops walking entirely. "Why the fuck would you want to see that?" he asks incredulously.

"Because I think it'll make me feel less jealous. I'm picturing supermodels, but really, they were just girls. And Josh Casey was an 18-year-old boy who was badly in need of a haircut and had terrible taste in music."

"I'm taller than he is," he mutters, unappeased.

I go on my toes to kiss his cheek. "Yes, baby, I know. Now let's go find some pictures."

Because I just unpacked, it doesn't take long to unearth my childhood photo album, but Nick's box of memorabilia is a little harder to come by, so it takes a few more days before we finally get around to the big *reveal*. When I show him the infamous Josh Casey of a decade ago, his shoulders relax. "Okay, you were right. I feel better."

"Your turn," I reply, nodding at the box. It will bother me, no matter who the girls are, that I wasn't his first for anything. But I think it will normalize it a little—as long as they're all not as attractive as Meg.

He digs into a large box he's brought up from the basement and stares at the contents in dismay. "I have no idea what half of this crap is," he says, handing me a pile of papers. "But the yearbooks may be at my parents' house."

I begin looking through the stuff he's handed to me. "Are you hoarding love letters from old girlfriends?"

"Doubt it," he says, retrieving another stack of miscellaneous cards and photos, "but you seem to remember my life back then better than I do, so you tell me."

My smile fades as I pick up a picture of Nick and Ryan. "You really were almost identical."

"Yeah, even my father confused us occasionally."

Was I really at fault that night I confused them? I know there wasn't a bone in my body that thought I was kissing Ryan until the horrible moment when he said *I wanted you first*. But should I have figured it out sooner? Did Nick continue to blame me in some quiet corner of his brain?

He comes to a sudden halt, staring at something in his hands, a half-second of hesitation before he shuffles the paper to the back of the pile.

"What's the matter?" I ask.

He glances at me and away, handing the paper to me. "I kept the flyer from Ryan's memorial service. I don't know why. I can't seem to get rid of it."

I don't want to take it.

But I find myself reaching for it anyway, and darkness closes in the moment it's in my hands.

∾

EVEN AS RYAN'S coffin is being lowered into the ground, I'm thinking about the party.

Nick sits beside me, crushing my fingers with his own, his face pale, empty. On the other side of him, his mother is bent low, shoulders shaking.

I did this.

It was so simple, time traveling back a few hours the night of the party. I stood there watching Nick and Ryan beat the shit out of each other—because of me—and it felt like the world was caving in. And it was so unnecessary, when I had the power to fix it.

It never really occurred to me that I shouldn't go back. I'd done far harder things with my mother over the preceding years. It was all so easy. Traveling back, convincing Nick to skip the party. And when I was in the treehouse with him, pulling his T-shirt over his head, it didn't feel like an act. It felt like the night we should have had all along.

Until the next morning, when I heard Ryan was dead. That's when I realized how wrong I'd been.

There's no one I can tell. Not Nick, who would never forgive me if he knew. Not Ryan, who will never hear my words, my apologies, again. And not my mother, because she warned me. Time and time again she warned me that when you go to the past to fix things, you risk making them worse. And she was right. I should have just left it alone. I have done a terrible thing, and I will never, ever do it again.

17

NICK

"It's going to be okay."

I've said this aloud so many fucking times, and I'm not sure if it's for her or for myself. I just know that repeating it a thousand times still won't make it true.

It's been several hours now. Me with my useless words. The only response—that rhythmic beat of the heart-rate monitor, the constantly bleat of the alarm on the IV. I can't get her latest MRI images out of my head. The tumor is swallowing her brain. The radiologist's face as he handed me his report said it all.

She is heavily sedated...I know this. I'm responsible for it. But no one is even sure she'll regain consciousness and Jesus, I need to see her open her eyes. I need to know she's still with me.

I squeeze her hand, tell her again that she's going to be fine. I'm grateful she can't hear the lack of certainty in my voice.

How did I exist without her? That two months ago I didn't even know her seems impossible to me now. And if she doesn't come back...I can't even think about it. I was such a dick the other day, when she suggested we sleep together. So appalled and so desperate for it at the same time I could hardly put two coherent words together. If I'd realized how little time we actually had left, I'd have given her everything. I just didn't know.

The staff mostly leaves us alone. None of them approve of the fact that I broke up with Meg and am now clearly with my patient, but they seem to sense I'm too close to the edge to be pestered. I should have handed her case to someone else a while ago, but no one is going to monitor her as carefully as I will. No one else will be as thorough as I'll be, will refuse to leave a single stone unturned. I dare any of them to even suggest it.

There's a timid tap on the door and then Sully, the only male nurse on the floor, pops his head in. "They sent me to deliver the bad news," he says with wary eyes. "There's a guy outside saying he's Quinn's fiancé. The hospital must have called..."

I don't even let him finish the sentence. "No." There's not a chance in the world that asshole is getting anywhere near Quinn right now.

He swallows. "I checked her file—he's still listed as her next-of-kin. I'm not sure what to say to him."

My blood boils at the thought of Jeff in this room when he knows she wants nothing to do with him. "Tell him I said to go fuck himself," I reply. "If he complains, let me know and I'll deal with him myself." *Gladly.* The only reason I'm not already out there is because I don't want to leave Quinn's side.

I hear shouting down the hall less than a minute later, and then the door is thrown open. Jeff storms in, freezing at the sight of me sitting beside Quinn. "Why the fuck are you here?" he asks.

I rise. Nothing seems to matter anymore. Not my job, not what happens after this. Only that Quinn walks out of this hospital again. "For the same reason I've always been here with her when you're not. Because I'm the only one of us she wants."

He lunges. There's a security button on the wall. I could have back-up here to deal with him in a matter of seconds. But my mind empties. This hatred toward him...it's been in me since the first night we met. And I want to expel all of it, right here, while I've got the chance.

He flies into me with his hands on my throat and the two of us topple to the ground. Within seconds, though, my fist makes impact, and I sling him off me, with his back to the floor. I could stop now, but it isn't enough. When he groans at the second hit and stops fighting back at the third, it is still not enough.

Security rushes through the door. I should have stopped two punches ago, but it's not until they grab me that I finally allow reason to intervene.

"You okay, Dr. Reilly?" asks one of them. They're still holding my arms but it's the way your buddy does when he's pulling you out of a fight.

I give him a stiff nod, breathing heavily more from anger than exertion as I rise.

The other security guard helps Jeff to his feet and starts pulling him away. "You're dead, motherfucker," Jeff says, turning back toward me when they reach the door. "I'm reporting you. You hear me? You're going to lose your job."

The words mean nothing to me. Maybe he's right, but I'm already back in my seat, my fingers twining through Quinn's, pleading with her to wake up.

∾

"Hey." The word is raspy and uncertain. My head, resting against her hand, jolts upright. She is heavy-lidded, but there's a weak smile on her face.

I haven't cried since my brother died but I have to swallow hard to keep it at bay right now. My jaw clenches as I try to get a grip on this illogical twining of grief and joy. "You scared the shit out of me."

"Sorry," she says. "You may need to get used to it." Her hand reaches out, brushes my cheekbone. "Is that a bruise?"

It's been hours since the fight with Jeff. I'd almost forgotten. "I had a little scuffle with your ex."

Her eyes open wide and she tries to sit up, but I gently push her shoulder back to the mattress. "It's fine. Believe me, he looks a lot worse than I do. How do you feel?"

"I feel great," she says dismissively. "Are you okay? What happened with Jeff?"

I smile. It's so like her to regain consciousness worried about *me*. "I told you it was fine. You're the one who's in a hospital bed. Let's focus on you."

She looks like she wants to argue but restrains it with a frown. "Did you already do an MRI?" she asks.

God, I wish she hadn't asked. Even her best-case scenario at this point is a shitty one, and I know she'll see that no matter what I tell her. I stare fixedly at the bed rail, gripping her hand tighter. "Your tumor has doubled in size."

She nods, lips pressed tight, trying to hold it together. "And what does that mean?"

It means you could be dead in a week, in a day. It means the staff will be shocked you even woke up. God, I can't tell her any of this. "It's close to the point where it's going to impact things—your memory, your gross motor function," I reply. "I'm surprised it hasn't already."

I watch this sink in, and then her fingers tighten around mine. "That's not how I want you to remember me," she whispers, "so when it happens I want you to promise you'll stay away. I'll go to my mom's when it gets to that point."

I sigh. If she thinks I'd ever consider that, she doesn't know me at all. "I am not fucking leaving you."

"But—"

"Ask me a thousand times and the answer will still be no."

"Such dedication," she begins, brushing at her eyes, trying to make light of it. "It really must be true—" She stops herself, flushing at the conversation she's opening up. A conversation she thinks would be ridiculous this early on. Except it isn't ridiculous at all. I've been dying to say it for weeks.

"Love," I reply, completing the sentence. My eyes hold hers. "Yeah. It is."

18

QUINN

Nick stays with me for hours, feeding me water through a straw like I'm an invalid. "I can hold my own cup," I scold. "Or do all your patients get this level of service?"

His lips twitch. "I'm pretty sure you're the only one."

I throw my head against the pillow. I feel fine and it's not like being in this room is going to extend my life, so I don't want to waste what's left of it here. "Can't we just leave?"

"Soon," he says, brushing the hair back from my forehead. "In the meantime, your food is on the way, and I was thinking if you're up for it, we could go down the hall to see Darcy. She's been asking for you."

"How is she today?" I ask.

A shadow crosses his face. I wonder if he can't think about Darcy without seeing my future at the same time. "Not good, apparently," he replies.

We just saw her a few days ago, and she wasn't doing great then. The possibility that she's *worse* sickens me. "Let's go see her now," I say, squeezing his hand. "The food can wait."

His tongue slides over his lip—his tell, the thing he does when he's worried and thinking something through. "Okay," he says. "Let me just get a wheelchair."

I roll my eyes. "I don't need a *wheelchair*."

"It's a long walk and you've had a heavy sedative," he says. I open my mouth to argue and he continues. "It's also hospital policy. So you're getting the wheelchair. I need to make sure she's awake anyway."

I love the bossy, no-bullshit doctor side of Nick. If I didn't have about fourteen wires attached to me I'd suggest he lock the door so I could show him just how much I like it. "Fine," I groan. "You win."

He kisses my forehead. "Be right back."

The truth is he's probably right. The sedative still must not be out of my system because I feel like I could sleep for days. Except each time I allow my eyes to close, I see Ryan's coffin being lowered into the ground and the grief on Nick's face. I remember my thoughts and my guilt, but I have no memory of actually time traveling. I just see two different experiences that occurred on the same night—one in which Ryan kisses me at a party, and another in which Ryan dies.

Am I really going to admit any of this to Nick? Am I really going to tell him that the version of Ryan's death he remembers is a result of the version I was responsible for? I can't. But I hate that he's hinting he loves me when he has no idea who I am and what I may have done. *Nick is going to make me do a bad thing*, I told the psychologist. Was Ryan's death that thing?

A searing pain in my arm sends my thoughts scattering. My eyes open and go first to the needle pressed into my skin before jumping to the person who wields it.

I suck in air, begin drowning in panic before I can call out.

It's a face I've seen in a thousand nightmares, always with

that long blond braid hanging down her shoulder. She has the face of an angel, but she couldn't be further from it. Words I mean to say stumble over my lips and vanish. The drug...it's slipping through my veins like a heavy blanket, smothering my ability to react.

She smiles. Sweetly, as if she actually cares about me. "Don't worry. You won't feel a thing."

My arms hang limply against my sides, refusing my commands to move as she pulls down the saline dripping into my IV and hangs an identical bag in its place. She speaks again, but I can no longer hear what she says. The fluid from the IV is so cold it seems to burn. And then everything goes black.

19

NICK

Darcy is asleep. Maybe it's for the best...as soon as I suggested a visit it occurred to me Quinn might see herself in Darcy's pale face, in the way she now struggles to form words and falls asleep mid-speech. She's gotten so much worse since that Connect Four tournament just a few days ago.

Since I'm here, I do a quick check of her vitals. Her blood pressure is low. I take a subtle look at her hands, examining their pallor, looking for the hint of blue beneath the nails that means the end is near. Nothing yet, but soon there will be.

I glance at Christy. "If there's any way her father can be transported, I think he might want to get here soon."

She blinks away tears. I'm not telling her anything she doesn't know, but it's no less hard to hear. "He's still in bad shape. They think it's another week at least," she whispers. "How's Quinn?"

I close my eyes. "Not good."

We sit in silence for a moment. Misery may love company

but there's little solace in it for me. "I know it's wrong," she finally says, her voice rough, "but it makes me glad they'll be together, her and Darcy. I know Quinn will look after her."

I flinch. I'm not at a point where I can discuss what happens to Quinn after she's gone, but even if I were, I wouldn't picture what Christy does—a heaven of clouds and harps and people walking hand in hand. She imagines Quinn taking Darcy to some heavenly zoo, buying her ice cream, tucking her in at night. I envy her belief, but I'm unable to share it.

Quinn has to survive. No other option is acceptable.

The halls are quiet as I head back, typical for a Sunday afternoon. A nurse is in Quinn's room when I push open the door, shaking down her saline as if she wants it to run faster, though the fluids were fine when I left.

I step inside. "Was there something wrong with the..." I begin, my words trailing off when I see her face.

The second our eyes meet, I know. I know who she is and why she's here. I can grab her, or I can get the line out of Quinn's arm. I don't even need to debate it—I lunge for the IV. The woman is long gone by the time it's out. I hit the alarm and the code team rushes in with security on their heels. But despite all the noise, all the chaos, Quinn lies there, unmoving, completely still.

20

QUINN

The doctor conducting the sonogram sees something. I can tell by the way his brows go up, and my heart starts to race.

"Is there something wrong?" I whisper.

He glances back at Nick, who is staring at the image like it's about to step off the screen and offer him the secrets of the universe. "Do you want to tell or shall I?" he asks Nick.

Nick swallows and points to one tiny dot of flickering light on the screen. "There's one heartbeat," he says, sounding awestruck. He points to a second light. "And there's a second one."

Twins. We are having twins, when we hadn't even planned on one baby just yet.

The doctor laughs at the look on my face. "Don't worry. You'll get used to the idea." I nod, grinding my teeth to hide my panic. He has no idea what this means, and Nick doesn't either. But I do.

It means the predictions are coming true.

It means we have to hide this, or she's going to take it all away again.

MY EYES BLINK OPEN. It takes a moment for the bright lights and the beep of the alarm to sink into my brain.

Hospital. I can't remember why.

Nick sits beside me with circles under his eyes and a day's worth of stubble, the only man alive who could make exhaustion look this good. "Hey," I whisper.

He startles. "Oh thank God," he says with a choked inhale. His lips press to the back of my hand.

I frown, trying to figure out why I'm here again. I remember Ryan's memorial service and waking up here. My stomach takes a nosedive as I recall Nick's news about the MRI. But everything after that is a blank. "What happened?" I ask. "I remember being here, but..."

And then I remember her face, her long blond braid, her pretense of care. I gasp, struggling to sit up. "It was *her*. The woman who—"

He places a gentle hand on my arm. "I know. She was here when I walked into the room."

"You caught her?"

His face falls. "No. I'm sorry. She changed out your saline with something, so I grabbed that first, and by the time I turned around she was gone. Security has her on camera and they found her scrubs in the closet around the corner."

I deflate immediately. "So we have nothing."

"No," he says. "This time we might have something."

NICK HAD the foresight to go through the pockets of the scrubs she left behind before security got to them, and in one of those pockets he found a receipt. It has no name on it, but there was a note: *Deliver by October 11*. And if there's going to be a delivery, it means that somewhere at Green Thumb Plants, just up the road from the hospital, there's an address for this woman. All we can do now is wait, impatiently, for the manager to return Nick's call.

I'm chomping at the bit to get out of the hospital and see what we can find out, while Nick is infuriatingly adamant that I stay right where I am. It's been nearly an hour and I'm completely fine—well, mostly fine—but he won't listen to a word I say. "You were just drugged with something we can't even identify," he says. "Until it's out of your system, you're not going anywhere."

I groan and throw my head against my pillow like a child. "But we need to investigate."

"They're closed by now," he says, "and *we* aren't going to be investigating anything. She just attacked you. I want you as far from this as possible."

I sigh. I'll deal with that little objection later, but first I just need to get out of this damn bed. "Fine, but I don't need to stay here. I feel great now. And I don't know if anyone's told you this, but my boyfriend happens to be a doctor."

He gives me a lopsided grin. "A doctor, huh? He must be brilliant."

He is, I think to myself, and it's unbelievably hot. That assessing look he gets on his face when he's mulling something over and his decisiveness during my time here would do it for me no matter what he looked like. "I don't know about that. I'm mostly with him for his body." I look at him from under my lashes. It's a longshot, but sex is the only strategy that might possibly overcome his irritating professionalism. "A body I could *thoroughly* explore if we were home."

He laughs, which means I've failed miserably. "Nice try. But you're staying here. It'll be fun. We'll order in dinner and watch a movie."

My lower lip juts out. "I'm not even vaguely interested in dinner or a movie right now."

"Well, our options are pretty limited otherwise," he says. "Connect Four? I'm no Darcy but I'd do my best."

I should probably give up and admit that I'm staying in the hospital tonight, but I've seen Nick when he's turned on plenty of times—rational thought abandons him when he's pushed far enough. I slide out of the hospital bed and climb into his lap, which would probably be sexier if I weren't still attached to a heart rate monitor. "There is only one thing I want to do," I reply, whispering the words into his ear. "And with that security guard right outside my door, I know for a fact it's not happening here. You know how loud I am."

He hardens underneath me. This attempt at seduction was more about manipulation than lust when it started, but at the feel of him there it no longer is. I'd forgotten that rational thought abandons me too. I lean in and tug his lower lip between my teeth and there's this ragged noise in his chest in response.

"Please don't tempt me," he pleads, sounding a little desperate. "I just need to know you're safe before we go home, okay? We're still waiting on the toxicology report, and at least here I know no one is going to walk in and kill you the second my back is turned."

"If this woman wants to kill me she doesn't have to walk in. She can just apparate or whatever."

He laughs. "Are you using terms from Harry Potter?"

I kiss his forehead. "I'm not sure what's dorkier... that I accidentally invoked a term from Harry Potter or that you recognized it as such. But anyway, you see my point."

He shakes his head. "No, I don't. She went to some pretty extreme measures to get in before. She stole scrubs and a security badge and brought in her own drugs...she wouldn't have gone to all that trouble if all she had to do was *wish* she was in your room and *wish* her way back out."

"I hate when you're right," I mutter, returning to my bed.

21

NICK

We get through a night in the hospital, barely. Quinn says something dirty to me pretty much every hour we're awake, and it's working. I'm so keyed up it hurts. But they still have no idea what was in those fluids she was given, and she's safest here no matter how badly I'd like to take her home.

I wake in the morning in the chair next to her bed and sneak out to my office to call the nursery again. Perhaps I'm investing too much hope in what we found, but I need this, something to focus on, something to help me believe there's even a chance she can survive.

I'm intercepted by Ed Philbin just as I reach the door. He can barely meet my eye as he asks if we can "have a word." I already know what he's going to say. I've been expecting it since I threw that first punch yesterday.

We walk into the office. I'm not sure if I should bother sitting down for this or go ahead and pack my shit. "I assume this is about Quinn's former fiancé?" I ask, taking the seat behind the desk.

He blows out a breath. "He's claiming you seduced a dying patient, Nick. It doesn't look good."

A few months ago, I'd be sick to my stomach right now. Instead, I'm numb. I can barely summon the effort to lie on my own behalf. "Quinn and I dated in college," I say flatly. "We picked things back up when she came to the hospital."

"Then you should have transferred her case," he says, leaning forward with his hands clasped. "Do you have any proof you dated before?"

Does a psychiatrist's interview with a five-year-old count? I imagine it does not. If our past was erased, all the evidence of it must be erased too, but if I admit I've got nothing I'm dead in the water. "Maybe. I can probably find some pictures."

"Look," he sighs, running a hand through his thinning hair. "You're a good doctor and I don't want to let you go. We're already understaffed as it is. But this guy is making a huge stink. He called board members at home yesterday. I'm going to have to put you on administrative leave until this is resolved."

This, too, is not the blow I'd have anticipated. I'd rather be home with Quinn right now anyway. "How long will that be?"

He averts his eyes. "I looked at her file," he says. "I think under the circumstances they'll let this go once..."

I wait for him to finish the sentence until I realize he's not going to. *Once she dies.* Those are the words he's not saying.

He rises. "Go home with your girlfriend. See if you can find some pictures. And...I'm sorry. We'll be here for you once this blows over."

I stare bleakly at the door when it shuts behind him. I don't give a fuck about my career right now, but Ed's certainty that Quinn is going to die soon opens this jagged wound in my chest. Am I being naïve, hoping we can track down the woman and stop this? Probably. But I am drowning, and this is what drowning people do: they grasp at any goddamn thing they can hold onto, even the things that don't float.

I pull the crumpled receipt from my pocket and dial Green Thumb's number. When I finally get ahold of someone in charge, I emphasize *neurologist* and *Georgetown*. Saying you're a doctor can be a lot like saying you're a cop—people almost feel like they have to hear you out. "We had a customer of yours come in," I tell him. "We only know because she left a receipt here. We're trying to get contact information for her."

"Ummm...she didn't give *you* her information?"

"Unfortunately, she took off before we could get it, but we just got results from her blood work, and there is a very serious issue we need to discuss with her. We're hoping you can help us out."

"So you just need a phone number?" he asks slowly, uncertainly.

I take a quick breath and try to rein in my eagerness. "Yes. That or an address. If you can even give us a name, we might be able to find her from that."

"Look," he says, "I don't know if I should just be giving out a customer's information. How do I even know you're a doctor?"

"You can look me up online." I spell my name, direct him to the Georgetown website. "You can send the information there if you're more comfortable."

He takes the order number off the receipt and then tells me he's only the assistant manager. "I'll have to talk to my boss when she comes in and let you know." Which is precisely what I heard from the person I spoke to yesterday.

"And when will that be?" I ask, straining to keep frustration out of my voice.

"She's at the beach this week," he replies. "She's back next Friday."

Six days from now. He wants me to wait six fucking days.

I've always thought of myself as an honest person. It's funny how the qualities you value in yourself go out the window when you really need something. "Look," I reply, "I don't want to pressure you, but this might be a bit of a public health hazard, so the sooner the better. And if any of your employees came into contact with her I think they're going to need to be quarantined."

I wait, holding my breath, until the guy gives a long, exaggerated sigh. "1649 Avon Lane," he says quietly. "But it didn't come from me."

"Okay. And what's her name?"

He tells me, and the pen falls from my hand.

I expected a name. I just didn't think it would be a familiar one.

QUINN IS awake when I return to the room, showered and grinning at me. "*Now* can we leave? Look how healthy I am. I could go run a marathon right now. That's how good I feel."

My mouth curves despite myself. "I didn't know you were a runner."

"Well," she says, "I could go run a marathon if running didn't suck."

My hand clasps hers and I pull her toward the end of the bed and have her sit. "I called the nursery. They told me who placed the order."

She freezes, her face gone pale beneath her tan. "That should be good news, but it obviously isn't," she says, watching my face carefully.

I flinch and then open my eyes to meet hers. "Quinn...her name is Sarah Stewart."

Her mouth opens. Closes. Opens again. "That's impossible," she finally says. "My *aunt*? The woman in here wasn't old enough to my aunt. She barely looked older than *me*."

I press my mouth to her forehead. "Rose told us they age slowly, remember?"

"But—" she begins, swallowing, and trails off as she comes to terms with the possibility that the hero of her childhood— the woman who exchanged a dreary life on the farm for a glamorous one in Paris—is the same person who now wants her dead. "Why? Why would my own aunt want to kill me? She's never even *met* me."

"It must be the Rule of Threes. She doesn't want you to have a child because that child would be the fourth in the line."

Her shoulders sag. "It can't be that. I'm not pregnant, obviously. She knows how unlikely it is that I ever *will* be. It must be the spark thing. She wants mine."

"I'll stop her before that happens," I reply. Though God knows I've got no fucking idea how. "I've got her address. I'll get you home and go check it out."

She springs to her feet. "I'll come with you."

"Not a fucking chance are you getting anywhere near her," I say, grinding my teeth. "She's already tried to kill you once that we know of, Quinn. I'm a big guy, but even I can't be sure you're safe around someone who can vanish in midair and reappear anywhere she wants."

"Well, you're sure as hell not going *alone*," she snaps.

I blow out a heavy, aggravated breath. Does she not realize how much danger she's in? Does she not realize having her there would only make things worse, and that I just want to know she's safe?

She rubs a finger over her lower lip and looks out the window, where the sun is shining and life isn't painful, *ending*, for the people who walk by. "Let's get out of here. Please. I don't want to think about this now."

"We will," I tell her. "Soon. Let me just take care of a few things first." After she agrees, I walk out of the hospital and head straight to my car.

Honesty, I've decided, is highly overrated.

OUTSIDE, the air is crisp, less humid than normal, the first hint that summer might be on the way out. It's start-of-the-school-year weather. When I was a kid, it always felt like a time for new beginnings, for optimism, but when I arrive at Sarah's pristine Georgetown home, all optimism fades. I'd expected, for some reason, to find the kind of place you'd see in a horror film —a creepy old Victorian, shutters hanging ajar, a broken window or two. But it couldn't be further from that. Like every other place on the street, it's worth millions. Confirming what I should have known all along: there is nothing this woman needs and therefore nothing I can bargain with.

I start up her walkway anyhow, but pause when I see the three newspapers in her yard. It means she probably hasn't come home since her little adventure in the hospital.

Fuck.

I'm not going back to the hospital empty-handed, and I'm sure as shit not setting this up so Quinn can return with me. Something needs to happen *now*. I glance around. The street is mostly empty, and even if someone's looking out their window, it's Sunday morning—I doubt anyone's going to pay much attention. I head down the small alley leading to the rear of her home and climb the stairs to her back deck, laughing at the futility of what I'm about to attempt. It is wildly unlikely a woman with this much money has left a door unlocked. It's also wildly unlikely she doesn't have a security system. I'm going to wind up in jail today, and then what? Who tracks this woman down while I'm behind bars? Jeff would be more likely to imprison Quinn in his home than help us out.

The door is locked—no surprises there—so I look for

something I can wrap around my hand to punch in the glass. I'm about to remove my shirt when I glance at the doormat.

She wouldn't leave a key, would she? It would be idiocy, and she doesn't strike me as a stupid woman. Yet when I use the tip of my shoe to lift the mat, brass gleams. It's as if the key was waiting here just for me.

I slide it into the lock, pausing for a moment to strategize. I'll only have a minute before the alarm goes off, and maybe another minute or two before cops arrive. So three minutes max, and I don't even know what I'm looking for.

I take a deep breath and push the door open. I'm as surprised by the lack of a warning chime when I enter as I am by what I find inside: Sarah lives very well. Not that I've ever given a lot of thought to what a time traveler's home would look like, but I guess I'd have expected antiques, lace doilies, needlepoint pillows, and creepy dolls. Instead I stand in a kitchen with thick marble countertops, gleaming fixtures. A glass table without a single fingerprint on it. Quinn's aunt is either OCD or has a whole lot of cleaning help.

I carefully place one foot after another, making my way through the kitchen, not sure what I'm looking for. I guess she wouldn't have left anything quite so obvious as a list of her diabolical plans. Just beyond the kitchen I find a small room that appears to be Sarah's office. Books and files are stacked to the ceiling, but I may not have to investigate any of it because there, atop the glass desk, is Sarah's planner. I slide it toward me, scanning the August calendar. A small sticky note rests on yesterday's date: **IAD to CDG, 6:30 p.m.**

Dulles Airport to Charles De Gaulle. The next three weeks are blocked out.

She is in fucking Paris for the next three weeks.

I slam my hands down on the desk. I don't know if Quinn even *has* three weeks to wait. I've tried to be optimistic, but my gut feeling is that if the tumor makes another leap like the last one, she will not leave the hospital the next time she goes in.

I flip through the planner, looking for any other sign of where she may have gone, and come up with only this—scribbled on the back of an envelope, an address: 37 Rue des Trois Freres.

I could go there. It's such a fucking longshot, but it's all we have. I can't imagine leaving Quinn right now, when anything could happen—these might be our last weeks together—but I can't not try. I can't.

I head out the back door, replacing the key under the mat. Shocked that I've gotten away with it. But next comes the really hard part: telling Quinn I'm leaving.

22

QUINN

Nick's "last-minute things" take forever.

Some of my impatience has to do with Sarah, but mostly it's the way the clock is ticking faster. Nick and I no longer have a year. We might not have a month, or a week. At the start of each new hour, I acknowledge the possibility that it could be my last. And I don't want to spend it here, especially away from him.

By the time he finally returns, I'm going nuts. I know he has other obligations, but how does he not see the urgency here?

"You ready?" he asks. His face is deadly serious, and there's a rigidity to his shoulders that wasn't there when he left.

I was irritated a second ago. Now I'm just scared. "Is everything okay?"

"Yeah," he says, but his glance flickers away.

He's quiet during the drive home, his fingers twined so tightly through mine it almost hurts. What happened after he left my room? There are so many things it could be—my prognosis or his job seem the most likely contenders—but I'm praying it's something simple. Maybe he's just eager to get back to work.

We get into the house and I turn to him. "Don't feel like you have to stay home with me today. I know you've got a lot going on." Every bone in my body wants to beg him not to go, but what I want even more than that is to fix this, whatever it is.

His tongue pokes inside his cheek. "About that," he says. "It's nothing to worry about, but I got placed on administrative leave."

I gasp. "*What?*"

"It's fine. Jeff complained to the board. I knew it would happen even before I hit him, and I just didn't care. I still don't."

I feel sick. It really happened, just like Jeff said it would. "God. I'm so sorry," I whisper, pressing my face to his chest. "Tell me what to do. I'll give a sworn statement that we were childhood friends. I'll swear we're not together."

He gives me a half-smile. "It's going to be fine. If they fire me, they fire me. I'll find another job."

"It's not fine. You really think I can't tell when you're upset?"

"It's not about the job," he says, sighing into my hair. He places his hands on my shoulders, holding me in place. "I went to your aunt's house. When I told you I had some stuff to do at the hospital."

My jaw drops along with my stomach. "How could you do that? Oh my God. Do you realize how badly it could have gone?"

His mouth curves into an almost-smile. "I'm 6'5" and she's not any bigger than you. What exactly do you think she could have done to me? Anyway, she wasn't there. I found a key under the mat at the back of her house and—"

"Oh my God," I groan, staring at the ceiling. "Please tell me you didn't break in."

"I didn't have to break in. There was a key, remember? But

my point is that I found her planner...and she's gone. She flew to Paris last night."

"Oh." I'm not sure what I thought it would accomplish, going after her. But that it's all amounted to nothing knocks the air from my lungs. "Wait. Why the hell would a time traveler need to *fly*? Couldn't she just, like, *wish* herself there?"

"I have no idea. Maybe there are rules. Maybe she just sucks at it. We know nothing. Which is why I'm going to Paris."

I stiffen. "*No.*"

"It's our only chance," he says, placing his palm against my cheek. "I have no idea how your tumor is going to progress, but we may not have time to wait for her to get back."

"Then I'll come with you."

"You can't," he says softly. "God forbid, but what if you had a medical emergency halfway over the Atlantic? You might need oxygen. You might need...Jesus, there's so much you might need if it happens again that I can't stand to think about it. And they can't do an emergency landing in the middle of the ocean. It's just for a day or two."

I stare at him, feeling completely helpless. I know I can't dissuade him, but I still have to try. "She's insane, Nick, and she can time travel. What are you going to do when she vanishes and appears behind you with a loaded gun? Use your medal-winning butterfly stroke to disarm her?"

He pushes the hair back behind my ear. "I'm so in love with you I can't even breathe when I imagine you not here, and I'll never be able to live with myself if I don't at least try to find her. So don't ask it of me."

I meet his gaze. His desperate, determined gaze. There is not a thing I can say to stop him. I press my forehead to his chest, trying to stave off tears. "When?"

"I've got a ticket on the six o'clock direct flight out of Dulles tomorrow. Tonight's was already full."

A sob swells in my throat and I can't contain it. "These could be our last hours together," I whisper.

"Don't," he says. His palms hold my face. "Don't even think it."

"But—"

His mouth closes on mine, stopping my words but not my thoughts or my desperation. The kiss is hard, punishing, as if it can somehow make the truth other than what it is, and my fervor matches his, fueled by the knowledge it might never happen again.

I'm still crying, even as need coils tight in my stomach. My hands tug at the hem of his shirt and pull it over his head. My fingers are greedy. It's not enough for them to trail over his shoulders, his biceps, his chest. They want to absorb him, consume him whole.

He grabs my ass and yanks me against him, hard, groaning as his mouth descends to my neck. My shirt is removed, my bra is released with a quick flick of his fingers. That old voice, the one that warns about the consequences of going too far, is silent. I no longer care what it means to give him everything. How could it possibly matter at this point, when it might be our last chance?

My shorts slide to the floor, and his follow, his hands clenched with need as they pull my hips toward him again. "Quinn," he growls. "I need more. I'm not going to stop this time."

"I don't want you to."

He lifts me onto the couch and is above me in seconds, fingers slick between my legs, confirming what I already know: I'm so ready for this. Beyond ready.

He grabs himself, sliding against me once and then twice before his cock sits right at my entrance. The tip presses, stretches me and I need more, everything. "Do it," I beg. He slides inside me slowly, with excruciating care. I know he's worried, trying to let me adjust, except I don't want him to go slowly. I'm so stretched and so full I can barely think, but I want more. When he finally bottoms out, he freezes there for a moment, a small, ragged noise at the base of his throat.

"Are you okay?" he grunts, eyes squeezed tightly shut, holding himself still.

God yes. I'd say this aloud but all that comes out is a moan. I arch against him, demanding more, and he gives it to me, slowly pulling out, coming back. We are sweating and slick, gliding against each other, mouths pressed to skin. My nails bite into his back and I clench him like a fist, holding him there on this high wire, pleasure so intense it's almost painful. "Don't," he begs. "You're so tight and I'm too close. I don't want it to end yet."

I don't either, but when he starts to move again, more forcefully now, I feel that sharp pluck in my belly and arch up. Swelling and tightening around him. He pulls my legs up, over his shoulders, hitting an angle that has me gasping and helpless. "Faster," I demand and he complies, his mouth on mine, the muscles of his back tightening beneath my calves. I dig my heels in and he thrusts harder, triggering an orgasm so violent I can't even hear my own noises. I'm deaf and blind as I give over to it, soaring through a constellation of stars, only vaguely aware that any world exists beyond the two of us. He slams into me and then his pace jerks, stutters. He comes with a sound that is pained and relieved at the same time.

His forehead lands against my chest. He's dead weight, pressing me into the couch. I welcome it. The last wave of pleasure recedes and when it does I finally find it—the deep contentment I've been chasing since the day I laid eyes on him. The satisfaction that's eluded me no matter what else we did, no matter how many times I've come.

"Holy shit," he gasps, still winded.

I barely feel capable of speech. "Yes." I exhale. "We're probably going to need a new couch now."

He falls to the side, his body loose with exhaustion, and pulls a throw blanket over us both. "Totally worth it. Christ, I needed that. I had no idea how badly until now."

God, me too. Everything we've done before, no matter how perfect, pales by contrast. I smile against his chest. "It was amazing. So amazing we probably ought to try it again."

"I don't see us doing much of anything else until I leave," he replies. "I've spent fifty percent of my waking hours thinking about this for months now."

I smile up at him. "Only fifty percent?"

He grins sheepishly. "I do have to think about doctor shit occasionally. And I thought it would sound creepy if I said ninety."

Is sex supposed to be like this? I'm not sure. It's not like I had complaints when I was with Jeff. It was fine. But it was never *this*. And I have no other basis for comparison. "Is it always..." I trail off, embarrassed by the question. "Was this normal?"

He laughs, leaning up on his forearm to press a kiss to the top of my head. "I can't speak for you, but no...for me, this was really different. Why?"

I sigh. I don't want to be the person who sees something supernatural about every single thing in my life that's different from the norm, because everyone has moments that are different—when you make a wish and thirty seconds later there's a shooting star, or when you're thinking about a song you really want to hear and it's the one that plays next. And yet... "I know that I want to be with you, that this is exactly where I'm supposed to be. I just sometimes wonder if the universe is trying to, I don't know, *incentivize* us. Everything is so heightened. We talked about there being some purpose to all this. I think this is a part of it."

His hands rake through my hair. "Yeah, it occurred to me. Or maybe it's just that this was meant to be."

I like his explanation better. And even if there's more going on here, it doesn't mean he's wrong.

MANY HOURS LATER, after we made it to the bed and exhausted ourselves into sleep, we wind up in the kitchen, naked still— the benefit of having a private backyard.

"I had no idea I was so hungry," I groan, pushing the remains of a second sandwich away from me.

Something flickers in his eyes and his smile fades. "You just got out of the hospital," he says. "And you barely ate yesterday. I shouldn't have—"

"Stop," I reply, climbing into his lap. "I know where you're going with that and just stop, right now. It was..." *our last chance.* "It was just something that had to happen."

"When you're in my lap naked, you make it very hard to have a real conversation," he says with a sharp inhale, hardening beneath me. He holds my face in his hands and kisses me before he pulls away. He is no longer smiling. I see grief in his eyes though he'd never admit the cause. "I love you, Quinn Stewart. And even if you can't say it back, I know you love me too."

My eyes well. "I—"

He holds a finger to my lips. "You don't need to explain anything. Just promise you'll wait for me. Promise you'll be here when I get home."

I press my mouth to his forehead. It's as close to a promise as I can get.

23

NICK

I arrive at Charles de Gaulle on Tuesday morning, exhausted and determined, and in no fucking mood for the line at Customs, which stretches as far as the eye can see. I should be home in bed with Quinn right now. For the briefest moment I allow myself to imagine the feel of her wrapped around me, all lush curves and smooth skin. Her face at rest, the graceful perfection of it—soft mouth, long lashes. My heart twists in my chest. I've been missing her since the moment I boarded the plane last night, staring at the cellophane-wrapped blanket in the seat next to mine and wishing it were hers. I'd have been content just to have her head resting on my shoulder, although an overnight flight under the cover of two blankets would have made for an interesting trip as well.

When I finally get through Customs and out the doors, I discover Paris is every bit as hot as D.C. and even more congested, if that's possible. The air smells more like gas fumes than anything reminiscent of art and haute cuisine.

Once I'm in a cab, there's more waiting to endure. The

highway is hopelessly clogged by morning rush hour, and only the motorcycles manage to make headway, whizzing through the narrow spaces between cars. It takes nearly an hour before we are finally in central Paris, with its maze of tightly lined streets, and another ten minutes to Montmartre. The bell tower of Sacre-Coeur looms ahead of us the whole way, a jagged cutout in the blue sky. I wish the sight didn't feel as ominous as it does.

"Vous êtes pres," the driver says. I don't speak French, but I can guess what he's saying. And I wish he were wrong, because 37 Rue des Trois Freres is not a hotel like I assumed. It's not even a business as far as I can tell—merely a bright red doorway with a street number beside it, otherwise unmarked.

I came here solely because we've run out of options, and staring at the simple, unassuming building makes me realize what a fool's errand this has actually been. If Sarah isn't on the other side of that door, and I doubt she is, we are fucked. I thank the driver and climb out with my overnight bag in hand, preparing myself for the possibility—a dwindling possibility—that I'm about to meet Quinn's aunt.

Everyone wants something, I remind myself. Even a murderous time traveler. I just need to figure out what she wants more than Quinn's spark. If it's in my power, I'll give it to her.

I knock, and after a moment there is shuffling, and the door opens. The woman who answers is old and stooped. She is definitely not Sarah, and seems an unlikely partner-in-crime for a time traveler bent on destruction.

"Bonjour," she says. *"Souhaitez-vous que je vous lise les lignes de la main?"*

I'm ill-equipped to have the conversation I need to right now. I nod, though I have no idea what I'm agreeing to. I just hope to God she doesn't start to undress.

She opens the door and I follow her into a small shop. Tiny

drawers line the walls, along with thousands of glass vials, leading me to wonder if witches are her customer base, because this definitely looks like someplace a witch would shop. Painstakingly I put together a sentence.

"Je suis désolé, je suis ici parce que..." I am sorry. I am here because... This is all I have. I don't know how to say *search* or *look* or *need to find* in French. I sure as hell don't know how to say *time traveler.* I begin fumbling with my phone, looking for a translation when she stops me.

"Why don't we speak English instead?" she asks. "Your accent is atrocious."

I laugh and sigh in relief at the same time. "Yes, I know."

She's still scowling. "I mean, it's truly, truly terrible. I barely even understood you. You should work on that."

I nod, torn between laughing and rolling my eyes. "I will."

"A foreign child on this soil for one day speaks better French."

I see she's getting hung up on this, so I decide to nudge her along to something I actually care about. "So the reason I'm here is that—"

"You want a reading, yes? Of your palm?"

In my sleep-deprived haze it takes me a moment to understand what she is asking. A palm reader? Why the hell would Sarah need a palm reader? Can't she just jump to the future and find out for herself? "Well, not exactly. I—"

"Let me read your palm first. You can clearly afford it."

I'm obviously not getting any help unless I comply, so I slump into the chair she points to, letting my laptop bag sag to the ground. I'm so tired I could fall asleep right here. I hold out my hand and she takes it, smoothing her calloused fingers over the lines.

"You're American," she begins, and I once more contain the urge to roll my eyes. I wish Quinn was here. She'd be every bit as cynical about palmistry as I am, even now that we've both watched people vanish in front of us.

"You're a swimmer." Lucky guess. Lots of people swim. Maybe she smells the chlorine. "And you're in love," she adds. Again, lucky guess. She had at least a fifty percent chance of being correct with anyone she said that to.

"A girl you've loved through many, many lifetimes." This feels like slightly less of a lucky guess. Her eyes brighten. "She is carrying your child. No, wait. I see two children."

Shock has me attempting to withdraw my hand, but she holds it in her tight, clawlike grip. "That's not possible," I say quietly.

She laughs. "Oh, I'm afraid it is, papa. As for the tumor..." I stiffen. Not a lucky guess. There's no fucking way she could have known. Her face grows sad and she withdraws her hand. "You never know. That'll be twenty euro. *Vingt euro.* You still need to learn French. You'll be spending a lot of time here, Nicholas."

My eyes widen. "How did you know my name?"

She looks at me reprovingly. "Well, I had to figure it out since you so rudely failed to introduce yourself. I am Cecelia, by the way."

Cecelia is definitely a hell of a lot more than a mere palm reader. I hand her a bill and with it, the photo of Sarah I got from the hospital security cameras. "I'm looking for this woman. Her name is Sarah Stewart. I saw something indicating she might visit you."

Cecelia slides the photo toward her, peering at it with a blank expression on her face. She nods. "Amelie, yes. She's picking up a shipment."

My hand flexes against the edge of the table. "Amelie? The woman I'm looking for is named Sarah. She's not French."

Cecelia nods. "Amelie Bertrand, *oui.* She is French."

I seriously doubt Quinn's aunt, who grew up on a Pennsylvania farm, speaks with the flawless accent of a native. But God knows this woman would be sure to comment on it if she did not.

"Maybe there's another woman who looks like her?" I insist. "This woman is American."

She looks vaguely insulted. "She's as French as I am. I've met her many times, the woman who does not age."

I inhale. I guess that means we're talking about the same person after all. "Do you know when she's coming in? Or where she's staying?"

She tilts her head, regarding me. For a moment I wonder if she's even planning to answer. "Sometime over the next few days, I believe. She is quite secretive, you know. This is why she comes to me when things could so easily be delivered."

"*What* could be easily delivered?" I ask, thinking of the solution in the IV bag Sarah tried to switch out. Toxicology is still wholly unable to identify it. They said it appeared to be herbal, but that doesn't mean it was harmless. I don't trust that Sarah does anything without intending harm, at least where Quinn is concerned.

She looks even more insulted than she did when I implied Sarah wasn't French. "I can't tell you *that*."

I press my fingers to my temples. "Look, the tumor you saw when you read my palm...it's my girlfriend. My supposedly pregnant girlfriend. And I think this woman could help. I just need to talk to her."

She rises, gathering items from the shelf behind her. "I do not know where she is staying. I will text you when she arrives, but if you plan to kill her, please do so outside of my shop."

My head jerks backward. "*Kill* her?" I ask. "I'm not planning to kill anyone."

She turns to me again and raises a brow. "Aren't you? If she has what you need to save your girlfriend, would you not do anything necessary to gain it?"

I stiffen. Would I? I've never pictured killing someone in cold blood, but if Sarah had what I needed, if killing her would accomplish it, would I? Yes, for Quinn I would. "If I need something from her, killing her wouldn't do me any good, would it?"

She smiles. "*Au contraire.* I think killing her would solve everything."

24

QUINN

I promised Nick that while he was gone I'd stay with my mother or Caroline. I also promised if I went to my mother's I would not drive myself, but I feel so healthy it's hard to take the whole thing seriously right now.

When I arrive the morning after Nick leaves town, my mother's eyes sweep me over, head-to-toe. "You're glowing," she says.

I'm guessing it's related to the sheer number of earth-shattering orgasms I've had over the past day, but my mother and I don't have the kind of relationship where I'd share that with her. "Yes, I...feel good."

I sit at the kitchen table while she moves around the room. "You want to explain why you're glowing?" she asks, her mouth pinched.

I heave a sigh. "It would seem Jeff's already told you."

She glances at me from the counter, where she's pouring me sweet tea, though I didn't ask for it. "You're dating your doctor, apparently." She returns her gaze to the glass. I get the feeling she's struggling to control her words. "I'm surprised at you, Quinn," she finally says. Her *surprised at* sounds an awful lot like *disappointed in*, but instead of feeling guilty, I'm irritated. Nick and I did nothing wrong, but we are getting endless shit for the decision to be together, a decision that truly has only hurt two people and will ultimately be in their best interest.

"I didn't cheat on Jeff."

She sets the tea down in front of me, so heavily it sloshes over the sides. "Even if you didn't, you need to realize that love means staying focused on the commitment you've made, not grasping like a child at the first shiny thing you see."

A thin seam of rage spikes in my chest. "That is not what happened, and you need to start remembering that *I'm* the one you're related to."

"Of course I remember," she says. "But you can't expect me not to say anything when I hear you were cheating on your fiancé."

"I wasn't cheating. And he's my ex-fiancé now. Who's been stalking me since we broke up, waiting in the lobby of Caroline's building, following me when I won't talk to him, forcing his way into my hospital room when I'm unconscious."

"Hospital room?" she repeats. "You were in the *hospital*? *Why*? Why didn't you tell me?"

I flush. I didn't tell her because I was a little occupied once Nick and I left. "I had another blackout. Anyway, a woman came in, wearing a nurse's uniform, and replaced my saline with something. Nick stopped the IV in time."

Her hand flutters to her chest. "My God. That's... insane. Why?"

My shoulders sag. "That's part of the reason I'm here. They didn't catch her but they did find a receipt she left behind and they were able to trace it." I look up. "Her name is Sarah Stewart."

I watch my mother's face, waiting for it to sink in. It does, first as confusion and then astonishment and finally denial. "Oh. But that's...no. You think it's your dad's sister behind this?"

"What are the odds she *isn't*? It seems like too great a coincidence, doesn't it?"

"Your aunt would have no reason to do this. She's never even met you."

I feel certain this will not be a productive question, but I have to ask. "Could there be something she wanted to inherit, maybe? Something in the family that would pass on to her instead of me if I weren't around?"

I want to see a light dawn in her eyes, some hint that what I've said rings a bell, but instead her arms cross and her brow furrows.

"That's ridiculous. Anything your father left to me goes to you if I die. Anything you have goes to whoever you want. He didn't leave her anything."

"So you have no idea why she'd try to kill me?"

She stares at the table. "It can't be her. It must be a coincidence. The woman's never even *met* you."

"Mom," I say gently, tapping her hand to get her attention. "This matters. For a lot of reasons. We think she might have some answers about the brain tumor. If there's something you're not telling me, please...I need to know."

She hesitates, and in that hesitation I realize she knows something. Something she has no plans to admit. She rises from the chair. "I know nothing about her and I've never met the woman." She opens the refrigerator. "So what should we have for lunch?"

NICK CALLS IN THE AFTERNOON, his voice groggy from being awake most of the last forty-eight hours. In typical fashion he's mostly worried about me, when he's the one in a foreign country pursuing a potential murderer. "How are you? Did Caroline drive you to your mom's?"

"Something like that," I reply.

"Quinn..." he growls.

"It's fine! I'm here safe and sound. You can punish me for it when you get home."

He laughs low in his chest. "I think you'd enjoy the way I'd punish you too much."

A small fire starts burning in my stomach. "Remind me of that when you get home. Did you find anything today?"

He sighs. "Yeah. The address I had? It wasn't a hotel—it was a palm reader who insisted on doing a reading. And it was unsettling because she got so many things right."

I groan. "Let me guess: she said you were American and wanted to be happy? The one palm reader I ever went to told me something was drawing me to Europe."

"What's wrong with that?"

"Who *isn't* drawn to visiting Europe? It's like saying you're committed to breathing oxygen."

He laughs but it fades away quickly. "She was slightly more specific, babe. She knew about your brain tumor. And she knew my name."

The fine hairs on the back of my arms stand on end. "Oh....I...wow."

"Yeah," he says. He takes a deep breath, releases it. "Cecelia —the palm reader—also said you're pregnant."

My heart begins to race. It's impossible. I'm on the pill, my period is due any second now and it's only been twenty-four hours. I'm not sure I could even have *conceived* anything yet. I force a laugh. "Wow, is it like some kind of vampire baby who grows at superhuman speed?"

It's disturbingly quiet on the other end of the line. "Maybe she got that wrong." He doesn't sound like he means it though.

It's too much to think about right now. And too ridiculous. I couldn't possibly be pregnant and even if time traveling exists, I refuse to begin believing in palm readings, tarot cards or anything like it. "Did she know anything about Sarah?"

"Yeah. She's met her several times but doesn't have an address for her."

I'm both relieved and disappointed. I guess I held some small hope this might work, but mostly I just want him back, and safe. "So then you're done, right? And you're coming home?"

He exhales. "Not exactly. This woman sells...I don't even know what she sells. It looked like an old-time apothecary, the kind of thing you'd associate with England in the 1600s. Anyway, your aunt is supposed to be coming in at some point. She's going to let me know as soon as she gets there."

With his words, my heart is hollowed out, empty. "*At some point?*" I ask. "That could be...that could be more than two weeks from now."

"I know," he says.

He sounds tortured by it. And I'm tortured by it. This might be all the time I have and he's the way I want to spend it. Him and only him. "Come home," I beg. "This isn't worth it. Please."

"Don't do that to me," he whispers. "You know I have to stay. I have to see what she knows and what she wants. It's the only way I can think of to help you and I won't be able to live with myself if I don't."

"And what happens when you find her?" I ask desperately, pacing the room. "She's more likely to kill you than she is to sit down and have a nice heart-to-heart."

He pauses. "Actually, Cecelia suggested that killing *her* would solve everything."

A startled laugh escapes my throat. "*Killing* her? Holy shit, Parisian palm readers are dark." He's silent in response. "Why are you not laughing? It's obviously a completely insane thing to say."

"Quinn," he says reluctantly, "it's...something to think about. Remember what Rose told us? That stealing someone's spark can strengthen yours? Well, maybe if you steal Sarah's it will cure this thing."

My mouth falls open. I can't believe Nick, of all people, is in favor of this. "Your career is dedicated to saving lives. You cannot actually be suggesting I kill a woman in cold blood on the *off chance* it might allow me to live?"

"She tried to kill you first, remember?"

"Nick," I breathe. "I...I don't even know what to say. We have no idea if she was actually trying to kill me and I just...*no*. I can't kill anyone. I'd never be able to live with the guilt."

"I could live with it," he growls.

It's easy to say when you haven't done it yet. I have though. I wake each morning sick about what I might have done to Ryan, and it wasn't even this version of me who's responsible. "No," I tell him. "I won't let you do that for me, if it would work anyway, and it wouldn't."

"I'm just saying it's something to think about."

I can't. I won't. If my desperation to stay alive is going to turn me into a monster, I don't deserve to live in the first place.

I wake early the next morning and come downstairs with my bag packed. My mother is already up, sitting pale and bleary-eyed, both palms pressed to a cup of coffee.

Her eyes go to my bag and her face falls. "You're leaving already?"

We haven't always gotten along, especially of late, but I hate that I'm disappointing her. "There's a doctor in New Jersey I need to talk to. Are you okay?" I ask.

"I was thinking we could spend the day together," she says quietly. Her palms press harder to the coffee cup. They are nearly bloodless. "We could go to Philadelphia and get lunch, go to the Barnes Foundation. You always loved that when you were little."

"I have this appointment, Mom, or I would."

She nods but I swear to God it looks like she's about to cry, and I think it has nothing to do with my tumor.

I ARRIVE at Dr. Grosbaum's house just before lunch. I've decided to keep the trip from Nick since he'd worry unnecessarily, and if it's okay for him to break into the home of a potential murderer with supernatural powers and not mention it until afterward, I can probably visit a neurologist with some offbeat ideas and not mention it either.

The sight of his house no longer scares me. It just makes me sad. How long has he been waiting for his wife to return? Will he die alone, still waiting?

He steps back in silence as I walk through the door.

"I owe you an apology," I begin, as I follow him to his office, but he waves my words away.

"Several universities thought the same things you did and were far ruder in their dismissal," he replies. "I'm accustomed to it. But I'm curious to hear about this time traveler you met."

We both take the seats we took a few weeks ago. My heart lurches a little at the emptiness of the chair beside me. Nick should be here. He should never have left.

"She was young," I reply. "Barely even a teenager. I saw her once in my head when I'd blacked out, and she insisted I hadn't blacked out at all, that we'd just passed each other time traveling."

He frowns. "But that's..." He stops, shaking his head. "And do you believe her? That you were time traveling?"

I nod. "Yes, but it only seems to happen when I pass out and maybe at night though I'm not sure, and *then* it's completely effortless. When I'm awake nothing happens. I don't know if I'm doing something wrong, or maybe I'm just not relaxed enough?"

He leans forward, tapping a pen against his lips. "Or perhaps your conscious mind fears it, so the ability sneaks around in the background instead. Time traveling PTSD, if you will."

"Why would I fear it?"

He shrugs. "Maybe you were raised in a very religious household? Or it had some negative association for you? I'm not sure."

The funeral. Nick's hand clenching mine and the certainty it was my fault. "Like maybe if I caused someone harm." I pose it less as a question and more as an admission of guilt.

He's quiet for a moment. "It's always a struggle for people with your gift. For all the good you can do going back in time, you risk causing just as much harm. What you don't realize is that any human's life is just as full of choices." He leans back in his chair and observes me solemnly. "Say you set up two friends on a date and they marry. People will pat you on the back, but you've also *deprived* other people of marrying them. The children they might have had with those other people are now not born. Every action we take, even the best ones, may cause harm. Time travelers just have the unhappy side effect of knowing what they've done."

My eyes flicker to his. "What if I'm the reason someone died?" I venture. I sound as guilty as I feel. "There's no good side there."

"You have no idea what would have come of that person's life," he argues. "If you caused a murderer to die early on, would you have done the world harm or performed it a service?"

Except Ryan wasn't a murderer. He was a brilliant, funny

boy who looked so much like Nick and had just as much potential. He might be a doctor now. He might have kids. And I took
all of it away from him. It makes perfect sense to me that I'd
have decided, long ago, that I would never risk using my abilities again. "I was hoping I could talk to someone about this. I'm
obviously not the only one of your patients with this, um..."

"Talent?" he offers. I was going to say *issue*, but I nod.
"Unfortunately, my files are organized by identifiers but there
are no names or contact information, for your protection."

My brow furrows. "*Protection?*"

He nods. "Even the fact that we sit here now, discussing it, is
a threat. Time travelers are like the rest of us in that there are
some good and some bad. And the bad ones...are very bad.
They wouldn't hesitate to kill anyone who showed signs of
unusual ability, something greater than theirs. And I suspect,
based on your ability to jump between different timelines,
you'd fall into that category. Which reminds me...the DNA
test."

"What will that tell you?"

"Right now I'm just trying to keep a database, determining
family lines, trying to see what makes some so much more
powerful than others. There are those of you who excel at
jumping back through time but struggle to change your location. Some can direct themselves anywhere, but can't quite
pinpoint time. And then there's someone like you, who can
jump back through worlds that no longer exist. It's...rare. No,
not just rare. It's unheard of."

A chill crawls up my spine. I think of that voice whispering
to me in a darkened room, saying my powers make hers look
childlike by contrast.

"Full disclosure," he says, with a heavy sigh, "I'm also trying
to get information about my wife. She was pregnant when she
got lost. I don't know where she went. I don't know how far
back she went. I just keeping hoping that...if I find a time trav-

eler with our DNA, it might mean our child survived. It might even mean she stayed there and led a happy life."

I sit with that, feeling heartsick. I could do this very thing to Nick if I jumped. "I'm so sorry."

He stares at his desk before finally raising his head to meet my eye.

"Make no mistake, Quinn: being able to time travel is both a blessing and a curse."

25

NICK

Two days pass. Two long days during which I do nothing but miss Quinn and imagine the worst. What if I come up empty-handed? What if something happens while I'm gone?

I walk for hours without seeing anything. I've been to Paris before, and there are places I'd like to go again, but right now this city is only a reminder of all the things I'll never be able to show Quinn—restaurants I can't take her to, museums she would love. A whole world I might be able to offer if I could just fucking fix this, which looks less likely with each hour that passes.

I've searched for the name Amelie Bertrand, but there are thousands, and ostensibly this one is cautious about giving out her address, though it seems she had no issue with giving it out as Sarah Stewart. With every new piece of information, the questions only grow.

∽

QUINN CALLS when she wakes up. We try not to talk about
Sarah, about the tumor, during these calls. I want just a few
hours of seeing what it might have been like to have a normal
life with her, and I think she does too. So she tells me about the
garden, about the bulbs she'll plant once the weather cools,
and the small blueberry bush she found in the back corner of
the yard. I tell her about Paris, about the things I'd like to
show her.

We talk about where we'd move if we had a family, whether
we'd put a pool in the back yard, where we'd go on trips. I'm
smiling throughout all of these conversations, but they cut like
a knife at the same time.

That night I go to a bar down the street. Though I've never
been a big drinker, I've become a regular here during my short
stay. The weight of missing Quinn, of worrying about her, is
killing me. I need to take the edge off. I'm on my second
bourbon when another American shows up. He's already
drunk at 10 p.m. and loud as fuck, which I'm not in the mood to
put up with.

"Check, please?" I ask the bartender. *"Billet, s'il vous plait?"*

"You American?" the guy shouts across the bar.

Fuck my life. "Yeah."

"Then you're from the best country in the goddamn world,"
he replies.

Drunk asshole. "If you say so," I reply, sliding a few bills to
the bartender.

"I do say so!" he shouts. "You got a problem with that?"

He's an idiot. Normally I'd laugh this off. But tonight I'm in
no mood. I'm angry. I'm bitter. What I want to do is blame God
or fate or whatever is responsible for this situation, and in its
place, he makes for an easy target. "No, but I have a problem
with you running your mouth about it in someone else's
country."

"I'll run my mouth wherever the fuck I feel like it," he says, climbing off his barstool and crossing to my side of the room.

"Yes. Obviously." I'm a big guy and aside from scuffles with my brother, I've never lost a fight. The sight of him moving my way leaves me more tired than worried.

He pushes me, and my fist slams into his face before I've even realized I'm doing it. I welcome the opportunity to tear something apart. It feels like the first thing I've actually fucking *succeeded at* in weeks.

He hits me back. I welcome that too.

My fist sinks into his stomach, and he gasps. I relish it. I even relish the sharp snap of pain when he hits my jaw.

I want all of it. I welcome all of it. Until the cops arrive, that is.

26

QUINN

I sit in our adorable backyard, lying on a blanket in the garden and looking at the stars. It normally brings me peace, but I'm unable to find it tonight. In part because Nick didn't call when he was supposed to. But there's something else too. It rests at the back of my brain, some small answer waiting to be recognized, a puzzle piece waiting to be put in its proper place. I have missed something big.

Something about Sarah.

It's not just that she wants me dead...it's that she's not making sense. Why would someone hell-bent on killing me leave the country right now? Shouldn't she be waiting here to hover over at me at the moment of my death and take whatever it is she plans to take? And why would someone who's been so careful and methodical in her planning—she's obviously been at this for a good long time—suddenly begin slipping up? Letting herself get caught by Nick. Leaving an address where she can be traced in the pocket of her scrubs.

I picture the key under her mat as Nick described it.

Gleaming and new. Who leaves a key under the mat when they live in a home worth a gazillion dollars?

It's too easy.

The address, the key, the journal left open with her dates of travel, an address. Sarah has left us a trail of breadcrumbs to find her, to chase her. She is laying a trap and Nick is going to fall right into it—if he hasn't already. Why didn't he call me? Panic, which was merely a whisper moments before, turns into a roar.

It's the middle of the night there but I call him anyway. It goes to voicemail. I call again. It goes to voicemail. He's too worried about me to have shut his phone off, and he's not a heavy sleeper. My hands palm the ground, press into it. I know I need to stay calm, but already I'm envisioning the worst. If Sarah's done something, how the hell will I ever find him?

FOR FIVE HOURS I remain awake, calling him, pacing through our house, sick to my stomach. Do I call the police? The state department? I can just picture how much attention they'll pay to a girl complaining that her boyfriend is in Paris and hasn't called her back. His parents might have better luck but they probably don't even know I exist. For all I know they still think he's with Meg.

When my phone rings, it's two in the morning. I open my mouth to speak and promptly burst into tears.

"Quinn," he croons. "Stop, honey. I'm so sorry."

"I was worried sick," I cry. "I didn't know if you were hurt, and your parents don't even know I exist, and I had no idea who to call, and would they even have told me if you were hurt? Would they?"

He laughs softly. "Yes, my parents know about you. I'm sorry

I put you through that. I kind of got arrested, so I didn't have my phone for a while."

My tears come to a sudden, shocked halt. "*Arrested*? For what?"

He sighs. "I got in a fight, in a bar. I know it sounds bad and you're probably now wondering if you're stuck with a violent alcoholic. All I can tell you is it was the first time since college that I've gotten into a fistfight at a bar. It's hard, being apart like this. I'm just not myself right now."

I curl up and press my face to my knees. This is insane, us being apart. We've waited our entire lives to get together, and once it happens we're separated by an ocean. "Then just come home. Please. I want you to stop anyway. I was thinking about it and Nick...it's a trap. It has to be. She's left us a trail of bread-crumbs straight out of *Hansel and Gretel*. The receipt? The key under her mat? She *wants* us to follow her."

"Maybe she wants *you* to follow her. But *you're* not, so we're fine."

I press my hand to my forehead. He doesn't get it. She can time travel. She's always going to be ten steps ahead of us. "Nick..."

"I'm sorry I worried you. It's the last thing you need right now. Seriously, I'm fine. Just a few more days."

"I don't think you're grasping how bad this could go. Sarah might not even be the only person you have to look out for. Grosbaum told me—"

"*Grosbaum?* You called him?"

I sigh heavily. *This is going to go over well.* "I drove up to see him."

"Jesus Christ," he says. "*Why?*"

"Why wouldn't I?" I counter. "He was right about every-thing, so I thought he might know something more. He thinks —" I hesitate. Telling him Grosbaum's PTSD theory opens up the topic of what I might have done wrong in another life. "He thinks I'm scared to use the ability, so it only comes out when I'm sleeping or unconscious and can't repress it."

"You're right to be scared to use that ability," he says. "Please tell me you're not trying anymore."

I could point out that there's nothing left to lose, but he sounds so despondent I decide not to argue with him. "I let Grosbaum do a DNA test. He wants yours too. I apparently have 'unusual' ability and he thinks your DNA is what would determine how powerful our child could be. Maybe that's why Sarah's trying to stop us."

"I don't want to brag," he says, "but I bet my DNA is fucking awesome."

I laugh, and then it fades away. "In this case it sounds like it would be a bad thing." I tell him about Dr. Grosbaum's missing wife. About those who target travelers more powerful than themselves.

"Fuck," he groans. "I wish I didn't know that. I thought we just had Sarah to worry about, and now it sounds like we have a whole universe of these people who could come after you. I hate that you are there, and I can't protect you."

Says the guy who just got out of jail and is hunting down a potential murderer. "You're the one in danger right now, not me," I reply.

"It's going to be fine," he says. "This will all end soon."

We hang up, and I walk out back to stare at our pretty garden, still flourishing in the warm August air. I'm glad something's flourishing. Nick obviously isn't, and I'm not either. I've felt a little worse every day since he left. We are not meant to be apart.

And I'm tired of him telling me it's fine that we are.

27

QUINN

I have a passport that's never seen the light of day. I still remember when it arrived eight years ago—how thrilled I was by the possibilities it offered. That was back when I still believed I'd be spending my junior year abroad. A week later I learned my father was going to die, and I threw it in a file and tried to forget.

Today, for the first time in all these years, I retrieve it. The cost of a last-minute ticket to Paris makes my stomach churn but right now, I need Nick and he needs me, and every other consideration is irrelevant.

I arrive in Paris just as the city is beginning its day—the tourists trickle while the Parisians move with brisk, impatient steps, dodging bikes and cars that zip down the street at twice the speed they should. The buildings rise on all sides, intricate and ancient and so amazingly *different* from home that if it weren't for the prospect of seeing Nick, I'd just want to start walking, drinking it in.

I arrive at the hotel and text Nick, who has no idea I'm here.

Me: What are you up to?

Nick: At breakfast. It's 3:00 a.m. there. Why are you awake?

I gather my bags and go in. After a brief and apparently persuasive conversation with the guy at the front desk, I'm standing inside Nick's room.

Me: Getting in shower. I like our room btw.

I take a selfie with his suitcase in the background and hit *send*, then go into the bathroom. As much as I'd like to stand under the hot spray for an hour or more, I hustle, because I imagine Nick's going to be here within minutes of getting that text. I've just finished shaving my legs when the door slams. Before I can turn off the water, Nick is there, pulling back the shower curtain, staring at me in shock.

His eyes sweep over me from head to foot, and I'm not sure how to interpret the look until he steps into the shower fully clothed and pulls me against his chest. "I'm going to kill you for flying," he says, his mouth buried in my hair, "but God, I'm so glad you're here."

I lift my mouth to find his. "Me too," I reply. "And you're wearing way too many clothes."

LATER, we lie in bed, a slight breeze blowing in from the open doors of the Juliet balcony, sunlight streaming in. "I still can't believe you did that," he says for what must be the seventh time. "I don't think you realize how badly it could have gone."

I smile. "Except it didn't. The guy beside me hogging the armrest was the worst thing that happened the entire flight."

He isn't impressed. "You still have to get back home."

I stretch my arms over my head. Given that I'm naked and the sheet's fallen to my waist, I'm assuming I can distract him once more into forgetting his worry. His eyes fall to my chest and his hand slides over my stomach to cup a breast. His brow furrows and his hand moves to cup the other one. "They feel...bigger."

"Maybe it's all the sadness eating I've done since you left."

He is absolutely still for a moment. "You wouldn't *only* gain weight there, Quinn."

I laugh. "I know what you're getting at but...you can't possibly believe I'm pregnant. Aside from the impossibility of it, we just wouldn't know this early. I wouldn't have gained weight *anywhere* yet. It's only been a week."

His frown deepens. "We've already established that nothing about this is normal. We've also established that it at least *seems* as if you got pregnant right away in the past, no matter what kind of contraception we used. And if you're not technically human, there's no reason to think a pregnancy would progress at a normal rate anyhow."

I feel the tiniest whisper of worry and banish it. "That palm reader is making you paranoid."

"Maybe," he says. "But you could take a test, just to be sure."

I grab his hand and press it to my sternum. "Stop," I whisper. "It's not possible, and we're in Paris. Together. Please don't ruin this for me right now."

I see the effort it takes him not to argue. He forces a nod. "Then I suppose I ought to let you enjoy a part of Paris that isn't this bed?" he asks, rising. "I'm telling you right now, it's the best part. And please don't argue with me or you'll destroy my self-esteem."

I take in the naked backside I've missed so damn much for the last week. "It's been an okay part so far," I tease.

He turns back toward me, arching a brow. "I know you didn't just refer to sex with me as *okay*."

"It was totally...pleasant," I counter, digging my nails into my palm to keep from laughing. "Just, you know, brief."

He kneels on the bed, his gaze dangerous. "Three hours was

brief?" he growls. "Then by all means, tell me what you'd consider *not* brief."

I smile at him as he hovers over me, supporting his weight on his forearms. "Three hours and fifteen minutes ought to cover it."

EVENTUALLY WE DO MAKE it out of the room, into the sweltering heat of Paris in August. "So what do you want to see?" he asks.

There's so much I want to see that I don't even know where to begin. I start throwing out names, ticking them off on my fingers as I go. "The Louvre, the Orsay, the Palais Royale, Notre Dame, Sacre-Coeur, the Jardins du Luxembourg, the..."

He laughs. "Sorry, I should have been more specific. What would you like to see *today*?"

I bite down on a smile. "You tell me. I've only been here on our honeymoon, so all I remember is the room."

"Which is precisely as it should be," he replies solemnly. "But I'll humor you since it's your first day."

He leads me to the path above the right bank of the Seine, where we end up walking mile after mile, solely because there's never a point when I'm ready to stop looking. As soon as the Eiffel Tower fades from view, we are looking at Les Invalides and the Alexander III Bridge, leading to the Champs-Élysées, but I'm not ready to stop.

All day he indulges me and my excitement never dims. We eat dinner at a bistro in Ste Germaine des Pres Nick's heard of. I'm so tired I'd probably collapse if we were home, but here I just want more and more and more.

We sit outside in a light breeze, under the hum of stars and streetlights, and I'm so happy I'm not even sure what to do with it all. I feel like a bottle of champagne that's been shaken hard and needs to explode.

"We should walk along the Seine when we leave," I suggest, though my muscles are burning from all the walking we did today. Fifteen miles, easily.

Nick shakes his head. "I'm putting my foot down. I don't know how you're still going when you've been awake for two days straight, but I'm telling you, any moment now the fatigue is going to hit and you'll be comatose."

"Never," I swear. "I'm staying awake the whole time we're here."

He laughs at me quietly. "I give it an hour."

In the end it takes less than that. By the time our meal is over, I'm leaning on him like a drunk just to walk to the Uber. I struggle to stay awake in the car but it's futile. My head jerks up as I try to regain consciousness.

His laugh is low and affectionate. "Go to sleep, baby," he whispers. "I'll make sure you get home safe." His mouth presses to the top of my head as he settles me back against his shoulder. "Superheroes need their rest just like everyone else."

It's the last thing I remember of our entire magical day.

NICK *and I stand next to a pay phone, outside a convenience store/gas station that is the only landmark for miles. The dry spring has stripped the ground down to nothing but beige earth. Only the occasional weed is there to provide it a hint of color.*

"You want me to stay?" Nick asks, pulling my hands into his. I want to say yes. I swallow the desire down.

An 18-wheeler lumbers into the parking lot, blowing dust into our faces, deafening us both with the squeal of brakes.

"Go ahead," I say, nodding at the market. "Get the food. It's just a matter of time before someone asks why we're not in school, and I don't want to lose our head start."

Nick laughs and runs his hand along my arm. "I don't under-

stand why you're so worried. Our cell phones are off. She's not going to stop us if she can't find us."

That's where he's wrong. She has a thousand ways to stop us, ways Nick can't begin to imagine. I know I need to explain this, and now that we're pregnant I finally can. But it also means admitting everything else: about my role in Ryan's death. The ways I changed not just my timeline but his as well. This time tomorrow we'll be married, if everything works out. If I wait until after it's done, he might not forgive me. But he might not forgive me if I tell him beforehand either. I can hardly blame him either way, given that I'm unable to forgive myself.

"Maybe I'm paranoid," I say, forcing a smile. "Humor me."

That dimple flashes and it makes my smile a real one. "Red Gatorade?" he asks. Since the moment the pregnancy symptoms hit, I've wanted nothing else. I nod and he holds my face in his hands, gently brushing my mouth with his own. "I'm buying you some carrots too. This kid must need something other than sports drinks."

Despair hits again as I watch him walk away. I'm too young to be a mother. I need help, and the one person I want to turn to has been at war with me since Ryan's death. I'm pretty sure she won't even speak to me once she knows everything.

I drop quarters into the pay phone and dial. My heart is beating faster than it should.

"Where are you?" she shouts immediately. She sounds less angry than she does desperate. It makes me feel even worse.

"I'm okay," I soothe. "Really. You don't need to worry. We're just going away for the weekend. We'll be back." It's partly a lie, but I can't tell her everything. If she knew, she'd just check to see which states allow you to get married under the age of eighteen without parental consent. And there's only one. She'll find us.

"I know you're pregnant," she says, and my stomach drops to the dusty cement at my feet. I lay my head against the phone booth's clear wall. How could she possibly know? I've been so careful. I didn't *even look up anything related to pregnancy on my phone.* "I've met the twins you'll have. They've visited me."

Twins. I sway against the phone booth like I've been hit. Twins who were able to visit her. I know what it means, if all of her Rule of Threes lore is actually true.

"They've been coming back for years," she continues. Her voice catches and she has to stop for a moment and pull herself together. "I didn't want to tell you because I wanted your life to be normal. I didn't want you to know what's ahead, but we no longer have that luxury."

Nick and I are having twins who time travel. It's impossible. Unheard of.

I struggle to find my voice. "No one knows for sure if the Rule of Threes is real. It's a legend."

"When the twins first visited, they didn't know me. Which meant I'd died when they were born. And I was fine with that. But Quinn..." She heaves a deep sigh. "After Ryan, after you let your spark fade... they came back. And now they don't know you."

The air leaves my chest without ceremony. It's just gone, and I stand here, holding the phone, unable to even form a response. Through the store window I see Nick in the checkout line. He smiles, holding up the red Gatorade.

If she is right, in five months I'll be dead. Will his smile ever light up the same way again? I'm leaving him to raise two daughters alone. I pull my hoodie up to cover my face and begin to weep. I'm going to ruin Nick's life.

"All you have to do is jump again!" she cries. "If you just get stronger, everything will be fine."

"So you die instead? I can't. You know I can't."

"If you refuse to jump," she says, "I will make the choice for you."

My stomach is bottoming out. I already know exactly what she's going to do. "No."

"I'm sorry," she says. "But if you'd never met Nick, none of this would have happened."

I reach desperately for the only threat in my power. "If you do this, I'll never forgive you."

"Of course you will," she says gently. "You're not even going to remember it happened."

～

MY EYES BLINK OPEN. For a moment I'm still seventeen. Pregnant and grief-stricken, waiting for Nick while the trucks blow past. Talking to a woman who seemed to be close to me—my mother, perhaps? Except she wasn't. She didn't sound like my mother, and even the way I felt about her was different. But who the hell could she have been?

Nick—an older version of him, an even hotter version of him—stirs beside me. His hand curves around my hip, keeping me close, protecting me, even in his sleep. The early morning light is just beginning to filter through the sheer curtains, the start of another day in Paris, but it won't be like yesterday. I know what he wants. Every time he's cupped my breasts, he's grown still, as if trying to restrain his thoughts. I guess he's indulged my desire to not know the truth long enough.

He wakes, pulling my back to his chest.

"We can do it," I tell him.

"I kind of assumed we would," he says, laughing a little as his hand slides down my bare hip.

I turn to look at him over my shoulder. "I was talking about taking a pregnancy test."

"Not where I thought you were going with that, but still a good idea," he says. He climbs out of bed and goes to his suitcase, from which he produces a box. "I bought them yesterday. I figured you'd give in eventually."

I take the box to the bathroom, half terrified and half... something else. I guess there's a part of me that wants it. That wishes I could dream and plan for a baby just like anyone else.

It's a selfish desire, one I try to ignore as I tear open the package. My best-case scenario is that I will give birth to a child, or children, who Nick will have to raise on his own. The worst case scenario is...much worse.

"How's it going?" he calls.

"I'm still urinating. The test doesn't work *that* fast, even for *tempore sphincter* or whatever the hell *shifter* was in Latin."

I hear a low laugh. "I'm fairly certain the word isn't *sphincter.*"

I finish and lay the stick on the counter before I exit the bathroom. "I'm too nervous to look," I tell him.

He nods, setting his shoulders. "I'm looking for two lines, I assume?" he asks.

I raise a brow. It's not that I don't realize he's slept with people before me, but that doesn't mean I have to enjoy the reminder. "Know a lot about pregnancy tests, do you?"

He gives me a half-smile. "Obstetrics rotation."

Of course. And how fucking ridiculous that I have room in my head for jealousy right now. "Yes. Two lines."

He walks in. I can't see his face as he looks at the test, but he stiffens, and I know right then what it says. He turns around, his face drawn, and hands it to me.

Two lines.

I sit on the mattress, too shocked to stand. We are silent, the two of us, dumbfounded. My mother calls at that very moment, and I let it go to voicemail. "It's just not possible," I whisper. "I've been on the pill without incident since I was 21. Seven years. And now we have sex once and ..."

Nick's mouth is a hard, set line as he thinks things I know he won't share. "It was a lot more than once."

"Fine, we have sex 700 times over the course of twenty-four hours, and I'm pregnant? It's just not possible."

He sits beside me. "There's something that defies the laws

of nature in almost everything about the two of us," he says heavily. "I guess this is no exception."

I swallow down the lump in my throat. "Am I...am I even going to live long enough?"

He takes my hand and squeezes it hard. "Yes. Because I'm going to find Sarah and solve this. But it means Cecelia was right, so I might as well tell you the other thing she said."

I take a deep breath. "That we're having twins?" I ask quietly.

His jaw drops. "How did you know?"

I was really hoping he'd tell me I was wrong. But this means my dream happened, and is happening again. "I dreamed about it last night—we were teenagers, and someone, maybe my mom, told me our twins had visited her."

He leans forward, hands braced on his thighs. "They visited her? How is that possible?"

The answer dawns on his face as I softly deliver it. "They time travel, Nick."

"Fuck," he says, staring straight ahead, his eyes empty. He rises and begins to pace with his hands on his head. "Jesus. I just...how are we going to keep them safe?"

He's thinking of Rose, as am I. Rose the wild teen with the absent mother and a father who had no way to keep her in one place. She, at least, had a grandmother to guide her. If I live long enough to give birth, who will my daughters have to turn to? "Nick, the other thing you need to know is that when they visited, they didn't know me. Which means either the brain tumor or the Rule of Threes is..."

"No," he says harshly. "Just because you saw something from another life doesn't mean it's going to happen in this one too."

I lean forward, pressing my fingers to my temples. "What I don't understand is how Sarah figures into this. In the dream last night, it was my mother or someone I was close to trying to stop us. But in London, and here, it's Sarah."

He shakes his head. "I don't know. But if only three of you can survive, maybe she's just trying to make sure she's one of the three."

I bury my head in my hands. We've done this twice before, and the odds are stacked against us even more this time around. "We shouldn't have done this," I whisper. "We gave in and we shouldn't—"

"I'm going to find her," he says. "And this time I will stop her. If we don't find her, we hide until they're born."

I don't have the heart to tell him this, but I'm pretty sure we tried that strategy before too.

~

WE BOTH LIE DOWN, not saying much. Because what is there to say? All I can think about is how badly I want this life I'm not going to have. I want to meet this product of the two of us. I want to hold them and raise them and I'm never going to get the chance.

My mother calls again. It's the middle of the night back home and I know I should answer but I just...can't. Not just because of this news I can't share with her, but because of what never occurred to me until just now: if she and Sarah and I all can time travel, and I'm having twins who can do it too, it's a death sentence for *two* of us.

"We never ate," Nick says. "I'm going to go downstairs and get you some food."

"I'm not hungry."

He pushes my hair away from my face. "It's not just you anymore, remember?"

He puts his shirt on, all those abdominal muscles flexing as he does it. I watch appreciatively, wishing I hadn't taken the test, wishing I'd just had one more day of enjoying this trip with him before we found out. I want to get us back where we were last night.

"You're looking pretty good there, Dad. Why don't you take that shirt off and come back to bed?"

A light flashes in his eyes, a half-second where he is considering the offer, and then he frowns. And continues to dress. "You need food."

I groan. "Argh. So you're going to be overprotective *and* turn me down for sex too. This is getting better and better."

He laughs, pressing a kiss to my forehead. "Believe me, once you've eaten I'll accept any offer you want to make."

He leaves and is back within minutes, carrying bread, cheese, jam, and juice. "It's all I could find at the moment," he says. "Eat this and then we'll go get a real meal."

It's more than enough food for four. My smile is wistful. I want this version of Nick, the overprotective expectant father. I want us to relish this, but how can we, under the circumstances?

My phone buzzes on the nightstand. My mother again. We both glance at her name on the screen but make no move toward it. "There must be something going on," I say, biting my lip. "It's not like her to call back-to-back like that."

"She's probably wondering if she can talk you into marrying Jeff again."

I close my eyes, wondering if Nick would be better off if I had. I've done nothing but cause him pain.

∽

EVENTUALLY WE MAKE our way out of the room, but Paris is no longer the same. We head to the Louvre, taking the path along the Seine, and all I see are children. Babies in strollers, toddlers playing in the grass. Nick sees them too. Every time a little girl passes, his worried eyes follow her.

He'd be the best possible dad under different circumstances. Under these, I'm not sure. "You've got to promise me you won't be like Rose's father," I say, squeezing his hand. "If I can stay pregnant long enough to have these babies, you can't be weighed down by everything after I'm gone. You need to put them first."

He comes to a stop in the middle of the path and presses his palms to his forehead. "Stop saying things like that," he says quietly. "You *are* going to make it. We are going to figure this out."

It's the least reassuring response he could give. It tells me that, much like Rose's father, he cares so much about my outcome he can't put anything else ahead of it, at least not right now.

We keep walking and exit the path at the Tuileries. Rodin's *The Kiss* stands outside. My favorite sculpture of all time, out in the open as if it's nothing special.

"I can't believe it's just sitting here, like any old thing," I whisper, as if the shock of it has stolen the air from my throat. I close my eyes for a moment, overwhelmed. Paris is like a life-size jewel box, and I'm standing in the middle of it all with the only person in the whole world I want to be with. How can there be this many wonderful things in the world? Nick, Paris, children—it would be too much good fortune for anyone.

"You alright?" he asks, his breath against my neck.

I swallow and nod, feeling a little choked up and a little terrified. "It's perfect," I reply.

"It's one of my favorites," he says, assuming I meant the statue when I really meant *this*, all of it. It is the high point, the moment when so much good fortune falls upon you at once that you know nothing else can ever match it.

Which reminds me it's all going to come to an end. Soon.

28

NICK

The call comes that afternoon, just after we're back from the Louvre.

Cecelia gives me an address. "You should hurry," she adds before she hangs up.

I lunge across the room for my shoes and Quinn jumps to her feet. "Was that her?"

"Yes. And you're not coming," I snap, shoving my wallet into my pocket.

She ignores me as she pulls her sneakers on. "You don't make the rules. I'm here and we're in this together."

I groan. I should have realized this would be a fight. "Not this, we're not. She tried to kill you, Quinn, and if you're there I'm going to be so worried about protecting you I won't be able to focus on anything else."

"At least tell me where you're going," she demands.

"You know I'm not doing that. You'll give me 15 minutes and then start to worry and come after me."

She folds her arms across her chest. "You know I could just follow you right now."

I gently push her to the bed and kneel in front of her. My lips graze her forehead and then her belly. "You have someone to protect. Maybe two someones. I need you to be safe, and this is going to be fine. It's a conversation, nothing more."

Her shoulders sag in unwilling agreement. In truth, I'm not sure it will just be a conversation. I press my lips to the top of Quinn's head, and hold them there, just a moment longer than I should. I hope to God it's not the last time I ever do it.

I GIVE the driver the address and he heads back toward the Champs-Élysées. I have no idea if this is going to be a polite visit or an altercation. Cecelia's words—*killing her would solve everything*—echo in my head. It's funny how the oath I swore about doing no harm becomes meaningless when Quinn's life is on the line.

We cross the Pont des Arts, heading toward the left bank. There's some legend about the bridge—lovers putting a lock on the bridge and throwing the key into the Seine. Quinn and I didn't do it. I'm wondering now if we'll ever get a chance, if doing it would have brought us some extra hint of luck we now don't have.

We arrive in a section of town that's seen better days. While most of Paris is old and charming, the houses here are only old, minus the charm. Their brick facades are crumbling and several of them lean precipitously to the right, one good storm away from annihilation. We stop in front of a stone structure that is easily 300 years old if not more. Given how well Sarah lives in Georgetown, I'm hard pressed to imagine *this* is where she stays in Paris. Even the driver seems to wonder if we're in the right place. "*Ici?*" he asks, with a single brow arched.

I nod and slide from the car, watching him speed off. With a single deep breath, I knock on the door. No one comes. I knock again, then try the handle. The door swings open into an entryway with a large kitchen just past it. The remains of breakfast sit on the counter—a pot of jam, a loaf of bread with the serrated knife still lodged inside it—almost as if whoever was here ran out in a panic, which doesn't bode well.

I'm trying to decide if I should wait outside or explore the house for clues when I hear a door shut below me. Someone is in the basement. Someone who may be hiding from me. I pull the knife from the bread, because this is clearly not going to be a friendly conversation, and go to the basement stairs.

She will have heard me creaking around up here so it's not as if I can surprise her, but if she's lurking near the bottom of the stairs in the dark she could sure as fuck surprise me. I flip on the light.

The floorboards creak underfoot as I descend into a basement straight out of every horror movie ever made: poorly lit, water dripping, crammed with dusty furniture strewn with cobwebs. "Hello?" I call. "Sarah? I don't want to fight with you. I just have questions."

I walk toward the back of the basement, to a second door. I brace myself as I reach for the knob, and the moment I do, feet skitter, flying up the stairs. There's an almost childish giggle as the basement door slams shut. I run up the stairs after her, not at all surprised to find the door is locked from the outside. Even when I throw my shoulder against it, it does not give.

I will need to call the police for help since I refuse to drag Quinn into this mess, and if they don't arrest me for breaking and entering...what then? How the fuck am I going to find Sarah if she doesn't want to be found? If she can disappear on a whim?

I pick up my phone and dial. Silence greets me: I have no signal.

The trap Quinn warned me about—I see it now. This was never about me meeting Sarah. It was about Sarah getting Quinn alone.

29

QUINN

Nick was right. Only twenty minutes have passed and I'm going crazy. If he'd given me the address I'd already be there, banging on the door. I text him but there is no answer, so I pace the room, taking deep breaths that don't help in any way, shape, or form.

I finish dressing, ready to leap into action. But what action can I even take? I should have forced him to give me the address. I should have followed him. I sink onto the edge of the bed and bury my head in my hands, tug my hair in frustration. What if he doesn't return?

It's at the 45-minute mark that I finally hear the chime of a text. I pounce at my phone, laying on the bed. It is from an unknown number.

Your boyfriend needs help.

And then there is a video. A doorway, and someone pounding on it from the other side. A stream of profanity from a voice that is unmistakably Nick's.

I can almost hear the sound of Sarah's trap slamming shut.

She played us both like clockwork. She knew he'd be desperate enough to do anything to save me, and I'd be desperate enough to do anything to save him. And we walked right into it like fucking toddlers. The wise thing, of course, would be for me to not take the next step, not go wherever she directs me. I already know I won't be doing the wise thing. I just can't.

I ask where he is and after a single, labored minute, the reply finally comes: *25 Avenue Montaigne. If you call the police, I will have no reason not to kill him. And as you must realize by now, I'll never be caught.*

I scramble to my feet. I know he asked me to stay. I know he wanted me to protect our child. But if only one of us is going to survive this trip to France, it needs to be him.

I'm unnervingly calm as I climb into the back of the car, because it's not Nick she wants, it's me. I have no illusions about surviving the day, but right now it just doesn't matter, and there's something freeing in the fact that I care so much about his outcome that I've stopped caring about my own.

We fly past the Seine, past all the wonders I gawked at yesterday, never dreaming my time here would be so fleeting. The phone rings—my mother again. Her timing couldn't be worse, and yet...do I really think I'm making it out of this place alive? It's me Sarah wants, not Nick. And my mother is back home in Pennsylvania, clueless. I'll never have told her goodbye.

I pick the phone up. "Hi, Mom," I say, swallowing down my sadness. We were very different people, and yes—maybe her fear of what I really am set me back—but she loved me the best way she knew. She deserves better than to be left alone in the world.

"I have to tell you something," she says, her voice quavery. "It's something I should have told you a long time ago."

"Mom, I'm so sorry but this might not be the best time. Sarah's causing trouble and it's sort of an emergency."

"She isn't your aunt," my mother says breathlessly, as if trying to expel the words before I can hang up the phone. "You were adopted."

For a moment I don't understand what she's saying. "*What?*"

"You were adopted," she weeps. "I-I wanted to tell you so many times but your father said no."

"But...that's not possible. I've seen my birth certificate." Even as I say the words though, things are clicking into place... that I tan while my parents both burned. Their stick-straight hair versus my waves. The green eyes when theirs were both brown. I was different in so many ways. I just tried not to see it.

"We faked it," my mother whispers. "Someone gave you to your father and he brought you home. We had no paperwork, nothing. We were scared the state would take you from us since we didn't do it all the right way."

"*Who* gave me to him?" I demand.

"I don't know," she says. "I asked him so many times and he wouldn't say. He told me you were our miracle and that there were some things you don't question. So I let it go."

That dream I had, about a version of my mother who time traveled...was that person my birth mother? Did she raise me once? I felt, in that dream, as if she loved me. As if I was her entire world. Which makes me wonder: did she give me up when my timeline was reset, or did someone take me from her? Under normal circumstances I'd need an hour or a day or a decade to unpack this, but the driver is pulling over, and the truth is it hardly matters. Not when Nick's life is in the balance. "I'm here, Mom. I really have to go. But thank you...for everything. I love you."

I hang up before she can question me. I just hope my final words were enough.

I climb out of the car, shocked to find I'm surrounded by mansions. And the biggest one of all says 25 Avenue Montaigne on a brass plaque outside its open gates.

I swallow hard and move toward it. The building is intimidating, formidable, older than any building we have at home. It makes no sense that I've been led here, and it worries me that it feels...familiar. Is this where another of my lives ended too?

There's a pounding at my temples I try hard to ignore as I walk through the wrought iron gates, half expecting to be tackled by security and somewhat surprised to make it to the front door unscathed. If Sarah is not a blood relative, then why the hell is she doing this? How would she even know I can, theoretically, time travel? Things make even less sense than ever, but there's not a doubt in my mind she's the one who took me from my birth parents.

My hand raises to knock, but I think better of it. I'm not stupid...I know I'm walking into a trap. And this bitch has Nick, so I have no intention of being polite. If there were time, I'd stop to laugh at how much in my life has changed. Obedient Quinn, who was marrying someone she didn't love, who wasn't willing to rock the boat no matter what it cost, is now someone ready to fight to the death. I've come a long way in eight weeks. It's a shame it took me so long to get here.

I open the door and find a foyer that looks like it belongs in a museum. The heavy carvings, gold-leaf sun and rays, suggest the place was built in the 1600s, during the reign of the sun king, Louis XIV—although I'm not sure how I know that. The brass lamps on the walls would be a more recent addition, but even they would have been added in the late 1800s. I take a few careful steps inside, my mind racing. The video sent to me showed a buttressed door, gothic. This place was built several centuries later. Which means Sarah has sent me to the wrong location. I step backward. That's when I hear the click of a gun, far too close to my ear.

"Quinn," says a voice, so pleasant, so melodic, you'd never dream it could belong to something entirely evil. "I was wondering when you'd arrive."

I allow my head to turn, just an inch, and watch as she moves around to my side of the column, the gun still pointed at my head. She is exactly as I remember—the long pale blond hair, the eyes a blue I've never seen on anyone else— an angel come to life. A terrifying angel who might, I now realize, kill Nick just because she can.

I swallow. "Where is he?"

"If you haven't noticed, I'm the one with the gun so I'll be setting the agenda." She nods at the door ahead of me. "Go downstairs."

I'm no ninja. I can't kick the gun from her hands as if this is a movie. Even if I were to disarm her, it's not like I could hold her at gunpoint. All she'd need to do is disappear. My only option is to run, which might not succeed, and which might be a death sentence for Nick. I glance from that door to the one behind me anyway, wracking my brain for another solution. "If you run," she adds, "Nick will be stuck in that basement forever. He'll die thinking you didn't care enough to come for him. I'll make *sure* that's what he believes."

My eyes narrow. "How do I know you're not going to leave him there anyway?"

"You have my word," she says with a saccharine smile. "He'll be freed the moment you've followed my instructions."

I've hated people before, but never like this. Never enough to kill. I would tear her apart with my bare hands if I could. "Do you actually think your word means anything to me?"

"Ah. I see your point," she says, tipping her head to the side. "However, you don't have much of a choice, do you? Follow my instructions and you might save him. Don't follow them and I assure you, you won't."

I take one last glance out the window. This time, not with any thought of running, but solely because I know I won't be seeing all these things again—sunlight, grass, flowers, the flash of a car as it drives past.

"Down the stairs," she barks, irritation straining her attempt at civility.

I glare at her as I begin to move. "Why are you doing this? Is this about my...spark, or whatever it is?"

Her eyes narrow. "Someone's been talking to you, I see. Move."

I climb down the stairs, rotting boards sagging beneath my feet. It is dimly lit, with only a dirty, cement floor—not a dungeon, but not far enough away from it to be all that comforting. "You see those shackles against the wall?" she asks. "Go lock yourself up."

I hesitate once more. The moment those shackles lock around my wrists I'm out of options. But I've been out of real options from the moment I heard she had Nick. "Time's running out, Quinn. If you try my patience I'll just kill you both."

That's all she needs to say. I go to the wall, grab the first shackle, and attach it to my wrist. "This seems like a lot of effort to go to," I say, glancing up at her. "Why not just shoot me?"

She gives me a bored look and nods at the other shackle. "It's more complicated than that, obviously, or I'd have done it long ago." Because she's going to stab me in the heart. It's really not how I thought I'd go, and the prospect would terrify me if I wasn't so scared for Nick instead.

I'm barely able to get the second shackle onto my wrist, one-handed, but it finally pops into place. "Okay, I did what you wanted. Now let him go."

She smiles, unhurried, untroubled. "He'll break the door down soon enough. He's very clever, your Nick, isn't he?"

I hang my head. He'll get back to the hotel soon and when he arrives I'll be gone, and he'll have no idea why. "Is he ever going to know what happened to me?" I ask quietly. "Or am I just going to disappear?"

"He'll know," she says. She raises her phone and takes a photo of me.

"Do not send him that," I bark.

"Why?" she asks, with the sweetest smile. "You look just as cute as ever. He's going to love it."

I press my forehead to my knees and take short, panicked breaths. He could get over this. He could return to his old apartment, his pretty ex-girlfriend, his old life and I *want* him to—but a photo like that will haunt him forever. "Please," I beg, my voice cracking. "I don't want that to be the last memory he has of me. He's going to blame himself and just...please. I'll do whatever you want."

She looks up from her phone, all blue-eyed and guileless. "But the photo has already been sent. Besides...how is he going to know he needs to save you if I don't show him?"

I strain against the shackles. "You lying *bitch*. You said he'd be free."

She takes a seat on the floor a few feet from me and sets the gun behind her. "As he will be. If he chooses to come here after you, that's up to him."

If I'd just listened to him, if I'd just stayed at the hotel, would none of this have happened? Probably not. Sarah was never going to free Nick. Even if he broke out of the basement, she'd find a way to catch him.

"Why? Why involve him at all?" I plead. "You've got me. Stab me in the heart or whatever it is you're going to do and leave him out of it."

"This is all your own fault," she says with a shrug. "It could have been avoided if you'd just done what you should have. Or if you just stayed away from him in the first place. Do you know how often I've had to go back in time to try to reset things? Countless. I'm tired of being nice about it." She stares at her nails, delicately flicking at dirt there. "It's such a shame too. I've seen your twins, you know. Beautiful girls. Their power, together, could be staggering. Which is a bad thing, to be honest." She smirks at me. "So this is kind of three for the price of one, isn't it?"

My twins. They exist somewhere out in the world at the moment, somewhere in the future. And when she kills me they'll just disappear. If Nick is raising them, he's going to lose them both at once. Maybe he won't realize they ever existed, but I think they'll remain inside him somewhere, a longing he can't explain, the same way I did. I curve forward as if it can ease the ache in my chest. "Why couldn't you have done this before I met him?" I cry. "Why do this now?"

She looks surprised, like the answer should be as obvious to me as it is her. "Lots of reasons. I mean, would you have shackled yourself to the wall for that boy you *were* going to marry? Of course not. You had nothing to live for until you met Nick, and you certainly wouldn't have flown all the way to Paris to chase the other one down."

I hate that she's right. I hate that she knows me so well when I have no idea who she even is. If Jeff were in Paris depressed, it wouldn't have occurred to me to come see him. And if someone trapped him, my reaction would have been pure logic. I'd have recognized I'm neither James Bond nor Bruce Lee, and I'd have called the cops despite her warning not to. "Why does it have to be Paris?" I ask, my lip curling. "Do you try to limit your murders to some distinct geographic area?"

She frowns at me. "Sarcasm is an unbecoming trait, Quinn. It needed to be in Paris because I want my husband nearby when this finally ends," she says. Her head tilts and the smile on her mouth is almost...affectionate? "He's waited a long time for this."

I doubt she's married to anyone I could actually appeal to, but my head swivels, looking for him anyway.

Her eyes follow mine and she laughs, as if I'm a child trying to read a book upside down. "He's here, just not in this time.

Some of us excel at traveling through time but not place. Places are difficult for me, while you were good at both, until you decided to give it all up. Such a waste. I understand you've somehow been able to jump back to previous lives too. I have no idea how, but that power you're hiding must be tremendous. It could have ruined everything if you'd just remembered a little more." Her mouth curves in disgust, and, seeming to remember her purpose here, she grabs duct tape off the desk and walks back to me. "I'd better muzzle you before he arrives. Not that he appears any more likely than you to care for his own safety."

I swing my head away but there is little I can do and in moments, I'm effectively silenced.

If I could, I would curl up on the floor and weep, but instead I lean against the wall, trying not to choke on my sobs. I still don't understand why she is forcing Nick to be here to watch me die, and I'm going to leave this world without ever knowing if he's okay when it's done. She is no longer interested in me. She returns the tape and gun to the desk—there's a knife there too, which I suppose is for me—and busies herself around the room, cleaning up, going through a stack of papers on a desk nearby, ignoring me completely.

Upstairs, the door hinges creak. My heart climbs into my throat, *beating beating beating* like a battle drum. A wary footstep echoes across the marble floor above us, then another, and another.

I want to shout into the tape but this will only gain his attention, so I sit, still and silent.

Sarah just laughs at me, in no rush to alert him to our presence. "I lured him all the way here and you know what I'm capable of. Do you really think if you stay quiet I'd just let him walk out? That farmer and his wife did you a disservice if they raised you to be so naïve this time around. I should have given

you to someone else. It's not nearly as much fun as it could
have been."

I thrash against the wall, in agony over what Nick is about
to see, and so frustrated by what she's done and all the things I
don't know. Who did she take me from? Does my birth mother
even know I'm alive? Did my father know I was stolen?

I'm about to die without the answers to any of it.

30

NICK

*I*f *you want to save her, you will come alone,* the text said, accompanied by a photo of Quinn chained to a wall. The picture sends me into a rage so fierce I can barely function around it. How could I have let this happen? I should have hidden Quinn, kept her locked up somewhere and guarded within an inch of her life. All that fucking education and when it came down to protecting her, I was worse than useless. I still am, but there's no choice anymore—Sarah has Quinn, which means she's got us by the throat.

I run to a main road and call a car, urging the driver to hurry in my pathetic French. *"Vite, s'il vous plait. C'est un...emer-*gency." I don't know the word for *emergency* in French. *Fuck.* I can't do anything here, can't control a single fucking thing, not even my ability to speak.

The driver seems to figure it out. My hands clench into fists as we fly back toward the sixth arrondissement, arriving at a home not too far from where I've been staying this entire time. Was Sarah nearby all along? Why is she going through all this?

She could easily have killed Quinn, if that's what she wants to do.

None of it makes sense, but whether it makes sense or not, I'm no longer thinking in terms of negotiation, of convincing Sarah to help us. As I reach the front door of the mansion Sarah directed me to, I've only got two goals: to save Quinn and to make Sarah pay for what she's done. Killing Sarah no longer seems extreme. It seems well-deserved.

I push the door open and walk inside. The place must have been spectacular once, though it's mostly empty now. I hear noise coming from the back of the house and creep toward it, over floors that squeak no matter how quietly I tread. I pass several doors until I get to a small salon and come to a stunned halt. The noise was just an open window. What stops me are the hundreds of photos hanging on the walls, every last one of Quinn. As a pink-cheeked toddler cradling a duckling. Her first day of kindergarten, with a wide, toothless grin. With rain boots on, ankle-deep in mud outside a barn. Her high school graduation, her prom. Every important event lovingly documented. It's as if Sarah has been stalking her since birth.

Or as if Sarah loves her.

31

QUINN

"Down here, Nick," Sarah sings, grabbing the gun from the desk. She sounds cheerful, like she's inviting him to join her potluck.

His legs come into view, then his chest, and with each step I'm futilely hoping he'll suddenly turn and flee.

He doesn't.

When he reaches the bottom step, he's so relieved to find me alive he doesn't even notice Sarah until the moment she raises the gun and pulls the trigger.

His eyes meet mine as it happens. One last, panicked glance as the bullet hits his leg. He staggers and falls. All my screaming is silenced by the tape.

This can't be happening. This is a dream. Wake up, I scream at myself. *Wake up*. But nothing changes. Nick's on the ground, bleeding. He's struggling to get to his feet, so Sarah walks to me and presses the gun to my head. "Shackle yourself and stop struggling," she says to him with a click of her tongue. "Surely you realize that the more you struggle, the faster you'll lose blood." She waits until he's shackled himself before she puts the gun in her waistband.

Nick grinds his teeth as he twists his leg to make the wound face up. "You fucking bitch," he says. "What do you want with us?"

She tips her head to her shoulder, amused by his anger. "This is a good start. I never dreamed it would all go quite this well. But don't worry. I'm going to give Quinn here one more chance."

One more chance to do what?! I already told her I'd do anything she wants. She's toying with us, as if this is fun for her, a lark.

She turns to me. "Just look at him. You could save him, you know, if you wanted to. That wound won't kill him. Not immediately, anyway. But now I can shoot him in the head from two feet away, and *that* will. And it's entirely your fault."

I struggle against the shackles, weep so hard I begin to choke, and she strolls over and finally rips the tape from my mouth. "Tell me what to do!" I scream. "Just fucking tell me! I'll do it. *Anything.*"

"Quinn," Nick groans. "Don't."

She crouches in front of me. "You want to save him? Then come get me. If you wanted it enough, you could have your hands around my throat in a moment. You just don't love him that much."

I thrash against the shackles. "I do!" I scream. "I do! I just don't know what you want!"

"If you love him so much, I want you to show me," she says, smirking. "Close your eyes and place yourself behind me. See that knife on the table? Picture yourself there." I think of that dream I had weeks ago at my mother's house. The voice telling me I'd be able to jump on the day when I needed it most. I couldn't possibly need it more than I do right now, yet there is nothing there. I'm as impotent as I ever was.

"I can't!" I cry. "I'm not like you."

"You can. You were once such a talented little time traveler. Remember? Remember how you rushed back to change Nick and Ryan's timeline? The way you swore you'd never wish for anything again after you messed up. You should tell Nick what you did. Go ahead."

My head is shrieking but I see it. I see the decision. I picture the moment I stood there, watching Nick and Ryan tearing each other apart, how I couldn't stand that I was at fault. "No," I cry, my eyes squeezed tight.

"The three of you were at a party and your brother was drinking too much. Sulking, as always, because he thought you stole Quinn from him," says Sarah without emotion. "He kissed her against her will and you caught them."

Nick's face is so pale, twisted with pain, but he stills at these words. My head falls backward. He's going to hate me, but maybe it's better that way, if she lets him live. Maybe hating me will make this easier when I'm gone.

"Tell him what you did, Quinn," Sarah says. "Tell him what you did, or I shoot him again and end this."

I turn toward him. He looks at me with absolute faith in his eyes, and he never will again. "I went back," I weep. "I went back and convinced you not to go to the party because I wanted it not to have happened. I didn't want it to come between us, and I was scared you and Ryan would kill each other. And Ryan went alone and got in that truck, and he died."

Nick's face gets even paler, and he stares at me in shock. He's just...blank. As if everything he felt toward me a moment before has seeped out along with the blood pouring down his leg.

Sarah turns back to me. "You didn't just stop time traveling, Quinn. You stopped fighting for anything you want, and I'm sure today's no exception. You're going to roll over again and because of it, Nick will die."

"I'm not! I just...please...I don't know how to do what you're talking about!" I plead.

Sarah groans in aggravation. "Enough! Enough of this nonsense. He dies." She walks toward the desk for the gun.

"Quinn," says Nick, suddenly still. "It's okay. Look at me." I comply, stunned by how calm he is, how resigned, as if there's no use fighting it anymore. That blank look on his face a moment ago is gone. His heart is in his eyes now, a heart that's entirely mine. "I love you. So much. And even if you can't say it back, I know you love me too."

Love. It's what holds Nick calm right now, in the face of his own death, worried about me instead of himself. It's what led him to give up everything to try to save me. And yes, it leads to bad things too—our tenant murdering his wife in a fit of jealous rage. Me accidentally killing Ryan simply because I wanted to prevent a kiss, a stupid fight. But ultimately, it's a beautiful thing, enabling the weakest of us to transcend our fear and our failings and our desires on behalf of someone else. And I never wanted to open myself up to it, not with him, because I knew it would lead me to this moment—the one in which the door I held so tightly, only letting a tiny bit of air come through, finally swings open. Love for him rushes in, brilliant and painful at once.

But something deadly is there too—and after way too many years, I'm finally able to welcome it. "I love you," I whisper. "And I'm not going to let you die."

My eyes go to Sarah, to the knife on her desk. I focus so hard that my brain shrieks in response, black oozing into the corners of my vision. But I do not let it go. I stare at the desk while she cocks the gun and points it at Nick's head.

There is a rush of air. Darkness flecked with tiny pinpoints of light. I ignore all of it and focus: *the knife on the desk, the knife on the desk.* I picture it in my head until it no longer seems like a picture, until it is real.

And I land. Free of the shackles, naked, on the floor behind Sarah. My brain begs for mercy, and I want to curl up in a ball at the pain, but I force myself forward to the desk, grabbing the knife. I don't know how far back I've gone, but when I glance at the wall I realize Nick isn't here yet. Which means there's one last thing I need to do in order to save him.

My vision narrows to only a pinpoint of light. I am half here and half in the place I go when I collapse, that land of darkness and absence. Sarah turns toward me just as I hear the door upstairs creak open. There is no time to think, to argue. I lunge, tackling her, with the knife in my hands. Her hands surround mine, and together we drive the knife into her chest. It hits bone first and then sinks in easily as we both fall to the ground.

My vision is gone, but I hear her speaking to me. "Good girl," she whispers. "You finally did it."

There's a question on my lips but it washes away along with everything else. I no longer hear Nick upstairs. I no longer see. The floor was cold a moment before and now it's...nothing.

I give into it, the inky blackness, and the pain begins to ease as night sweeps through my veins. *Nick*, I think, just before the blackness obliterates thought. *I found you before. I will find you again.*

32

QUINN

It's just after 4:00 a.m. when my mother calls.

She knows London is six hours ahead. She wouldn't call right now unless it was an emergency.

Despite that, I don't want to pick up the phone. Over the past months I've been remembering so many things from a life with Nick that isn't this one. Warnings. I'm not sure what happened, but I know she tried to keep us apart somehow, and I know the pregnancy is why. That's why I've kept it a secret this time.

"What have you done?" she asks. She sounds as if she's been crying.

She knows. Why did I think we could hide this from her? I press my hand to my stomach. The twins are so big I can no longer see my feet when I look down. "I don't know what you're talking about," I reply coolly.

"You know exactly what I'm talking about. Your twins visited me, Quinn," she says. "I know everything. And I know they're born a month from now."

My twins time travel. Which means if the Rule of Threes she's harped on forever is real, one of us will die, and it will probably be me since my spark has faded.

"Did you know?" I whisper. "Is this why you always pushed me so hard to time travel?" *In my entire life it's the only thing we ever really fought over. She's begged and argued for well over a decade, but I always sensed a danger in it I couldn't put into words. Maybe the danger was what I did to Ryan in that other life I remember. Or maybe the danger is that when I give birth to twins, it will kill either my mother or myself—and I couldn't let it be her.*

"Yes," she admits. "I'm sure you've figured out by now this isn't the first time we've been through this. You and Nick grew up together, until I changed things, and you got pregnant in high school. I did the only thing I could to save you."

I rest my hand on my stomach. I already love my daughters. It's far too late for her to convince me to take it all back. "Leave me alone. It's my life and you have no right to decide how I spend it."

"I'm your mother. Do you really think I'm going to just let you die? I'll reset your timeline and we'll try it again."

I remember this panic. It's what I felt in that dream, the one where I was standing outside a convenience store, talking to her on the phone. Looking at Nick inside and knowing we were going to be torn apart. Except it wasn't a dream, it really happened. And she really did exactly what she threatened to do.

"You will fail again," I tell her. "No matter how many times you try to keep me from Nick, I'm going to find him."

I hear the sound of something shattering. She's breaking pottery, which is what she does only when she's at her angriest. "Your love for him is your Achilles heel. You won't act on your own behalf, but for him there's no depth to which you won't sink. And don't think I won't use that to my advantage."

I stop breathing. "Use it how?"

"By making you take my spark," she replies calmly.

I sink onto the bed. "You can't make me do that."

Her voice is steady now, determined. "Of course I can. I'd just have to convince you to kill me."

33

QUINN

I'm cold.

Ice pricks the surface of my skin, pins and needles that begin at my neck and work their way down my arms. A hand is holding mine, and then I find it pressed to something wet and warm. Sound then...the gurgle of strained breathing.

"Good girl," a voice whispers. "Good girl. You finally did it." She sounds as if she is proud of me, like I'm a child who's taken her first steps.

My eyes open. It's Sarah clutching my hand, pressing it to her chest.

Images explode in my brain. Scenes in which this woman I thought I hated was the person I once loved most. I'm a child playing in the woods behind my house and Nick is there too.

"I think I'll marry you when I grow up," he says. She's the one who smiles at me in the darkness when I tell her this. She's the one I'm hiding from in London, because I know she will stop me somehow if she discovers I'm pregnant with twins.

My mother. The woman who kept changing the timeline, refusing to let me die. Who begged me to kill her in order to save my own life.

"Mom?" I cry. The word is choked, horrified. I want to stop this, save her, but I still can't seem to move. "Oh my God. What did you..."

She squeezes my hand. "I couldn't lose you. I did the only thing I could think of." She sounds tired, winded. "The brain tumor—I'd altered too much of your life and your brain couldn't...keep up. You wouldn't kill me if you knew who I was. So my brother agreed to raise you."

She gave me away. And made me believe she was the enemy.

That bad thing I knew I was capable of, the thing I've dreaded my entire life—it wasn't time travel, and it wasn't causing Ryan's death. It was what I've just done—I've killed my mother to save Nick and myself.

"I'm so sorry," I weep, clutching her hand. "I'm so sorry."

Her eyes flutter open. "It all worked out the way it was supposed to. Just keep the twins safe, because this will change everything."

The ice eases from my hips, and then outward. I try to sit up, but she clings to my hand. "Not yet," she whispers.

"I've got to get help," I plead. "Tell me what to do."

Tears roll down her face and she smiles up at me. "You just did everything I needed you to."

"But—" My eyes squeeze shut. It's too much. It's happening too fast. "Why is it so hard for me to remember you? How could I not have known who you were? Just please...stay." I feel so much inside me right now, all this love from another time, for her, and I have no place to pin it because the little I can remember of her is so dim.

"You shouldn't have remembered anything at all, sweet girl.

You just loved Nick too much to let him go, the same way I did your father." Her palm rests against my cheek. "I have to tell him it all worked out. We both love you so much."

And then her eyes flutter closed for the last time.

～

"Quinn," says Nick. The word comes out as a low, pained gasp.

He's frozen, standing at the bottom of the stairs. I look down to see that I'm naked, covered in blood. "I'm okay," I whisper but he's already crossing the distance between us in two bounding steps. He drops to the ground, pulling me into his lap, and as he does, my mother starts to disappear. First feet, then limbs, then the rest of her. I lean my head against his chest and weep.

"Are you hurt?" he asks. He sounds desperate, panicked.

I shake my head, crying so hard it's difficult to speak. "She saved me," I finally whisper. "All she ever wanted was to save me."

～

We are in a private room in the hospital waiting for MRI results. It's sterile and brightly lit, silent aside from the clamor in the hallway. It couldn't be further from the place we left a few hours ago.

I remember very little about leaving the basement. Nick dressed me and carried me out. There was still no trace of my mother. I hope that means she got wherever she was trying to go.

In spite of witnessing the way her body disappeared with his own eyes, Nick still doesn't entirely believe my version of events—my mother has been the villain in his mind for so long he can't bring himself to see her otherwise. "But she *did* try to kill you," he insists. "Remember the hospital? *And* you say she shot me. So something's not adding up."

I get it...my faith in her is absolute because I remember her —not everything, but enough to know she loved me more than anyone alive. He doesn't have the benefit of those memories though. "We have no idea what she gave me in the hospital. And she shot you in the leg. If she really wanted to kill you, she could have."

He frowns but doesn't argue. "And you really time traveled? You're sure?"

I nod. It was all so fast I'm not even sure what happened myself. If Nick hadn't found me naked I'd still be wondering if I hadn't imagined the whole thing.

There've been enough revelations in one day to last a lifetime. Not just about the twins, or that I can time travel, but that my parents were not actually my parents, and the man I thought was my father was actually my uncle. That we were related is something I'm sure my mother didn't know. I understand why my father kept it to himself—if he was helping Sarah with her plan, he couldn't risk anyone telling me the truth— but my mom won't. She'd be so hurt if she learned it now. When I call later, I'll thank her for raising me, for caring for me so well that I never knew I wasn't hers. But the thing about my dad is a secret I will take to the grave.

"I still can't believe Sarah was your mother," Nick says. "It's weird you didn't remember her at all."

It hurts, the empty space where her memories should rest. There's this ache inside me for her, even though the lives before this one are almost entirely a blank. "I shouldn't even have been able to remember *you*," I tell him. "She didn't seem to know I could do it, until recently. But yes, if I'd remembered any more than I did it would have all been for nothing."

"How did she know it was happening at all?" he asks. "It's not like we told a lot of people. Was she spying on us?"

I know the answer to that question, but he definitely isn't ready to hear it. "No, she wouldn't do that." I glance at the clock. "Why is this taking so long?" I ask. "I know I'm fine. Can't we just leave and have them call us with results?"

Stabbing my mother cured me, but like everything else, it's harder for Nick to believe than it is for me. He pushes my hair back from my face, two frown lines between his brows. "Please don't get your hopes up just yet."

My hopes aren't just up. I'm *certain* this worked. I have never felt better in my entire life than I do at this moment. There's an energy coursing through my blood, like some combination of sugar and heat and excitement. I feel powerful.

And even if I'm not powerful, at the very least I am now brave enough to tell him the truth. Another gift from my mother. She forced me to tell Nick what I did to Ryan so I'd finally understand that he will forgive me. It might take a while, but he will. "We need to talk," I say, swallowing, "about why I stopped jumping in the first place."

He raises a brow. "*Stopped*?"

I nod. "The first time we were together, in high school? Something happened. It's been coming together bit by bit over the past few weeks."

He squeezes my hand. There is such blind, absolute faith in his expression, and I really pray I don't lose it once he knows everything. "I'm the reason your brother died."

He goes absolutely still. "My brother died in a car accident."

"We were all at a party," I say. I can no longer meet his eye. "You went to get the car and I walked out of the bathroom into this dark room and he kissed me. I only realized he wasn't you just as you walked into the room and caught us. I never would have gone along with it if I'd realized. But I was drunk and in the darkness...he was your height, he had your voice. I had no clue."

"How far—" he begins. He sounds gutted. "How far did it go?"

I haven't even gotten to the bad part and he's already destroyed. "Not very. It was just kissing and when he tried to... when he tried to do more I knew it wasn't you. You were never aggressive like that."

His jaw ticks at the corner. "And then what happened?"

I tell him the rest. How the two of them got into a fistfight unlike anything I'd ever seen before, both big enough to do damage and so evenly matched that neither would back down. I tell him how I panicked, watching it, until it occurred to me I could fix it.

When I conclude, his body is rigid, his tone neutral only by force. "I don't see how that makes you responsible for Ryan's death."

"If we'd been there, he wouldn't have gotten in Tyler's truck. I wanted to tell you the truth, but I just couldn't," I admit. "I was too scared you'd hate me afterward."

I see emotion filter through his expression at long last. A flash of surprise. "You really thought I'd *blame* you?" he asks.

"Who else could you possibly blame? I'm the reason we weren't at that party to give Ryan a ride home."

"I blame *Ryan*," he says angrily. I jolt a little at his tone and he tugs my hand into his. "I'm sorry. I'm pissed off right now but not with you. I've spent over a decade thinking I should have gone to that party, but it wouldn't have made a difference, would it? He was still getting in Tyler's truck no matter what I did."

"But—"

"No. Ryan did a shitty thing. You can't tell me he didn't know he was tricking you, grabbing you in a dark room like that, and I'd kick his ass for it all over again if he was here now.

What this tells me is he was going to ride with Tyler no matter what."

I look at him with wide eyes. Maybe I should just accept his forgiveness and move on, but I don't think he really gets it. "If I hadn't tried to change things, he might have come home with us."

He laughs, but the sound is harsh and unhappy. "Are you kidding me? Do you actually *remember* my brother, Quinn? He was stubborn, and he hated to lose. If we were fighting over you, I guarantee there's no way he'd ride home with the two of us from that party. And maybe he'd still have gone with Tyler and maybe he wouldn't have, but my guess is that nothing you did changed anything for Ryan."

I shake my head. "You're taking this way better than I expected."

He pulls my hands into his lap, holding them between his. "I've been sick with guilt about his death for over a decade. And now you've just given me the original story, and it's one in which I am not the villain, and you aren't either. But Quinn, even if you had been at fault, there's nothing you could do that would make me stop loving you. I just wish you'd known that when it happened."

I realize, suddenly, that he can't remember what I said to him in the basement. He's said he loves me so many times now, and here he is still patiently waiting for me to come around. "I love you," I whisper. "I should have said it a long time ago."

His palms slide to either side of my face, and his lips brush mine. Our foreheads rest against each other's, noses touching. "I knew," he says with a small grin. "But I'm glad you figured it out too. It would be awkward to propose to a girl who can't even admit she likes you."

I pull back. "*Propose?*"

He bites down on his lip to keep from laughing. "Have you forgotten we're having twins already?"

I guess I should have known this would come. He's the kind of guy who steps up, always. But this isn't like our other lives, when we'd been together a while before it happened, and he shouldn't have to marry a semi-stranger until he's actually ready for marriage. "You don't have to do that," I tell him. "It's still really early and I'm just not that old-fashioned."

He laughs and pulls me into his lap. "Do you honestly think I'm asking out of obligation? I've been planning this since the night I drove to your mom's house."

I smile, warmth spreading through my chest, and press my mouth to the corner of his jaw. "Okay, but you are not allowed to propose to me in a hospital room."

There's a sharp tap on the door, and the attending walks in. His eyebrows raise for a moment at the sight of us, me in Nick's lap, our mouths a hair's breadth apart. But we're in the city of love, after all. I figured they'd *expect* it here. I sheepishly rise and take my seat.

"*Bonjour,*" he says. "You're American, yes?"

We nod, and Nick grabs my hand hard, channeling all his fear into it. "You've got the scans?" he asks.

The doctor nods, shifting uncomfortably. He's frowning, and my heart starts to tap in my chest, faster and faster. I really believed what my mother just did would save me, would save all of us. *All the effort she made, the years she put in, what she gave up...it cannot be for nothing.* But the look on his face alone is crushing my hope into a million pieces. Nick's shoulders go rigid, bracing for the worst. "The staff, uh, they tell me you are a neurologist?" he says to Nick.

Nick nods and glances at me. Fear is written all over his face. His hand presses tighter.

"We do not have your images from before," the doctor says, moving to the light board, "but I am confused." He hangs the scans up, one and then the next. "You said she had a brain tumor, but we see nothing there."

I'm not a doctor, but even I can see that each image shows a perfect, tumor-free brain.

Nick's utter shock turns to something else. He swallows hard, stares at the floor as he tries to compose himself. "I guess," he says in a choked voice, squeezing my hand, "that you were right about your mom after all."

34

QUINN

When I wake the next morning in the hotel, I'm alone. A note on the nightstand from Nick tells me he's off finding "breakfast for the four of us." I lie back, smiling at the ceiling. It was a long time coming, and a lot of sorrow on the way, but I think we're finally getting our happy ending.

I called my mother—the one who raised me in this life—last night. She was so relieved by my news about the tumor that she didn't even ask about the emergency I'd mentioned earlier on the phone. She *did* ask if I'd consider going back to Jeff now that I'm healthy again and I laughed. I haven't told her about the pregnancy yet—it's best to give her surprises in small doses —but given that I'm carrying someone else's kids, I seriously doubt Jeff would want me back even if I were willing.

I hop into the shower, eager for this last day in Paris with Nick, and just as eager to get home and start our lives. He's returning with two full bags of something fragrant and newly baked when I emerge.

"When you said you were buying food for four," I say, tying the sash of my robe, "I didn't realize you meant it literally."

He grins, a little sheepish. "I got carried away. You'll probably need to get used to it." He hands me a Styrofoam cup. "Caffeine-free."

I accept the coffee and blow on the steam coming from the lid, while he opens a bag and pulls out a variety of pastries. "Why do I feel like you're buttering me up?" I ask.

He exhales. "I grabbed something from the desk at Sarah's yesterday," he says. He goes to his laptop bag and hands me a manila envelope with my name on the front. "Things were so heavy at the time that I thought I should wait. But since I'm not sure what's in there, you probably need to take a look before we go home. I can give you some time alone to go through it if you want."

I take a seat on the bed, patting the spot beside me, and then I carefully unclasp the envelope. Inside, the stack of papers clipped together is nearly an inch thick. I remove the letter on the very top and hand the rest of the pile to him. In a way I don't want to read it. This is the last thing I'll ever receive from my mother, the last piece of her I'll hold. But I hope, at the same time, that it will help me remember her.

To my Beautiful Daughter —

In this envelope you'll find deeds to some of my properties, and my lawyer will pass on the rest soon. Needless to say, it is all yours now. I have taken care of things so there will be no questions about my disappearance. And there are some photos here to help both of you, but I've broken my own rules to acquire them. Once you begin time traveling, you should take pains not to be photographed.

And now for the hard part. I've had a long time to think about what I would put in this letter, and yet now that it's finally time to write it, I'm at a loss. There are no words for how much I wish I could be there during this next stage of your life, how much I wish I could be a grandmother to your girls, but I'm so grateful you've made it where you are that it's hard to want for much at the moment.

Never regret what happened. Your daughters needed you, not me. There will be times, I know, when you will question this, but you shouldn't. Remember, I saw the outcome of them growing up without you and I know exactly how it would have turned out. They would have come far too soon, leaving one of them very ill and one of them bitter, with a father who never quite recovered from losing you. You will change all that. You will give all of them the life they are meant to have. There's more, but it can wait. Come back to see me and let me know how it all turned out.

All my love,
Mom

I can't say it helped me remember her, but there's still hope. Eventually I'll go back and get reacquainted with the mother I don't remember and, perhaps too, with the father I never met. I brush at my eyes and turn to him. My voice is raspy. "Anything there?"

He starts shuffling through the papers. "You have property," he says. "You have a *lot* of property. Greece, Paris, London, Brazil, California...Jesus, it goes on and on."

My breath releases in an audible huff. After an entire lifetime spent worrying about money, I'll never have to worry about it again. I wonder why she never shared it with my father —*uncle*, I correct, though he will always seem like my dad—but realize she probably tried and he was just too proud to take it. "I suspect that's the tip of the iceberg," I say quietly.

He presses his mouth close to my ear. "So you're telling me I fell in love with an unemployed student and it turns out she may be an *heiress*?"

My lips tug upward. "I hope you'll be able to live with it."

"I'll manage," he says with a grin, which fades when he shuffles through the last of the papers and comes to the photos.

Photos of us, together. In a previous life.

"What the hell?" Nick whispers.

In the first, we are in the treehouse—I'm sitting between him and Ryan, and all three of us are grinning wide, missing teeth. The second is the two of us at the lake as teenagers. The shot is taken from behind, but our faces can be seen in profile. The third is of us dressed up for a dance of some kind, maybe in college. Me with regrettable hair and him all arms and legs in a tux that doesn't fit quite right.

"Are they photoshopped?" he asks.

I smile, marveling at my mother once again. "No. There are elements here you can't fake. So even if someone wanted to argue that we'd Photoshopped it, any expert would testify on our behalf that it couldn't be done."

"But how? If you can't even time travel with clothes, how the hell can you time travel with photos?"

I shake my head. I have no idea. While some of my memory has returned, time traveling and its rules remain, for the most part, a complete blank. "I don't know. *Now* do you believe my mother wasn't evil?"

His smile fades. "I'm getting there, but there's something we need to discuss. What she said, about going back to see her—" He sighs. "I know you're going to want to go, and I know I can't stop you. I shouldn't even ask. But...I can't get Grosbaum's wife and my grandmother out of my head."

"Grosbaum's wife was probably doing things I wouldn't," I argue. "Your grandmother too. I'm not looking to go to China in the 1600s or something."

"You have no idea what they did," he counters, "but you *do* know they had more experience at it than you. Quinn, I..." He stops, jaw grinding as he runs a hand through his hair. "I couldn't fucking stand it if you were stuck somewhere. Not knowing if you were safe. I couldn't. I feel like I just got you back."

I swallow. I'd feel the same way if our situations were reversed. "I know," I reply. "And I swear I won't go crazy with it. But I do need to go see my mom, somehow. There are things I need to learn and not just out of curiosity."

He leans forward unhappily, elbows to thighs. "Like what?"

"We are going to have twins who *time travel*, Nick. And they're especially good at it, according to my mother. We can't go into it blind."

His eyes close. I wish I could give him the simple life he'd have with someone else. A life where his girlfriend can't be stuck in another time, where his children won't be in danger. Except he didn't want that life in the first place. I already know he'd choose this one with me, dangers notwithstanding, a thousand times over.

"Then at least promise me you'll wait," he finally says. "It's bad enough to worry about you, but the thought of you somewhere pregnant kills me. What if something happened? Even if you survived you'd have children you couldn't bring back and I'd never even know if you were okay."

My stomach churns. I hadn't thought about that. The twins could be stuck somewhere with me for well over a decade before they came into their powers. Nick would miss their entire childhoods. "But Darcy..."

He shakes his head. "I already know what you're going to say and believe me, I want to go back and change what happened to her as much as you do, but you can't risk three lives to save one. Even if it's hers."

My mouth opens to object and no words come out. He's absolutely right. I just don't want him to be.

"Quinn," he says, pushing my hair back from my face, "even if you managed to go back a few years, where would you even go? You might be able to find Sarah, but if you couldn't...what then? I didn't *know* you. There's a small chance you'd fix things and a huge chance you'd make things worse."

I picture it, me meeting Nick a few years back—I'd be a stranger to him. A naked stranger, begging him to listen to my story about time travel...it could ruin everything. But saving Darcy was my one goal other than saving myself. And now I'm going to abandon her.

"Maybe we'll find Rose," says Nick. "Maybe Sarah left names in her office of people we can talk to."

I nod. I know it's the responsible decision. But it feels like the wrong one.

35

QUINN

On the way to the airport, we take a quick detour... back to Cecelia, the palm reader who must have helped my mother with her plot. She opens the door, and when she sees me her eyes fill with tears.

"Ça *fait longtemps,* Quinn," she says, placing a hand on my face. *It's been a long time.*

"*Je suis désolée,*" I reply, glancing from her to Nick in alarm. "*Je ne pense pas vous avoir déjà rencontrée.*" *I'm sorry. I don't think we've met.*

Nick gawks at me. "Since when do you speak French?" It's only his question that makes me realize I *am* speaking French. Fluently. The words tripped off my tongue without fore-thought. "I...have no idea."

"And unlike you," says Cecelia to Nick, brushing away her tears, "her accent is flawless. Come in, come in. You have questions."

We follow her inside. We take seats at a small table while she puts her dogs out back. I look around the room—Nick was right. It does look like something out of the 1600s. "Wow," I whisper to Nick, directing his glance upward. "Look at how they did the ceiling."

I hear a low laugh from the base of his chest. "Only *you* would visit a psychic palm reader to learn about your time traveling mother and be fascinated by the ceiling of her house instead."

Cecelia comes back into the room and takes a seat. "I suppose you have many questions."

I don't even know where to begin, but Nick does, apparently. "Did you know the plan all along?" he asks. There's a hint of accusation in his voice—I think it's going to be a long time before he gets over what we went through—but it doesn't seem to bother her in the least.

She smiles. "Oh yes. That was my niece you chased out of the basement. Don't worry. She loves helping."

Nick shakes his head. "Why all the insanity though? Why make us come to Paris?"

Sadness flickers across her features for a moment. "Sarah wanted to be near Quinn's father. She worried, in her weakened state, that she might not be able to master traveling through both time and place. That basement was where he died."

It saddens me that my father is dead, and I'll never know him, but not as much as it might under other circumstances. The truth is I had a father, a good one. And I would never want to change that. "Did you...know him?" I ask.

Her eyes go a little brighter. "Not well, but yes. He was a wonderful man."

"I don't even know his name."

She twists a ring on her finger. "All good things in time, Quinn. You'll learn everything when you're ready for it."

The temptation to argue with her is strong. Why do I need to be *ready* just to learn my own father's name?

"Things could have gone wrong so easily," Nick says. "If just one of those steps hadn't worked or if it had gone on a week longer, Quinn might have died."

"Sarah would have just changed the timeline again," Cecelia says. "In fact she had to change several things...Nick's little scuffle at the bar went a lot worse the first time. She went back and had the cops appear before it could go too far. But you did cut it very close with that tumor, didn't you?" she says, turning to me. "We bought you more time with the herbs in your IV, but the future seemed to change on a daily basis. Anyhow, it all worked out. Your mother will be pleased."

My head jerks. "*Will* be?"

"I have no doubt she jumped to the future too. You'll see her again there, as will I."

My pulse takes an excited leap. I thought we'd have to struggle to find someone to help Darcy. Perhaps we won't. "Then can you also...?"

She shakes her head. "No, no. It's quite rare, you know. My grandmother and aunt could, but the ability to reproduce among your kind seems to be dying out rapidly. Fewer and fewer of you are born, and your survival...well, you know."

"I'm having two time travelers by *accident*," I reply quietly, pressing my hand to my stomach. "It can't be *that* hard to reproduce."

"Twins among your kind are unheard of," she says softly. "They are special, your girls. Your mother and I, we both thought they must have a purpose."

"What kind of purpose?" Nick asks with an edge to his voice. His chair slides backward. Already he's thinking he needs to find a way to protect them from whatever lies in their future. I'm pretty sure he can't.

She shakes her head. "I don't know. That's for them to discover." She looks back at me and her eyes soften. "The last time I saw you, you were an infant. Before your mother gave you away. Oh, how she wept when you left. But I've followed your life through all the pictures her brother sent."

I swallow hard. It hurts a little, that he knew and kept it a secret. I know he did it for me, and that hurts in another way. I wish I could thank him. It had to have been so difficult to keep it all to himself. "Did he know? That I could jump?"

She nods. "Oh yes. He believed you would learn to time travel when you became a teenager, that you'd save yourself."

"But I didn't," I reply, feeling that all-too familiar grief in my throat. All the stories he told me as a kid...they were allegories. He was trying to convince me not to fear it. Perhaps it's why, at the end, he pushed me so hard to marry Jeff. He thought he could save me by keeping me from Nick instead. "He never lived to learn that it all worked out."

"You can go back and tell him," she says.

Nick tenses at that but I lean forward. Even if I can't time travel right now, we've got to find someone who can. "We have a friend, a little girl. We need to find someone who can go back in time to warn her about something, but I can't risk trying it while I'm pregnant. Do you know of anyone who can help us?"

She shakes her head. "There is much secrecy, you know. You can only tell someone with whom you share blood."

"But...you're discussing it with me now. And my mother discussed it with you."

Her smile is gentle. "A mystery for another time, *mon cheri*. You have a plane to catch, yes?"

We nod and rise reluctantly, thanking her, though the visit was hardly enlightening. When we reach the door, she stops and grabs my hand, whispering to me in rapid-fire French. Saying words she already knows Nick will object to.

He waits until we're walking to the car before he asks what she said.

"You won't like it." I can't say I liked it much myself.

"Tell me anyway."

I sigh, turning to face him while he opens the car door. "She said it's not just the twins who are powerful, that my gift is meant to be shared."

His jaw flexes. "You're right. I don't like it."

She predicted his reaction too. "And she also said overcoming my fear was only half the battle. Overcoming yours is the other half."

His mouth is set in a grim line. "Quinn—"

I open the door, shoulders sagging in resignation. "I know. I know what I promised."

I think of Darcy. I'm still not sure it's a promise I should have made.

36

QUINN

By the time we land at Dulles, Nick's received an email from the hospital board, who examined our photos and deemed that the relationship was not a breach of ethics. Unfortunately, this means they expect him to report to work the next day.

I lean my head against his shoulder as we ride home from the airport. "I was really looking forward to a few days with you, where no one has imminent death hanging over their heads."

He pulls me closer. "We can get away for a few days next month. Let me just get all my patients taken care of and put in for leave."

"Doctors get to put in for leave," I pout. "Students do not."

I see a quick flash of his dimple. "I bet your professors would understand if you missed a day or two because you were on your *honeymoon*."

I laugh. He's relentless—this is at least the fifth time he's brought up marriage—but I sort of love it. "What would everyone say? I just called off my last engagement a month ago."

"I don't give a fuck what they'd say," Nick replies. "When we hit our 50th wedding anniversary, they'll know they were wrong."

"You really pick the most romantic places to discuss this," I reply as the driver turns onto our street. "Hospital, cab ride. I'm assuming you'll propose while I'm peeing or vomiting next."

"Those weren't proposals." He grins. "Believe me, when I propose, it'll be memor—"

His words are cut off by a low groan. *My* low groan.

Jeff is sitting on our front steps.

"What the fuck?" Nick snaps.

"My mom." I smack my head. "She must have told him when we were getting in."

"I think it's time you have a conversation with your mom about who she's providing information to," he says. "Stay in the car. I'll deal with this."

"If I'm capable of stabbing my own mother," I reply, climbing out after him and ignoring the driver's gaping mouth, "I'm capable of dealing with Jeff."

Nick turns toward the walkway and sets the bags down in front of him. "Get off my property," he says. His voice is flat, calm, but somehow far more threatening that way. "I've already kicked your ass once and I'd be more than happy to do it again."

"I want to talk to Quinn," Jeff says, moving toward us.

I step forward and Nick gives me the side-eye. "You never listen," he mutters.

I glance up at him, trying not to smile, before I turn back to Jeff. "Say what you have to say."

Jeff's eyes shift to Nick. "I don't want *him* here."

Nick growls in response. "If you think I'm leaving you alone with her, you're out of your mind."

Jeff visibly struggles to control his temper. I wait impatiently, already knowing exactly what he will say. I've heard it so many times now that a part of me doesn't feel capable of listening to it again. "I just want to know why you—" he begins.

I can't do it. I can't listen to him even one more time. "I'm pregnant."

He actually steps backward, as if he's been struck. "Bullshit," he whispers.

I pull my T-shirt up just enough that he can see the swell of my stomach. A swell that's never been there before. Even *I* can't imagine why I'm showing so soon, but today it's come in handy. Because I see, in his shock, that this is the one way to make Jeff give up.

He stares so intently that Nick finally tugs my shirt back down. "Whose is it?" he asks mutinously.

"I think you know the answer to that," I reply. It's been months since we slept together.

The ugly words he wants to say are flashing across his face. But I know how he was raised—I'm going to be a mother, which creates a line he won't cross.

He swallows. Holds his ground. Then marches past us without a word.

Nick stares him down until he's in his car and driving away. "I think that's the end of it," I say, turning toward him. "Which is a good thing. You've got to be sick of getting in fights on my behalf."

He wraps an arm around my waist and pulls me close. "I will very happily fight for you and our family until my dying breath," he replies, his mouth near my ear. "And if our daughters are anything like you, I'm guessing I'd better plan on it."

37

QUINN

Nick is up bright and early the day after we get home, trying to get back on schedule.

I watch him pack his gym bag, smiling to myself. These tiny moments with him aren't something ephemeral, they're something I might get to live again and again. It seems like too much good fortune for one person. "We could have sixty more years like this."

He looks over and grins. "I was just thinking the same thing. Although it was mostly to convince myself I'll have plenty of opportunities to climb back in bed with you."

I stretch my arms overhead. "You should totally climb back in bed with me," I reply throatily.

His eyes move over me, linger on my curves under a single flat sheet, before he forces himself to look away. "You should be sleeping in while you can," he says. "And you're not eating enough either. Red Gatorade is not food."

The craving for Gatorade—and absolutely nothing else—is

new. Maybe the twins are going to be athletes. "I feel like a million bucks. I'm *pregnant*, not dying."

His eyes close and he smiles. "You're going to be a complete pain in the ass about this, aren't you?"

I laugh. I was just thinking the exact same thing about him. "Fine. Go to work. I can't wait to hear what your colleagues have to say when they find out you're dating an undergrad."

"I think the bigger news will be that I *knocked up* an undergrad," he mutters, knotting his tie. He presses a kiss to my forehead. "I hope you plan to rest today. You've been through a lot the past few weeks."

Argh. I suspect he will not approve of my plans for the day. "I was thinking I'd go by my mom's place in Georgetown to see if she left any files. There may be someone I can contact to help Darcy."

He frowns. "I just get through suggesting you rest, and you respond by telling me you plan to break and enter?"

"It's not breaking and entering if it's *my* home."

He arches a brow. "The title wasn't in the papers she left us. So do you have a single way to prove it's yours?"

"Yes," I say, petulant as a child, "but I may need to break and enter to find it."

His mouth twitches but he flattens it out just in time to look stern again. "Just wait," he says. "I'll leave early today and we'll go over there together. I don't need my pregnant girlfriend walking into another deadly trap alone."

I climb to the edge of the bed with the sheet wrapped around my chest. "How can you still be so suspicious? I'm *healed*."

He sighs. "Look, it's not that I don't trust Sarah. But I don't trust what we'll find there. I don't trust that there isn't some new fucked-up thing that's going to make shit go haywire."

"Like what?"

His raises his hands, exasperated. "I don't know! That's the problem. What if she's got some magic portal to the future you don't even know you're walking into?"

I laugh so hard that I collapse back on the bed. "Did you really just say you're worried about *magical portals*?" I glance down at my stomach. "I'm so sorry to tell you this, little embryos, but your father is a total dork."

"How is *that* any more unlikely than time travel?" he argues. "Just wait. I'll try to come home for lunch and we can go then. But just so we're clear, if there *is* a magical portal that pulls you away forever, I'm going to be very annoyed."

"If that happens you can say *I told you so* all you want."

He glares at me. "If you're pulled away forever you won't be able to hear me say it."

I grin at him over my shoulder as I head to the bathroom. "Precisely."

~

AFTER HE LEAVES I finish unpacking, carefully placing the knickknacks I bought Darcy on the kitchen table so I don't forget to bring them to her this weekend. I hold the Eiffel Tower snow globe in my hand, watching the flakes settle along the banks of the Seine. She's never going to see that. All my dreams came true in one fell swoop, while not a single one of hers will. She's never going to travel, or fall in love, or have children. I understand Nick's point about the dangers, but it's just so fucking wrong that I'm not even going to *try* to help.

I walk to the store, but once I've done my shopping and returned home, the silence of the house eats at me. No—not silence—*guilt*. Because maybe our caution is for no reason whatsoever. We don't know what Grosbaum's wife was *really* doing when she disappeared. Maybe she decided to go to medieval England during a vicious bout of the plague. Maybe she met some real-life version of Lord Darcy and decided to stay. And maybe if I took baby steps I could build up to jumping a few months, back to the day I saw Rose. How badly could I possibly mess things up? I'm not even sure I'm capable of doing it outside of really extreme situations.

I should at least see how hard it is.

Am I breaking a promise to Nick if I just try it? One *tiny* jump, an hour back in time? Yes, probably. But if it was up to him, I'd go through the rest of my life encased in bubble wrap, and while I agree that any major attempts at time travel should be avoided for the time being, I just don't see how much harm this could possibly do.

I ignore the twinge of guilt I feel, and try to remember what I did in Sarah's basement. I close my eyes, just like I did then, and picture the upstairs hallway, maybe an hour earlier. I squeeze my eyes tight, clench my fists, try to make my mind go there.

My eyes open to discover I'm still standing downstairs like an idiot. Absolutely nothing has happened. So perhaps all my angst over not helping Darcy is unnecessary, and finding a friend of my mother's is our best bet.

I've finished unpacking the groceries and started a load of laundry before I decide I should try again, once more. A smaller jump. Maybe five minutes.

I picture the hallway, focusing on it as if nothing else exists. I picture the divots in the hardwood, the way the balusters are slightly loose and in need of paint. At last I feel the rush of air in the darkness, see a night sky flecked with light. Fear and triumph twine together in my stomach, but I ignore them both, and I land exactly as I pictured—naked in the upstairs hallway. The clock in the bedroom says I've gone back only a few minutes, just as I planned.

"Now to see if I can return," I say quietly. I'm slightly unnerved by the idea of jumping down a floor, but I ignore it. I close my eyes and think of the kitchen.

Nothing happens. I'm just standing naked in the upstairs hallway, five minutes back in time. *How does this even work if I'm unable to return? Does Nick come home to an empty house, or am I here, just five minutes behind?* I don't want to find out.

I close my eyes and try harder. I imagine the smell of bananas starting to ripen, freshly ground coffee beans on the counter, empty Gatorade bottles in the recycling bin. I hold onto it and don't let it go, and at last there's a rush of wind. I land precisely where I pictured, with a ridiculous smile on my face. It's hardly going to change the world, my ability to go up and down the stairs this way or move forward in time by a whole five minutes—but it's a start. I could build up to a week, and then two weeks, then three. I'll tell Nick so it's not as if I'll be lying, and maybe if I get good enough at it, if it starts to come as easily as it did long ago—the prospect of going back a few months to find Rose won't seem so terrifying to either of us.

I try it twice more. It comes to me more effortlessly, and though I'm tempted to keep going, I decide I've pushed it far enough for now. I get my clothes on and make a smoothie. I'm about to take it into the garden when I hear my phone ringing in the bedroom. I turn toward the stairs, wishing I *could* just jump for it. It would certainly make getting around here a lot more efficient. *With my luck*, I think, *I'd end up going back a year and give the old tenants a heart attack.* I laugh to myself as I picture landing naked upstairs on a summer night in a different year.

By the time I realize the air is rushing around me, it's too late to take it back.

38

NICK

I move through my morning rounds, wishing I could have gotten the day off. Quinn starts school Tuesday, and even though we have the weekend, I wanted just one idyllic day with her after the upheaval of Paris.

My first stop is Darcy's room, which I enter with a heavy heart. She went into a coma while we were in France—a fact I haven't shared with Quinn—and while it's always hard for me to lose a patient, this one hits harder than most. I can't believe she's never going to open her eyes again. She's never going to correct me when I try to discuss *Teen Titans* with her or crush every opponent at Connect Four.

I know I should have told Quinn when I heard, but she'd been through so much with Sarah that I decided to give it a day or two. I suppose, selfishly, I also didn't want to tell her anything that might encourage her to time travel. But I cringed, watching her buy souvenirs for someone who will never be able to see them.

Christy's face as I enter the room is blank. I've seen this look from patients' families too many times before. Exhaustion and distress, at a certain point, don't just weaken you. They empty you. "There's not much longer, is there?" she asks, her voice flat.

My lips press together. "I don't think so, no."

She looks at her lap, and when she speaks again her voice is choked. "Her father's on a plane home...I just wish he could have seen her while she was still conscious."

I flinch. I know it's selfish, what I'm asking Quinn to do. And standing here, I'm no longer certain I've made the right call. She has a gift, and maybe it's meant to be used. If it were anyone but Quinn, I'd probably insist it should be. Except I just got her back. I can't stand to lose her all over again.

I FINISH my rounds and call Quinn to suggest we meet at her mom's house. Mostly it's to appease my guilty conscience, but who knows? Maybe we'll find something there. Sarah must have known someone else who time travels. As thoroughly as she seems to have planned for various outcomes, I have a hard time imagining she didn't leave Quinn with some backup.

The phone rings but goes to voicemail, and I have to force myself not to panic. *She no longer has a tumor. I can't freak out every time she doesn't answer her phone.* I go see my next few patients, but I'm only half here. The other part of me is wondering where the hell she is and why she hasn't called me back.

An hour passes. I call again. She still doesn't answer.

39

QUINN

I land in my upstairs hallway, but it's nighttime, and the bass is so loud downstairs that the floorboards vibrate beneath my feet.

Oh shit.

From where I stand I can hear people outside in the garden. A girl is shouting something about beer I can't quite make out.

I want to be wrong. Please God, let me be wrong. Let me open our bedroom door and find Nick there, asleep.

He's not. Instead I find a mattress on the floor and two beanbag chairs where our beautiful king-size bed should rest. There are clothes everywhere, as if three suitcases exploded at once.

The air conditioning tells me it's summer. Aside from that I have no idea how far back I've gone, although I hear Rihanna's voice coming through the speakers, a song that's only a few years old, so it couldn't be far.

I've got to get home. What if I can't? My heart pounds in

terror at the thought and I force it out of my head. Right now, I'm naked inside a stranger's home. First things first.

I grab a pair of denim shorts and a flannel shirt off the floor and throw them on quickly. Rihanna stops singing and Bruno Mars takes her place, a song I think only came out last summer. If I'm right, it's just 2017.

Which means I could, potentially, save Darcy.

I know what I promised Nick, but this was an accident, and the opportunity to save her has basically fallen into my lap. I can't *not* try. For most of my life I blindly did what my father told me. When he died, I let Jeff assume that role. I love Nick, and I trust his opinion more than I did either of theirs, but I'm done letting someone else make my most important decisions.

I creep down the stairs, though with the volume of the music, it's not as if anyone could possibly hear me. Avoiding eye contact, I push through a wall of bodies toward the front door. I'm almost there when someone grabs my arm.

I've begun to mount a defense about the stolen clothes when my eyes go to the tatted-up college kid who's grabbed me. I seriously doubt it's *his* shorts I'm wearing...these things barely cover my ass.

"Hey," he says, as if we're friends. "Where are you going?"

"Home," I reply, pulling my arm from his grip. I take two large strides and get out the front door with him on my heels.

"Slow down," he says. "I just want to chat." I keep walking, fully intending to ignore him and possibly run if he keeps following, when it occurs to me I have no fucking idea where Darcy even lives.

I whirl around so fast he's forced to take a step backward. "Can I borrow your phone for a second?" I ask. "I left mine at home. I just need to look something up."

He unlocks his phone and hands it to me. "It's an iPhone 7?" I ask.

"Yeah," he says, smirking. "Why? Would an iPhone 6 not be fancy enough to borrow?"

I laugh out of relief more than anything else. An iPhone 7 means it's definitely 2017, because the house wasn't occupied in 2018 until we moved in, and the iPhone 7 didn't exist in the summer of 2016. "I'm not that picky. Just curious."

Christine Whitley, Washington DC, I tap out on the keyboard. Safari returns a gazillion listings for Christine Whitleys who live nowhere around here.

Shit. With a heavy heart I start to return the phone, and then one more possibility occurs to me. Her candle company— I close my eyes to picture the business card she gave me. *Heart in Hand Candles*, it said. I type the name and an address comes up immediately. *Thank God.*

They live in Cleveland Park, just a few miles from here. I could walk, but I want to get this done as fast as possible so I can get home to Nick. I hand Skinny College Boy his phone. It's annoying that he stopped me and even more annoying that he *followed* me, but he does not look dangerous.

"You go to Georgetown?" I ask.

He nods. "Business major. You?"

I make a split-second decision. "Do you have a car? Can you give me a ride? I need to get to the Giant in Cleveland Park."

"I have a motorcycle," he offers. "Just to warn you though, I don't have helmets." I shrug and follow him, already imagining how I will explain this to Nick later: *Yes, I know I said I wouldn't jump but I did. And then I stole some clothes and got on the back of a motorcycle with a stranger who followed me out of a party. Oh, and —fun fact—we didn't wear helmets. How ironic would it have been if I'd died of a head injury right after recovering from a brain tumor?!*

I doubt he'd find it as amusing as I do.

I climb on the bike behind him, not allowing myself to dwell on the stupidity of this venture. He takes off so fast that I'm forced to cling—intentionally no doubt. My nose is pressed to the back of his shirt, which smells like weed. So this terrible idea just got worse, something I didn't realize was possible.

We arrive in Cleveland Park a few minutes later. If I'd realized just how close we were and just how poorly he drives, I'd have walked. "We still have all of our limbs," I say with a shaky laugh as I climb off. "What a pleasant surprise."

"You want to get a drink before you go?" he asks.

I flash him a smile. "I'd love to but I'm pregnant, so I probably shouldn't."

He's still staring at me, jaw gaping, as I turn and walk into the store.

～

FIVE MINUTES later I'm walking back out with a note clutched in my hand. Customer Service lent me pen and paper. Unfortunately, I wasn't able to consult with them on how best to explain to someone that I've traveled back in time to warn her about her daughter's brain tumor. As badly as I longed for subtlety—a casual mention of a case similar to Darcy's, a newspaper clipping—there just wasn't time. I went for candor instead and I pray it will work:

Your daughter's headaches are more serious than your doctor realizes. She needs an MRI ASAP. Go see Nick Reilly at Georgetown.

I leave the store, my feet stinging as they slap against the rough pavement. I wish I'd stolen shoes, because God only knows what I could catch. I cross Wisconsin Avenue, narrowly avoiding broken glass, and turn onto Porter. Darcy's house is two blocks down the road, a tiny Cape Cod. There's a purple bike dumped in the yard, chalk fading on the sidewalk in front. It takes a second to realize the bike is Darcy's. I've only known the version of her that exists in 2018—pale and bald and far too thin. I'd almost forgotten she wasn't always that way. *Please let this work*, I pray, hand pressed to the mail slot for only a moment before I push the paper through.

One job done.

Now I've just got to figure out how to get home to Nick.

I SIT in the grass a few blocks away, hidden by darkness, attempting to focus. I think of our little house, our bed. I think of Nick mowing the lawn on a Saturday morning, shirtless. Small flecks of grass clinging to his skin. There's a flutter in my belly but it's cut off by a thought—*Am I going to wind up back in the house on Saturday morning instead? What then?*

What if I can't get home? Just considering the possibility is enough to make my stomach bottom out. My muscles go stiff, my heart starts to race. Like test anxiety, but with much higher stakes.

I close my eyes and try to focus again. When I open them, nothing has happened. I'm still sitting in the grass, in the oppressive summer heat, the screech of crickets almost painfully loud.

Our house. Go back to our house. I try again. I picture Nick lying in bed, his profile sharp in the morning light. The sound of birds outside, the twitch of his mouth as he starts to wake, his hand curving around my hip the way it does, as if discovering a lost favorite toy. Even if I wind up there a few days off, it'll be close enough. *Go.*

But the air remains still and stagnant, clinging to my skin like something tangible. The tightness in my chest threatens to strangle me. *How long have I been gone? Is Nick back from work? Is he worried?*

I try again, but all I can see is him—brooding, desperate. When he finds my clothes in a pile, the glass I was holding shattered, he's going to panic. He's going to sit there thinking how unlikely it is I will find my way back. Which introduces another terrible question: *What if I get home too late?* What if it's two years from now and he's with someone else?

I bury my head in my hands, realizing how right he was when he begged me not to jump. This is no longer about just me—it's three of us he loses now if I can't make it back. And *then* what??

I try to focus, I try to make myself jump again and again, ignoring my terror. Hours pass and nothing works. I try small steps, like I did this morning: five minutes later, a minute earlier, and my repeated failures make desperation tighten in my gut. If I knew my mother's address in Georgetown I could ask her what to do. But I don't. How could I have let this happen? How could I have been so unprepared for it?

Daylight is now only an hour or two away. I pull my knees to my chest and press my forehead against them, thinking. I'm not sure how long I can walk around D.C. barefoot and filthy and penniless, before this whole thing gets worse. I could go see Caroline and pray last year's Quinn doesn't show up at her door at the same time, but it won't solve the real problem. And how would I ever explain the problem to her anyway? I can't tell her the truth. I don't remember how to time travel, but some sort of ancient knowledge now rests in my gut—telling people you're not related to has consequences. Terrifying ones. I would die before I'd do that to her.

The inky black of the sky has begun to soften to the east. Daylight right around the corner. I just wish I could rest. I wish I could lean on Nick for a minute, feel his chin against the top of my head while he tells me things will be fine, that he's going to fix this somehow. Nick is my wall—but I can't lean on a wall that hasn't been built yet.

Or can I?

Nick is here, in D.C., newly back from London. I can't ask him to hold me, to reassure me, but it might be enough just to see him. He's religious about his morning swim, so I know where he'll be. It's not without risks—if he meets me now as a barefoot, disheveled girl wearing too few clothes, it will change things when we meet later on. He won't think of me as someone intriguing who knows way more than she should. I might instead become the creepy girl who lurked outside the Georgetown pool the summer before, looking like she was coming off a bender at Coachella.

But I need to see him, so it's a risk I'll have to take.

I break into a run, down the long hill to Georgetown. Past the cathedral, past the stores, until I'm sprinting through the very neighborhood where we house hunted a few weeks ago. It's light outside when I finally arrive on campus, winded and sweating. I stake out my spot in the parking lot beside the gym, and collapse on the curb, debating with myself about what I'll do when I see him. *Could I tell him? Would it change things?*

For the next fifteen minutes, I wait. My heart leaps each time I see a car swing into the lot, and plummets when, again and again, that car is not Nick's. He should be here by now, and the idea that today might be the day he skipped makes me long to weep, which I'm on the cusp of doing at the precise moment his car pulls into the lot.

He stops about twenty yards away from where I sit. I watch as he steps out, and it's just so *him*: his preoccupation, the slight frown on his face, the morning stubble, the way he slings his bag over his shoulder. It's so perfectly, absolutely him that I can't stay where I am.

I don't know what I can possibly say to make him remember me, make him believe a sweaty, half-naked girl is someone he'd ever want to move in with, but there must be something. I jump to my feet. He'll know he's mine the same way, as I watch him get out of his car, I know I'm his. He has to.

I step off the curb and have taken two steps into the lot when the passenger door of the Jeep opens and a woman climbs out, dressed to run, pulling her hair back into a perky ponytail as they chat on opposite sides of the car.

Meg.

The shock of it forces me backward, knocks the air from my chest.

You don't arrive at the gym with a *friend* at 6:00 a.m. They're together. They were together last night. They slept together, woke up next to each other. In this timeline, she is the last person he kissed and she's the person he will sleep with next. It's her he wants right now, not me. My stomach churns at the thought.

She walks around to his side as she puts her headphones in, placing her hands on his shoulders and going on to her toes to kiss him goodbye. He doesn't linger on it the way he does with me, but it hardly matters. I'm watching the father of my children kiss someone else after spending the night with her. As he heads toward the gym—never looking my direction once —I sink to the curb and allow myself all the sadness and desperation I am feeling, face buried into my grass-stained palms.

I just want to be home. God, I wish I was home. It's a mantra that plays on repeat in my head. The desire to press my head to Nick's chest is so strong it's almost real. I can feel the way his arms would wrap around me, smell the soap and chlorine on his skin. I imagine his relief when I land, the way we'd cling to each other and thank God it turned out okay.

Air rushes around me, and then there is absolute darkness.

I land on a hard floor, falling to hands and knees at the suddenness of it. For a moment I'm too scared to open my eyes, but when I hear Nick shouting my name and the thunderous clamor of his feet flying up the stairs, I finally look around me. *Home.* Relief surges through my blood like a drug. It's nighttime here, but I'm home with him and nothing else matters.

He reaches the hallway, wild-eyed, and drops to the ground,

pulling me to his lap and rocking me like I'm a child. "Thank fucking God," he says. His voice is rough. "Thank God."

"I'm sorry. I'm so sorry," I tell him, weeping hard enough that I'm barely coherent. "I didn't mean to. It just happened and I couldn't get home..."

His arms tighten around me. "I know." He buries his face in my hair. "You scared the shit out of me. Are you okay?"

I nod. I can feel the panic in him still, like a stain he can't wash away. "I need to clean up," I whisper after a minute. "I was barefoot all night. My feet are a mess."

He gently lifts my foot and stiffens. "You've got some cuts."

His voice is flat, purposefully emotionless. He picks me up like a child and starts to carry me toward the bathroom.

"I can walk," I argue, but he ignores me. His profile is so rigid it looks cast in steel as he sets me on the counter and inspects my feet.

"We'll get them cleaned off first," he says, running the water in the tub. "Stay here."

I watch him stalk off, suddenly unsettled. What the hell is happening here? He was relieved when I came back—beyond relieved—but now it feels like he doesn't even want me around.

I limp to the tub and rinse my feet, watching as the water goes from muddy to clear, and then I push down the plug and step inside, sighing as the water begins to fill around me. He returns with a first aid kit and Gatorade, which I chug as if I've been wandering the desert.

"You're dehydrated," he says with a harsh exhale, not meeting my eye.

I'm not sure if I want to snap at him or burst into tears. I've just been through one of the worst nights of my life and he's acting like I did something wrong.

"I didn't do it on purpose," I tell him. "It just happened."

"I know," he says, jaw clenched tight. "I saw all the shattered glass where you dropped your drink." Maybe his disapproval isn't aimed at me, but I feel it anyway. And I can't entirely blame him—inadvertently, I risked my life and our children's lives as well.

I stare at my bent knees, at the water rising beneath them. "What time is it, anyway?" I ask. "Were you waiting long?"

He runs a hand through his hair, not quite looking at me. "It's about midnight. I came home when you didn't answer the phone this morning and found your clothes on the floor." He continues to look away. Those hours were just as hard on him as they were on me and he's trying not to blame me for what I put him through, but he can't help doing it anyway. I feel this distance between us like a physical thing, made of air yet impossible to reach through entirely.

I hold out my hand. "Come in with me."

He swallows. "You need to rest and if I get into that tub you know it'll lead somewhere."

"Please," I say quietly, staring at the water. After another moment's hesitation I hear his clothes hitting the floor and then he climbs in behind me, sliding his long legs on either side of mine. I lean against his chest while he pours the body wash in his hands, lathering it up before he washes me off. Feet, legs, arms, back.

He buries his face in my hair. "I'm sorry," he says. "I hate what you must have gone through. I hate that I'm mad about it when I know it wasn't your fault. But we need to find a way to make sure it doesn't happen again. Especially not when you're pregnant. I feel like tonight took a decade off my life."

My stomach sinks a little. The truth is, it was absolutely my fault. I should never have been trying to time travel in the first place. "It was stupid. I'd been practicing a little. Just going from the kitchen to the upstairs hall, thinking maybe I'd get good enough that we could help Darcy, but—"

"Darcy?" he asks.

I turn back, glancing at him over my shoulder with a raised brow. "Yes, Darcy. Who else would I be trying to help?"

"I don't know what you're talking about."

I slide away so I can turn toward him, staggered. "Darcy Whitley. Your patient. Seven years old? Brain tumor?"

He looks at me blankly before his eyes open with recognition. "Oh, right. How the hell do *you* know about that? I only saw her once, and it had to be a year ago."

My eyes fill for at least the tenth time since I got home. "Are you saying she's not your patient? She's fine?"

He shrugs. "Yeah, I assume so. She just had a little glioma, if I recall correctly. It was no big deal. I referred her to neurosurgery. I'd have heard if there was anything else going on."

It worked. I take a quick breath as the relief hits, but once it's gone my throat tightens a little, happy and sad all at once. This, I realize, is what it's going to be like to time travel. I may do good things, but it means losing people too, losing shared experiences. Darcy no longer knows me, and I'm the only one who will ever remember sitting beside Nick at her birthday party.

"It was a big deal. You won't remember, because I changed her timeline," I whisper, hugging my knees. "Today when you went to the hospital, Darcy was a dying patient without much time left because the first doctor they saw blew off her headaches. So I warned her mother tonight. During that visit you barely remember, you saved her life."

He frowns. I get it, the way it's impossible to grasp that something has happened when you don't remember it, but he also has faith in this—and in me. "No," he says. "You saved her."

Either way, I'd do it all over again, even if it means the memory of Nick with Meg is stuck in my head forever. It's stupid that seeing him with her is still bothering me, but the problem is that even if it took place in 2017, it *feels* like it was minutes ago.

"What's wrong?" he asks, wrapping his hands around my ankles. "Are you just tired or is it something else?"

My head droops. I could choose to keep pretending things are fine, but not telling him things just doesn't seem to work out for us. "I saw you," I say quietly. "I ran from Cleveland Park to campus, thinking if I could just watch you walking into the gym I'd feel better. And then Meg got out of your car." I press my face to my knees. I don't want to cry in front of him over this and it's completely unfair to make him feel guilty over it. I just don't know what else I can do. "You'd just spent the night with her, obviously. It was sunrise. And I know it was a year ago or more but it feels like it just happened."

"Jesus," he says. "I don't know what you saw, but no matter what it looked like, I was never in love with her. Never even close."

It helps, a little. "I know. It just felt real. It feels like it just happened."

He slides toward me and his hands cradle my face. "In my whole life it's only been you. You're the only person I've ever been in love with, and tonight when I contemplated the idea of life without you, I finally got what Grosbaum must have gone through, because I'd have waited forever just hoping you were coming back."

He kisses me. A real kiss, one without any blame or terror. His lips are gentle on mine, as if I'm so fragile I might shatter right here in his hands.

I'm the one who needs more, and demands it. I climb over him, placing a knee on either side of his hips so there is no distance between us. With a guttural noise, his hands twist in my hair, and the kiss grows hard and desperate. I slide my hands over the broad shoulders, the perfect chest I missed so much, and then lower.

"Quinn," he groans, his mouth still against mine, "we really shouldn't. You should rest."

I rise, move him against me, watching his weak attempts at restraint falter.

I start to sink on top of him but hold myself aloft instead. "Are you sure we shouldn't?" I taunt.

"No," he grunts, arching upward. His head falls against the back of the tub as he bottoms out inside me. "*Fuck*. That's so good."

He watches as I move, his eyes heavy, his mouth ajar, his hands slipping over my chest. With each thrust he drives the memories of Meg a little further from my head.

"Faster," he pleads quietly, grabbing my hips.

"I can't in this position. My knees..." I begin, and find myself lifted and carried to the bed, with him still inside me. He lies me on my back and pulls my knees over his shoulders, hitting an angle that never fails to drive every other thought from my head. "Oh God," I moan.

He watches my face, desperate to come, waiting for the tell-tale arch of my spine. I see the strain in him, in his shoulders, in the tendons of his neck. He slips his fingers between us and I go off like a rocket. He follows, my name a pained whisper falling from his lips.

After a moment he carefully removes himself and flips to the side of me.

He opens one eye. "I told you that would happen."

I grin. "Are you saying you regret it?"

He pulls me against him, dragging a blanket over us and tucking my head into the crook of his shoulder. "As long as we're in the same place, I'm never going to regret anything again."

40

QUINN

The following week, just before my classes begin, Nick and I have our first obstetrics appointment. He's already in the waiting room when I arrive.

"Decaf latte," he says, placing a Styrofoam cup in my hand as he leans down to kiss my forehead.

I smile at him. "You're spoiling me. What happens when the novelty wears off?"

He tips my chin up with his index finger. "The novelty of you is never going to wear off. But you know how to scare the shit out of me if I ever start taking you for granted."

"I have less stressful ways to remind you that you like me," I reply, and I get his dirtiest smile in response.

"Once this is done we should go home so you can remind me again," he replies.

A few minutes later we are called back, and I go through something I only vaguely recall in the past...the cold jelly spread over my stomach, the smooth paddle sliding over it. Nick is watching the screen so avidly you'd think he expects one of the babies to speak to us. He finds what he is looking for and stares at it awestruck.

"You see something?" I ask.

His smile goes wide. "Yeah."

"I see two somethings," says the doctor triumphantly. "You're having twins, Mrs. Reilly."

I try to pretend I'm surprised, and I don't correct him on the name. I guess I'll be Mrs. Reilly soon enough.

41

QUINN
TWO WEEKS LATER

I've finished getting ready, though I'm wearing clothes Caroline will undoubtedly find lacking because they don't cost ten million dollars. "You're sure you don't want to come?" I ask Nick for the third time.

Nick kisses my forehead. "Go have fun with your friends," he replies. "I'll see you when you get home."

Between school and the pregnancy and my unending obsession with Nick's eight-pack and biceps, there hasn't been time to see Trevor and Caroline since we got back from France. I'm excited to have drinks with them, even if I won't be drinking, but I wish Nick was coming with us. When we're apart it feels like something is missing, and the world becomes nothing more than a series of stories and experiences to dissect with him later. "I'm not sure how much fun it will be watching them drink margaritas while I sip water."

"I thought you were meeting someone Trevor is dating."

"The senator," I reply, grinning, "in *theory*."

"Trevor is dating a *senator*? You said he prefers criminals."

"Let's not kid ourselves. *Senator* and *criminal* aren't mutually exclusive terms. But no, it's just some legislative aide. He and Trevor do this roleplay in which he's a senator who trades political favors for sex. And thus the nickname."

Nick shakes his head. "That was slightly more than I needed to know about Trevor's sex life."

"Admit it. You'd love to play senator with me."

He gets that smile on his face—slow and dirty, his eyes a little feral. "Senator Reilly has a nice ring to it." He pulls me in for a kiss. I can feel his cock pressing against my stomach as if it's knocking on the door to beg entry. I really wish I wasn't already running late.

He sighs as he pushes away, glancing downward. "Now see what you've done?"

I bat my lashes. "Oh, *Senator Reilly*, I'm so sorry, sir," I reply, my voice high and breathy as I grab my keys. "If there's any way I can make it up to you, let me know."

"Not helpful," he growls at my retreating back.

TREVOR'S MARGARITA looks like the most delicious thing I've ever seen in my life—the dollop of foam on the top, the frosted glass, the neon green that couldn't possibly come from nature. Pregnancy is a miracle of life, blah blah blah. I'm still allowed to miss margaritas.

"It tastes like piss, I swear," says Trevor, catching my glance.

I laugh. "Right. That's why you ordered a second one."

Just as I expected, they made me change clothes for this, Trevor insisting the jeans I wore were unacceptable because "we are not dock workers," whatever that means. The outfit is of Caroline's choosing, a white, Tom Ford wrap dress, cut low and flaring out at the waist. It seems like a lot of effort for what is definitely going to be a short evening, but I'm not complaining. *Senator Reilly* is going to enjoy this look a great deal when I get home.

"Look at your boobs," Caroline says, shaking her head. "They're stupendous. You've gone up at least one cup size, if not two. You know I really don't want kids but *wow* you're making me think twice."

"There are easier ways to get boobs," says Trevor, rolling his eyes before he turns toward me. "But speaking of kids, when's Nick going to make an honest woman of you?"

I shrug, feeling the tiniest prickle of worry that I instantly push aside. "We're not in any rush. There's enough going on." The truth is I *do* want him to ask but he seems to have just forgotten about it. Maybe I shouldn't have shot him down those first few times he brought it up.

"Watch out," says Caroline. "Remember Daniel? He was—"

"Oh, *here we go*," says Trevor. "Now she's going to tell you a warning story about the time *she* was a mother of twins too."

"Shut up, Trevor. Anyway, he was always saying he wanted to marry me and then it turned out he was *already married*."

I laugh. Their stories appalled me before, but now that I'm with Nick, the stories seem too terrible to even be real. "I'm pretty sure I'd know if Nick was already married, given that we live together and haven't spent a night apart in weeks."

Trevor gets a text and his face lights up. "It's showtime. The senator is down at the waterfront." He and Caroline exchange a quick glance and then they both wave frantically for the bill.

"What are you not telling me about this guy?" I ask, looking between the two of them.

"Nothing," they reply in unison, which makes it that much fishier.

"Neither of you can lie for shit. What's the deal? Is the senator someone I know?" I ask, and then I gasp. "Oh my God. It's *Jeff*, isn't it?"

Trevor rolls his eyes. "As if. I don't have a straight bone in my body, but if anyone could bore me out of homosexuality, it would be him."

We head down Wisconsin Avenue toward the river. I remember the days when I'd look at all the bars we are passing longingly, a desire for the years of being a wild, single college student I missed out on. Now they do nothing for me. Going to any of them would feel like a punishment if I could be home with Nick instead.

We cross the street to the waterfront just as the sun begins its slow slide over the horizon.

"Hey, isn't this where you went dancing with Nick?" Trevor asks.

I glance at the couples shuffling over the waterfront's travertine tiles. "Yeah, right before—" my words falter at the sight of a tall, broad-shouldered hunk in a suit cutting through the dancing couples. Nick. My heart is doing pirouettes in my chest. "Hey!" I shout, moving as fast as I can in the four-inch heels Caroline forced me to wear. "I thought you said you didn't want to—"

He drops to one knee. His face is every bit as sweet, as earnest, as it was when he was a teenager. He looks at me as if I hold his entire world in the palm of my hand, as if I'm his to crush or to keep. He reaches into his pocket and pulls out a black velvet box.

The couples around him have mostly stopped dancing. Caroline, standing on one side, and Trevor, standing on the other, push me forward until we are in front of him. "Since I couldn't ask your father, I asked them instead," Nick says with a shy smile. The dimple blinks into existence.

"You have our blessing," says Trevor.

Caroline kisses me on the cheek. "I'd totally let him get me pregnant," she says as Trevor pulls her away.

I'm so astonished all I can do is stare: at Nick, at the box, at the dancers and setting sun. It feels as if my brain is moving a little more slowly than normal.

"Marry me," Nick says. People around us are listening, so his voice drops to add, "in this lifetime and any others we find ourselves in."

He pops the box open and I gasp. It's *my* ring, the oval diamond I remember from London. I reach for it and he pulls the box back. "You have to actually agree before you get the ring, greedy girl."

"But how...where did you find it?" I ask.

He grins. "My grandfather gave it to me when I went to see him. I'll tell you about it later. *After* you answer."

Goose bumps crawl over my arms, but they're the good kind. The kind you get when you're so thrilled and astonished at once that you have no idea where to begin. "Yes," I whisper. "In this lifetime and all the other ones, I will only want you."

IT'S LATE. We both should be asleep, but I'm way too giddy for that. Every five seconds I'm holding my ring up so I can see it in the moonlight. "It's even more perfect than I remember."

He laughs. "You said that before."

I said it during our celebratory drink with Trevor and Caroline. My explanation of how I could *remember* a ring I'd theoretically never seen before made little sense, but fortunately they'd had enough to drink they didn't notice. "That was awkward. I'm going to have to be more careful in the future."

He runs a hand over my hip. "Don't you think you ought to just tell them the truth?" he asks. "As weird as they are, they do seem to have your back."

I shake my head. "I couldn't. You know the rule...you can't tell anyone who isn't related by blood."

"That *can't* be true. Grosbaum knew about his wife. He talked to us about it."

"Anyone can have a theory about anything and discuss it. That's all Grosbaum did with us. His wife was pregnant. That's what made them related by blood. Your grandparents were the same… your grandmother never said a word until she was pregnant, right?"

"Then what about Rose?" he argues. "She told us everything and time traveled in front of us more than once."

My mouth twitches. I've dropped so many hints since we got back and he hasn't picked up on a single one. "For a smart man, you're occasionally very slow about some things."

"What are you talking about?" he asks, but his body tenses beside mine.

"Rose is a blood relative. *Our* relative."

He freezes. "But for that to happen she'd need to be—" he groans. "No. *No. That* was not our kid."

My hand slips through his while he grapples with the fact that the juvenile delinquent we met drinking with erstwhile rock stars, is one of the tiny blinking shapes he just saw on an ultrasound a few weeks ago.

"She said she had a younger sister who can time travel, but her mom was dead," he says. "That can't be you."

I smile gently. "Her sister is younger by about five minutes, I'm guessing. And her mother was dead because we hadn't changed our future yet."

He flinches. "You can't possibly know that. You're just guessing."

"Don't you remember how she laughed when we asked if her parents knew she was there and said 'kind of'? The way she completely softened when she saw you because you were the parent she knew? Nick, think about it. She had your smile. She looked at you like she knew you."

He groans. "I'm not saying it doesn't make sense. I'm just saying I desperately want you to be wrong."

I'm not. I figured out while we were still in Paris what Grosbaum began to tell me in that last meeting before he stopped himself: you can only run into someone during the process of time traveling if you share their spark. I'm not sure how I know this—little facts just seem to appear in my brain now, from another time—but I'm certain of it.

"The girl we met that night grew up under entirely different circumstances than our daughter will. So the girl you met is not who our daughter will become." I also suspect if something is going to go wrong, my mother will find a way to let me know. Cecelia did tell me, after all, that she jumped to the future too.

He looks over at me balefully, intent on being unhappy about this. "Even good parents have kids who go off the rails. And that kid was born *wanting* to go off the rails."

I push his hair back from his face. "We managed to overcome changing timelines and jealous exes and a brain tumor. I'm pretty confident we'll be able to handle *parenting*."

"I wouldn't be so certain. She was doing *shots*, Quinn," he says, tugging at his hair. "With guys in a *band*." I'm getting a glimpse of a whole new side of my fiancé—Nick as a father. It's going to be interesting.

I climb over him, planting my knees on either side of his hips, linking our hands together. There's generally no better way than this to make him forget what he's worried about. "Do you have faith in me?" I ask.

He shifts beneath me, trying to cling to his fear, while certain parts of his anatomy push to pursue a different type of conversation entirely. "Of course I do."

"Then you'll just have to believe me when I say that I know it's going to be alright." I've spent my entire life riddled with uncertainty. But I feel certain about the twins in a way I've never been before. "Nick...this is supposed to happen. And we were meant to raise them. It's all going to be perfect."

Actually, I guess it already is.

THE END

NICK AND QUINN'S WEDDING: surprise guests and surprising revelations. Turn the page for the bonus epilogue

To understand where Quinn and Nick are heading, you need to see where it all began. Turn the page for a sneak peek at Sarah's story, ACROSS TIME.

THE WEDDING

A PARALLEL BONUS NOVELLA

1

It's a silent sort of island.

Lush and mountainous, with cliffs that tower over the sea beneath. The kind of place you'd expect to find very few people, even fewer homes—and absolutely no churches like the one that sits on its shores, its stone facade wind-blown until it's nearly as white as the sand it overlooks.

I stare at the picture on my laptop, the one that's popped up unannounced while my mother yammers at me by phone. I never believed in anything even vaguely magical or supernatural before the past few months, but the more I open myself up to the possibility, the more I see it around me, in the smallest things I'd have called coincidence before—and there's a hum in my blood as I look at the photo that tells me I can't call this a coincidence either.

"I just don't know what people are going to think," my mother is saying. She's used this phrase no fewer than twenty times since I told her Nick and I are getting married. She thinks it's "unseemly" to get married so soon after I've called off my engagement to someone else, but that it's even *more* unseemly to be visibly pregnant during my wedding. "I can't go telling everyone that you're marrying someone new so soon after you broke up with Jeff. But if you wait any longer everyone will know you're pregnant, and that's almost worse."

I wasn't listening all that carefully in the first place, but now with this photo staring back at me, I barely hear her at all. The church—how the hell did they build it? It's surrounded by cliffs and water for miles. There is absolutely no way they could have gotten limestone there in the quantity necessary except by ship, and no ship could have docked anywhere in the vicinity of that cove without crashing into the cliffs.

Nick, sitting across the room, is watching my face. His eyes sharpen as they flicker from me to the phone in my hand, and he rises. He was protective before. Now that I'm pregnant he treats me like Murano glass. If he could bubble wrap me, he absolutely would.

My mother is saying something about Abby and Jeff—no doubt about how insensitive I'm being, but I'm not really listening closely enough to be certain. "Mom, I have to go. I'll call you back."

Nick runs a hand through his hair as I hang up, trying to mute his frustration. "I know she's your mom and I'm trying not to get involved, but I'm getting pretty sick of her upsetting you," he says.

I bite my lip. "For once it wasn't her," I reply. "But come look at this."

He walks over and leans over my shoulder.

"Wow," he says. "That's amazing. Where is it?"

"The Isle of Eader. It's somewhere to the north of Saint Lucia."

Nick rests his hands on my shoulders. "I wish we had a church like that around here," he says. "That looks like the perfect place to get married."

He says the words and something begins to seep into my blood—contentment and certainty. The same things I felt when I ended up with him—as if some piece of me floating in space had finally found its way home. I reach back and cover his hands with mine. "Yes," I reply. "It does."

A WEEK LATER, we are on our way.

All I can see outside the window is water, in every direction, but there are storm clouds ahead, the kind a little plane like ours shouldn't be flying through. I bite my lip. We are traveling to an island neither of us have ever heard of, a place we could barely find on a map, to see if it's a good spot to hold a wedding. And by the look of those clouds in the distance, we won't even make it there without taking our lives in our hands. "Was this insane?" I ask.

He grins. "I'm just happy you didn't break up with me at the airport."

I raise a brow at him. "That joke will never grow old for you, will it?"

"It's one of the best things that ever happened to me. You can't expect me just to forget." He presses his lips to the top of my head. "But are you okay with this? Obviously it's going to have to be a very small wedding if we do it here."

That part doesn't bother me at all, actually. It was just the two of us when we married before, and really, the journey that got us to this point was ours alone. No one outside could possibly understand what we've gone through to make this happen.

"Oddly enough the only person I'd actually want here is Sarah." My throat swells a little at the thought of her. My biological mother gave up so much to make this possible. My memories of her are filmy, scattered, but love for her sits inside me as solidly as it must have in other lives. I've always missed her, I think, the same way I always missed Nick. I just never knew what to blame for that sense of loss, so I blamed myself. "Are *you* okay with the fact that it'd be a small wedding?"

"If it were up to me there'd be no one there but us. I could do without another night listening to your mother comparing me unfavorably to Jeff, among other things."

I smile at him and lean my head on his shoulder. "She never compared you unfavorably to Jeff."

"No, she just brought up the fact that he's your hometown hero *ten times* during a one-hour dinner and said something about football being more *manly* than swimming."

"You should have reminded her that you're the one who knocked me up with twins the first time we slept together. That's fairly manly."

"I thought about it. Speaking of which, have you found anything?" he asks, nodding at the laptop in front of me, where I've been combing over the files I downloaded from Sarah's hard drive. In a little over eight months, I will give birth to twins who will eventually be able to disappear at will. If there's a way to control them, to keep them safe, I felt certain Sarah would have let me know, but after hours of searching, I'm beginning to have my doubts. "All garbage so far. It's bizarre—mostly term papers, really badly written ones with no names or dates." I turn the open laptop toward him.

"A history of the liberation of Paris at the end of World War 2," he reads. "She had a home there. Maybe it was just idle curiosity."

My lips press together. I didn't give it too much thought before but now that I am, it's not adding up. "Why save all of it though? I wonder if maybe she was there?"

"She told you she wasn't good at traveling from place to

place. France during the mid 1940s seems like a bad area to visit if you can't really control where you're going to end up."

He's right, and while I don't remember everything about her, I know she was never reckless. "I just don't know why she'd save all this crap and not leave a single word behind to help us out. Maybe she thought I'd just travel back in time to see her."

His jaw shifts. I feel dread at the prospect, but I know he feels something ten times that. "She must have known you'd have babies at home. And that you'd refuse."

My nod is small, symbolizing my desire to agree with him and my inability to do so. Because the truth is that if we don't find something soon, if I don't figure out how to protect our daughters, there won't be any other option. I push the laptop toward him. "Feel free to take a look if you'd like. This stuff is all blurring together."

"What I'd like to find is some information about your dad," he says. "You had to have inherited a mutated gene from him too, so it's possible he still has family who time travels."

I push a hand through my hair. "I haven't really been looking. There's only one reason that palm reader would have been reluctant to tell me who he was."

Nick frowns. "What are you talking about? I can think of a thousand reasons she wouldn't want to tell you."

Nick wants to see the best in me. He's incapable of believing anything bad—even telling him I played a role in his brother's death didn't make a dent. I'm less able to see things that way. "Come on. He had to have done something bad. And I mean really bad. She probably thought I'd be better off not knowing that half of my DNA."

He laughs. "Don't you think you're sort of jumping to conclusions? Maybe it's because he died tragically, and you'd already been through too much. Or maybe his family doesn't know about you and she needs to prepare them first. Your mother loved him. How bad could he have been?"

I exhale slowly. "Well there's nothing in my mother's files so far and I have no idea where I'd even start looking for him."

"Sarah said he died in that house, and that he died before you were born. So I'd say we start by looking up the address of her house in Paris and see if anyone died there around that time."

I guess he's right. And maybe it's better to just know whatever terrible thing my father did than to sit here stewing about it. Until I know for certain, all the worst things are possible, and perhaps the truth is only moderately terrible—maybe he was just a petty criminal or went to jail for tax evasion. "I'll look it up when we land." I glance out the window. "*If* we land." The clouds ahead of us are a charcoal so heavy, so dense, they look drawn into the sky with a heavy hand, and we're heading straight for them. I've always been a nervous flyer, but this situation would make anyone uneasy. I don't know a lot about planes, but I know this tiny eight-seater was not cut out for the storm we're heading toward.

Nick's hand tightens around mine. "Why the fuck isn't he trying to go around those clouds?" he asks. "I'm going to talk to him."

He reaches for his seatbelt just as we hit our first bump and I grab his hand. "Don't," I beg. "It's too late. You need to stay belted in."

"It'll just take a second, hon," he argues, but before I can even reply we hit a bigger bump, and then another, and finally knock into a wall of clouds so hard that I can feel the plane shudder and slow in response. Nick's arms encircle me like a vise, though there's nothing he could do to protect me at this point. My head is pressed to his chest and I can feel his heart hammering just as hard as mine. We bounce again and the plane wobbles and seems to still. For one breathless moment I wait, ready to feel us freefall from the sky. But instead we bounce again and then leave the clouds entirely.

The island appears just ahead of us, bathed in sunlight, even more beautiful than in the photos we saw. There is not a cloud in the sky.

Nick and I exchange a look. Nothing about our desire to get married here has been normal. But what just happened seals it. Something has driven us to come to this island.

I just hope it's something good.

2

We land in the middle of nowhere, on a tiny landing strip surrounded by trees. If I hadn't already decided as we ploughed through that storm that we couldn't hold our wedding here, I know it for certain now.

"There's not even an airport," Nick says, quietly astonished.

I tuck my passport back into my purse. "There's no way we can hold a wedding here."

He wraps an arm around me and sighs. "Yeah, I guess we're back to the drawing board, but I'm not going to complain about two days alone on a tropical island with my gorgeous fiancée."

I smile up at him. "I'm not complaining either. Although I *am* wondering how the hell we get to our hotel. I'm guessing Uber doesn't have a thriving business here."

He raises a brow at the Range Rover sitting in the grass beside the tarmac. "I think that's probably ours. The hotel set it up."

"They sent a Range Rover?" I ask. "Good grief. How expensive is this place?"

He picks up our bags and starts toward the car, grinning at

me over his shoulder. "I thought we agreed it was best that I leave you in the dark about the cost of this trip."

It's exactly what we agreed, because while I have a great deal of money coming in and am about to marry a guy who makes a very good living, I still have a hard time stomaching the kind of prices Nick doesn't blink an eye at. "You can tell me."

He shakes his head and leans down to press a quick kiss on my mouth. "Not a chance. We've got two nights here and I'm not spending them camping on the beach because you think the hotel room is unreasonably priced."

He puts our bags in the back and we climb in. The hotel has already programmed their address into the GPS, so we follow its commands, heading down one long road and up another, toward the island's eastern side.

Our hotel is built into the cliffs, impossibly chic even from the outside. Staff members step forward before I even have time to gawk or—again—ask Nick how much it cost. We are hustled forward to the check-in desk, where a girl stands—smiling at us so broadly I actually look back over my shoulder to see if she's looking at someone else. There is no one there.

"Welcome, Doctor and Mrs. Reilly," she says. "This is a great honor."

Nick's gaze flickers to mine—*a great honor?*—and then he smiles a little awkwardly. "Uh, thank you. We're excited to be here."

He tries to hand her a credit card and she waves him off. "That won't be necessary. Your trip has been paid in full."

Both of us still. What she's saying just isn't possible. We didn't tell a soul about this trip. Not our friends, not our parents. "Paid in full by *whom*?" I ask.

She glances at her computer. "Cecelia Boudon? She's upgraded you to the presidential suite as well."

"Are you sure?" Nick asks. "I don't think we know anyone by that name."

She raises a brow. "That's what it says here. There's a gift bag for you as well," she says. "Let me get it from the office. I'll be right back."

The second she's out of sight I turn to him. "Did you tell someone?"

He shakes his head. "Not a soul. And I definitely don't know anyone who could have afforded the presidential suite. That room costs fifty grand a night."

My jaw drops. "Fifty *grand*? For one night? My God that's…"

"Insane," he agrees. "For once I agree with you on that. Do you know anyone named Cecelia? The only person I can even think of is that palm reader in France, but obviously it couldn't be her."

The girl emerges and hands me a gift bag full to bursting, and introduces us to a bellman who will take us to our room. We follow him from one hall to the next, until he at last opens the door.

We step in after him and stop, staring in shock. The room looks like a celebrity's vacation home straight out of *Architectural Digest*—plush white linen couches and glass tables, and the entire seaward wall is missing so when you face forward all you can see is water and the green peaks of the mountains on the other side of the island. Outside there's a huge deck with lounge chairs and a fire pit. But it's missing one very critical item.

"Where's the bed?" Nick asks, just as my mouth opens to ask the same question. Not that we're above having sex on the couch. God knows it's happened enough times back home.

The bellman opens what I assumed was a closet door and nods. "Right this way sir," he says.

We follow him into what turns out to be an elevator, and then emerge into a room even more astonishing than the one we came from. A huge bed, gleaming ebony wide-planked hardwood floors, another open wall looking on to the mountains, but this time the deck ends with a private infinity pool at its edge.

"This..." I begin and then trail off, looking at Nick to complete the sentence.

"Is unbelievable," he concludes.

The bellman hangs his head with a bashful smile. I realize only now that he seems to be struggling to make eye contact. Nick tries to tip him, and he waves his hands. "I could not accept," he says. "It's an honor to have met you." And with that he turns and gets onto the elevator, closing the door behind him.

"That was strange," I whisper. "But at least it was the good kind of strange?"

Nick nods, looking around us. "Definitely the good kind of strange." His gaze reverts to me, and he tips my chin up to plant a light kiss on my mouth. The sun bursts out from the clouds all of a sudden, and we stand in a beam of light. Something about all of this—the weather, the island, the church, the room—feels preordained. It's possible I'm reading into things too much, but whether it's something supernatural or not, I plan to enjoy every moment of it. "We need to figure out who the hell got us this room."

I nod, reaching for my phone. As amazing as all this is, it just makes no sense...and I'm tired of things making no sense. I type the name Cecilia Boudon into the search engine—and the palm reader's face is the first thing I see. Except it's an entirely different version than the one we met—almost unrecognizably so, with salon-perfect hair and jewels and a Chanel suit that fits her trim figure in a way that only comes with tailoring. "It's her," I gasp.

Nick pulls my back to his chest and looks at her over my shoulder. "What the hell?" he whispers. "She looks completely different." I click on the image and her Wikipedia page opens, proving that this situation is even weirder than we thought:

Cecelia Boudon, widow of philosopher Jean Marc Boudon, is reputed to be among the wealthiest women in France. She is the founder of HSD, one of the country's largest purveyors of electronics, and the first company to bring televisions and microwaves to France. Boudon used her earnings to become one of the country's most successful investors, recognizing the value of stock in Microsoft and Sony long before those companies became household names. Her mansion, on Rue d'Exupery, is considered one of Paris's most magnificent homes.

"So it was all an act," I say quietly. "The house, the palm-reading thing. It was all an act. But why?"

"Maybe she thought I wouldn't go barging into her mansion?" Nick suggests. "Or maybe there are details about her she didn't want us to know."

I scroll down to the next paragraph. **Born Cecelia Durand, the daughter of a stage actress and a farmer...**

"Durand," Nick says. "That's the name your mother was using in France. I assumed it was just a pseudonym...but maybe not. Do you think you might be related?"

I look at the woman in the picture. I see nothing in her face that reminds me of my own, but she's nearly seventy—I'm not sure I'd recognize much with that kind of age difference. "I guess she'd be the right age to be my grandmother?" I say. I glance back down at the phone. The rest of the article really only discusses her investing prowess, but a final line at the end rules my theory out. "It says here she had no children." I put the phone down.

"Maybe your father was illegitimate. It would have been a bigger deal back then than it is now."

I turn toward him. "Or maybe he did something terrible and she didn't want to be associated with him."

He laughs again, tipping my chin up to find my mouth. "Hon," he says quietly, "there is no way your father was evil. I know you and I'm telling you it's not possible. The only reason you think that is because of how your parents reacted to your abilities as a kid."

I close my eyes and press my face to his chest. He's probably right. I just wish I knew for sure. "I don't want to think about this right now," I tell him. "Let's just enjoy this trip."

Nick's hands curve around my neck, thumbs pressed to the corners of my jaw. "Are you tired? Do you want to lie down for a while?"

I go on my toes to pull his mouth back to mine. "I tell you I want to enjoy our trip and you ask me if I need to rest?"

"It seemed more considerate than immediately suggesting you take off your clothes."

I tug at the button on his shorts. "You're pretty considerate when our clothes are off too."

He pulls my shirt over my head. "I'm going to be especially considerate today."

WE'D INTENDED to explore the island on our first day, but we never make it out of the room. Between school and Nick's job, time like this—time where we have no responsibilities and can just enjoy each other—has been rare. And as far as I can tell, there's nowhere to go really, anyhow. I've seen no sign of restaurants or stores. It's bizarre—you'd think on an island this size there'd be some kind of tourist industry—but I sort of prefer it this way. This room, this view and Nick are pretty much all I require to be 100% content.

We swim and lie in the sun gorging on the fruit the hotel sent up. We've both agreed that the island is too hard to get to for a destination wedding. But it's a shame, because with every moment I spend here, I just want more.

I emerge from the bathroom at dusk but stop for a minute and just watch him. He's on the balcony staring at the ocean, clad only in swim trunks. I take in his broad, tan back, his narrow hips, the long, lean line of him. We were supposed to drive down the mountain to go see the church, but the church is the last thing on my mind.

I walk up behind him, press my palms and my mouth to his sun-warmed back. He shudders. The good kind of shudder, his body tensing slightly as if preparing to pounce. I go on my toes to kiss his ear and the soft skin below it, feeling that delicious tension in him grow. He turns and pulls me to him, the palm of his hand beneath my jaw, soft mouth pressed to mine. A small groan, low in his throat.

Every once in a while it strikes me all over again: *I am marrying Nick Reilly. Me.* I've been blessed in so many ways, but sometimes it seems like winning him is too good, too much luck, for any one person.

And I suppose I'm pushing it, but I really wish I was marrying him here.

THE NEXT DAY we force ourselves from the room to go explore the island. It's mostly wild, and half the roads consist of only gravel or sand. We follow the GPS mile after mile down a sand road, under the impression that it is leading us to the beach. It leads, instead, to a dense wall of trees.

Nick wants to return to the room, but I object. "It's right on the other side of these trees," I insist. "I mean, look at the map. There's absolutely no way that the beach isn't right there."

"I'm not walking my *pregnant* fiancée through a fucking forest in the middle of nowhere in search of a beach. Didn't you ever watch *Lost*? Do you how much awful shit can live in a forest?"

"The beach is right there," I reply, hopping out of the car. "What could possibly go wrong?"

Nick follows. "On a weirdly uninhabited island that is shielded from bad weather and has absolutely no infrastructure but somehow supports a hotel worth *millions*?" he grumbles. "Yes, it sounds like a completely legit place where *nothing* weird happens."

We find a sand path so narrow and overgrown we have to walk single file. He insists, naturally, on going in first. After five minutes, the path widens and then suddenly stops at a wide beach with powder-fine sand and water so clear and calm you can see to the bottom.

"Quinn," I say aloud to myself, imitating Nick's voice, "you were completely right about this place. I'm sorry I was being such a pussy."

He turns back to me with an incredulous look. "Did you seriously just call me a pussy because I was worried about protecting my pregnant wife?"

"Girlfriend," I correct. "And technically, I didn't call you a pussy, because *I* would never use that word. I pretended you were calling yourself one."

"That does it," he says, swinging me over his shoulder. "You're going in."

I squirm. "Don't you dare throw me in! I'm pregnant! I'm fragile!"

His laugh is low and slightly sinister. "Too late to play that card." He ploughs forward until we are waist-deep and pretends he's going to throw me but then, at the last minute, sets me gently down in the water instead.

"Thought you were going to throw me?" I tease, wrapping my arms around his neck as he sinks lower into the water. He grabs my ass and pulls me tight against him.

"I had second thoughts at the last moment."

I wrap my legs around him and feel something rigid pressing against my abdomen. "Did those second thoughts involve your penis?"

He laughs, his mouth moving down over my neck. "Pretty much all my thoughts involve my penis to one extent or another. But yeah," he says, sliding my bikini bottoms to the side. "This one was particularly penis-oriented."

WE STAY on the beach longer than we probably should, but given that we no longer need to go look at the church it probably doesn't matter. We exit the water and stand side-by-side, staring out at the view. It was a hard trip to get here. I can't imagine we'll ever come back, especially given that we'll have twins eight months from now. My throat tightens at the thought. "I wish I knew we'd be coming back here."

He wraps an arm around me. "We will. As soon as the twins are old enough to be left at home, we'll come back."

I hear a noise in the distance. It sounds like the giggle of a small child. We both look back toward the woods.

"It sounded like a kid," I whisper.

"Great," says Nick. "Mysterious giggling ghost children who live in the forest."

He swings me back over his shoulder and heads for the woods.

"Are you serious right now?" I demand. "I'm pretty sure I can handle a child on my own."

"What if it's some crazy supernatural ghost child, like the twins in *The Shining*?" he counters.

I seriously doubt a crazy supernatural ghost child is going to be so intimidated by Nick's size that it would really make much of a difference, but I love that his first thought is about protecting me at all costs. I can't wait to see him as a father.

Nick sets me down when we finally get to the car and opens my door, where we find flowers resting on my seat. Calla lilies and peonies, my favorites, tied in a thick satin bow, like a bridal bouquet. It's the kind of thing Nick would do, but I can't imagine how he'd have pulled it off here, and the astonished look on his face suggests he's as in the dark as I am. "What the hell?" he breathes. "We're in the middle of nowhere."

"This just gets weirder and weirder," I say, climbing into the car with the bouquet in my lap. It's as if someone around us knows more about our future than we do and wants to help us along.

Or as if someone wants us to choose this place for our future wedding despite the difficulties involved.

"Let's go look at the church after all," I tell Nick when he climbs in.

He glances at me. "I thought you said it was too hard to get to."

I shrug. "It is. I just...I don't know. I feel like we're supposed to go see it."

THE CHURCH IS BACK on the other side of the island, not far from our hotel. Because it's built at the base of a cliff, we can't drive there and instead need to park on the top of a scenic over-look and walk down the steep staircase built into the cliff wall. The area is every bit as wild and uninhabited as the beach we just left, but to our surprise, the doors are wide open.

I hesitate, though I'm a little more scared of angry priests than supernatural ghost children. Nick grabs my hand and we walk in together. The church is even more massive inside than it appeared, airy and light. It seems less a temple to God than it does a temple to nature, to the beauty of the limestone that crafted it, the bare stone floors, the roar of the ocean, dust motes in a stream of sunlight. We seem so small within it, and yet it feels right, as if we belong here, as if we too are part of what makes this place alive. The breeze whips around us, and I picture it, marrying him here. I'd want it to be exactly like this—just us and the sunlight and the ocean behind us. Not my mother clucking her tongue about what people will think, not the few people who choose to weather the long trip while talking behind their hands about how unseemly it all is. Even Caroline and Trevor, my closest friends... they aren't a part of this really. I'm not sure I believe in God, necessarily, but there is something holy in this place, something bigger than the two of us, and yet exclusive to us in the same moment.

A side door opens and a small man walks into the room. He looks nearly as old as this church, his body wizened, his skin darkened by years under the sun. He moves toward us with surprising speed, given his age. "I'm so happy you've finally come," he says, beaming at us like a grandparent might. And as if he was expecting us. "It's a marvelous place for a wedding, is it not?"

Nick's hand tightens in mine. I know his thoughts are along the same lines: *how did this guy know that's why we were here? Was it our age? A lucky guess?*

"We'd love to get married here," says Nick. "But I think logistically it might be difficult."

"What logistics?" the priest asks. "You're already here. We have no licensing requirements on the island."

"It was a long trip too," I explain. "I'm not sure we can ask everyone to travel that distance, and there'd be no place to hold the reception."

"And you very badly want this reception?" the priest asks. Again he asks in a way that implies he already knows the answer...and he's *right*: I *don't* want a reception. No one alive really understands what we've gone through to get to this point, and in an ideal world, it would just be the two of us. Here, in this holy place. And afterward, alone. On the deck of our hotel room, the balmy breeze swaying our hammock to and fro. I suspect Nick would be okay with that too, but his mother and mine would not be. "Our families would be very upset if they weren't invited," I explain.

"Well, I'll let you think about it," the priest says, clasping each of our hands in turn. "I'm here if you change your mind. And if nothing else, you must come back to baptize the twins."

My jaw drops. He is already walking away. "How did you know about the twins?" I call after him.

He turns back to me with a smile. "Quinn Stewart Durand, I know more than you can begin to imagine."

He walks into his office and closes the door while Nick and I stand there, speechless. Nick runs his hands through his hair.

"He called me Durand," I whisper.

"And he knew about the twins," Nick says. "We've only told a few people. And certainly no one here."

I bite my lip. "I know we should be weirded out, but I'm sort of...not?"

"Yeah," he says, clasping my hand. "Me neither. And that's probably the weirdest thing of all."

WE SPEND our last night in Eader out on our deck. We order room service and dine under the moonlight, watching as the waves crash against the cliffs across from us. We swim and lie in the hammock together in a blanket. He rolls me on top of him. "We can't possibly have sex in a hammock," I argue.

He puts one foot on the floor to brace us. "Watch and learn, Mrs. Reilly."

Eventually we rouse ourselves just enough to shower and

go to bed. When I wake in the morning Nick is sound asleep, flat on his back, one arm stretched over his head. And completely naked. It's extremely hard not to wake him up, but in an act of supreme selflessness I instead climb from the bed and go to our deck, leaning against the railing to watch the night sky give way to morning, the sun bursting out over the peaks to the east like a ripe peach begging to be pulled free.

I love my life with Nick back in D.C. but there is something about this place—it feels like home in a way nothing else ever has. I picture a different kind of life here with Nick, one I spend barefoot and free, one where our daughters tumble out onto a wide white beach each morning and run wild.

Nick comes up behind me, clad only in boxers, and rests his hands on my shoulders, pushing my hair aside to press his lips to the side of my neck. I lean back against his chest. "Do we have to leave?"

He wraps his arms around me. "Unless you want to give birth to the twins on an island which appears to have no medical care, I think we do. But I had a thought—how do you feel about eloping?"

I turn to face him.

I wrap my arms around his neck. "I feel pretty good about that."

～

WE WEAR the clothes we brought to go to dinner, before we discovered there'd be no place to go. Nick is in a white button down and suit pants, I'm in a white sundress. I bring the bouquet that was left on my seat yesterday. The flowers, which I placed in water last night, still look as fresh as they did when I received them.

I emerge from the bathroom in my dress, no make-up but the tan I've gotten since we arrived and a touch of lip gloss.

Nick walks toward me slowly, placing his hands on my arms. "You have no idea how lucky I feel right now."

I have some idea. I go on my toes to kiss him. "I just need to put my hair up and we can go."

Nick runs a hand through it. "Leave it down. I want you to look exactly the way you do at this moment," he says. He pulls my hands to his mouth and kisses both. "This, just as you are right now, is who I want to marry."

THE PRIEST DOES NOT SEEM at all surprised to find us at his doorstep at 8 AM on a Monday morning, but why would he be? He seems to know everything before we do. He throws the massive doors of the church wide before he begins, securing them with bolts so they remain open during the ceremony. It's oddly perfect. The beach and the sea behind us feel, to me, every bit as holy as the inside of this church.

He brings us to the altar. I set the flowers on the pew behind me and join hands with Nick. He's smiling at me in that way of his—shy and pleased, unable to keep that dimple of his in check. He is so unspeakably beautiful. I swallow down the lump in my throat.

"Will you, Quinn Stewart Durand, take this man to be your wedded husband? Will you love him, comfort him, honor him and keep him, in sickness and in health, in sorrow and in joy, so long as you both shall live?"

"I will," I whisper. My voice is slightly hoarse. It's a struggle not to cry.

"And will you, Nicholas James Reilly, take this woman to be your wedded wife? Will you love her, comfort her, honor her and keep her, in sickness and in health, in sorrow and in joy, so long as you both shall live?"

Nick's eyes hold mine. "I will."

"By the power vested in me by this church," the priest concludes, "I now pronounce you man and wife."

Nick's mouth twitches upward. "Where's the part where I get to kiss the bride?"

The priest laughs. "She's your wife now. You are free to do as you wish."

Nick cradles my face in his hands. "I'm going to make you the happiest woman alive, Quinn. I swear it."

"You already have," I whisper. He leans down and when our lips meet, there is only him. There is no priest, no roof over our heads, nothing but him and the wide, wild world around us, a breeze—fragrant with sea myrtle and sandalwood—drifts around us like a blessing.

Finally I drop back to my feet. The priest waits, marriage decree and pen in hand, at the altar. I take the pen and sign, and then hand it off to Nick just as something at the back of the church catches the light.

A long blonde braid swaying as a woman exits the church, while a man I've never seen stands just outside waiting.

I know her. I know her in my soul before I even put it together, but then she turns and smiles at me over her shoulder. Sarah, my mother, younger than she was when I last saw her. Two small girls on either side of her—one blonde, one brunette—grasp her hands. The brunette turns back and gives me a big, cheeky smile just before she's pulled away. I get just enough of a glimpse to see that her eyes are an astonishing gray. *Rose.* Or the twin who told us her name was Rose, anyway.

They are gone before I can even utter a word. And a wiser part of me knows that I am not meant to meet them just yet. I can't imagine how the twins were able to time travel here at such a young age. I can't imagine how my mother managed to be here when I saw her die with my own eyes. But I suspect it means our lives are about to get far more bizarre than they've already been.

Nick finishes signing and the priest hands us the certificate. "In this marriage, you will be blessed beyond measure, and you will produce daughters who will be a blessing to the world. Protect them. Protect each other. Go forth," he says, "and begin the life you were meant for."

The life we were meant for. A life that will involve time traveling twins, a supposedly dead mother stopping by for surprise visits.

"You ready, Mrs. Reilly?" Nick asks.

I look up at him. At the pleased, sheepish smile, his heart in his eyes, and I know that as long as I have him by my side, we can handle whatever our lives throw at us.

"Yes," I reply, taking his hand. "I'm ready."

For more about the next book in the series, Across Time, turn the page, or find it on Amazon here.

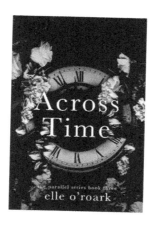

To learn where Quinn and Nick are heading, you need to see how they began.

When Sarah Stewart finds herself stuck in pre-war France, fifty years before her time, her biggest problem isn't the threat of WWII...it's Henri Durand, the infuriating and over-protective Frenchman upon whom her survival depends. Henri challenges everything Sarah holds true—particularly her hatred of the gift that brought her there in the first place. As the bond between them grows, Sarah will begin to wonder if the life she's returning to is actually the one she wants, and if her connection to Henri might be strong enough to surmount any obstacle...even time itself.

www.amazon.com

ACROSS TIME

When I pictured pre-war France, I envisioned sun-dappled fields of lavender that would capture me like a fragrant cloud. But that is Provence, not Saint Antoine, and I've landed indoors despite my best efforts. I hit a hay bale so hard I flip over it—I'm pretty sure I'll never master a graceful landing—and I know before I even open my eyes that I will find hay wedged into my hair, my mouth and...other parts. This hay has now hit more bases than Mark ever has.

On the bright side, the barn I've landed in is not the modern one I saw only moments before. It's old enough that the wood has warped to let sunlight into open spaces. I see no trucks, hear no machinery.

As I force myself to stand, I feel the deadening fatigue setting in, my head fogged as if I have one of those colds that puts you to sleep for days. My limbs are growing heavier by the moment, weakness setting ever faster into my bones. A cow not four feet from me bellows a warning, and I can't even summon the energy to jump in surprise.

And I'm hungry. My God I'm hungry. *If I could just eat*, I tell myself, *I'd have the energy for this*. I spot an apple sitting on a stool five feet to my left—small and dull, barely fit for livestock, but right now it might as well be a large pizza with a side of cheese fries.

I grip the stall door and take one small step on trembling foal legs, but catch movement outside before I can take another and dive back down to the hay, trying not to cough as I inhale the dust around me.

It's a man who's entered. I can tell by the heaviness of his tread, the certainty of it. He moves through the barn and a bucket clangs against the metal hinge of the stall next to mine. There is a moment of silence, during which I hear no movement, no breath. "*Ici*," he says—to the cow I assume—and then mutters something else in French that I don't quite make out as he sets the bucket down.

The steps recede, and after a moment of silence I rise, forcing myself, one foot in front of the other, toward that apple. I've never wanted anything more in my entire life. Just as my hand closes around it, the man steps back inside the open barn door, this time pointing a gun straight at my head.

He is about Mark's age and handsome—a lock of dark hair falling over his forehead like some old Hollywood film star. Though I freeze in surprise, it's hard to picture him as a killer. I'm more bothered by my nudity than I am his gun.

"*Pourquoi etes-vous ici?*" he demands. He wants to know why I'm here.

Good question, I think. *I wish I knew*. I'm too exhausted and unsettled to form a reply in French. "Can I... Give me your shirt."

His eyes flicker downward. I guess he didn't notice I was naked until I pointed it out. My hair covers my breasts and my hands cover the rest, but he looks unsettled anyway. "I think not," he replies in perfect, British-accented English. "In order to give you my shirt I'd have to put down my gun."

It's illogical, but his British accent sounds sort of posh and

James Bond-ish and puts me at ease. Granted, lots of villains in James Bond movies have British accents too, but they generally don't look like this guy.

"I'm looking for Marie? Marie-Therese Durand?" I explain. "Do you know her?"

I wait for a sign of recognition. Instead his eyes narrow and he raises the gun higher, pulling back the hammer. "There is no one here by that name," he snarls. "You need to go back where you came from."

I sway on my feet again and grab the stool to hold myself steady. "Please lower the gun," I whisper.

A hint of softness passes over his face before he blinks it away. He grabs a horse blanket hanging off the wall and throws it at me. "Are you ill?" he demands.

I somehow manage to catch the blanket and wrap it around me, but the effort of standing up on my own is getting to be too much. With each moment that passes I feel a bit further away from him, as if I'm sinking fast in a deep, dark lake.

"No. Please just let me talk to Marie-Therese and then I swear I'll go." I meant to sound stronger, more forceful, but it feels as if I'm speaking to him from under water.

"Again, there is no Marie here," he says. "So you can go right now. Don't think for a moment I'm reluctant to use this gun."

I don't entirely believe him, but even if I did, I wouldn't have the energy to obey. I'm barely remaining on my feet.

"Please," I beg. "I can't...I'm too—" I reach for the wall and use it to stay upright. If I allow myself to fall asleep right now, I'm not certain I will ever wake up.

Footsteps approach and from around a corner comes a shockingly lovely girl about my age. I recognize her from the photo I found, the one that led me here, and my hunch is confirmed: she is a time traveler. Our looks are what set us apart, and though I'm blonde and fair, while she's brunette and olive-skinned, there's a similarity between us as well, in the symmetry of our features and in our eyes, which are backlit, as if a fire shines just beyond the pupil.

"Mon Dieu," she whispers, staring at me as if I'm a ghost. She hisses at her brother in rapid-fire French and he lowers the gun.

My mouth opens to tell her why I'm here. But I pitch face first to the ground instead.

AVAILABLE ON AMAZON

ACKNOWLEDGMENTS

When you publish two books only a few weeks apart, the acknowledgments come out looking pretty much the same, so I'll use the space here for the few who weren't at the end of *Parallel*:

—My author buds, who are some of the nicest people I've ever met.

—Maïwenn from Maïwenn Blogs, for her very cheerful translation assistance.

—All the amazing people who came out in support of Parallel's release. You know you are. When we meet, the margaritas are on me.

ABOUT THE AUTHOR

Elle O'Roark (who writes contemporary romance as Elizabeth O'Roark) spent many years as a medical writer before publishing her first novel in 2013. She holds bachelor's degrees in journalism and arts from the University of Texas, and a master's degree in counseling psychology from the University of Notre Dame. She lives in Washington, D.C. with her three children.

Made in United States
North Haven, CT
03 July 2023

38530560R00173